Vanished

shed

E. E. COOPER

KATHERINE TEGEN BOOKS
An Imprint of HarperCollins Publishers

Katherine Tegen Books is an imprint of HarperCollins Publishers.

Vanished
Copyright © 2015 by HarperCollins Publishers
All rights reserved. Printed in the United States of America.

Library of Congress Cataloging-in-Publication Data
Cooper, E. E.
 Vanished / E. E. Cooper. — First edition.
  pages cm
 Summary: "A teen girl must race to solve the mystery left behind in the wake of one
friend's disappearance and the suicide of another"— Provided by publisher.
 ISBN 978-0-06-229390-9 (hardcover)
 [1. Friendship—Fiction. 2. Missing children—Fiction. 3. Mystery and detective
stories.] I. Title.
PZ7.1.C65Van 2015   2014038820
[Fic]—dc23   CIP
                                                                                                        AC

Typography by Carla Weise and Joel Tippie
15 16 17 18 19 PC/RRDH 10 9 8 7 6 5 4 3 2 1
❖

First Edition

TO BOB,

who believes in all my impossible things

**But it's no use going back to yesterday,
I was a different person then.**

—Lewis Carroll, *Alice's Adventures in Wonderland*

CHAPTER ONE

Temptation is a tricky thing—just ask Eve. That girl got a bad reputation over a single apple. Tossed out of the Garden of Eden because of one teensy bite. Talk about harsh. It's not like she took out the whole tree. I understood why she did it, though. Even when you know the risk, there are things too tempting to walk away from even if you know you should. For Eve, the possible sweetness had outweighed the dangers. I could relate. For me it was worth it, despite the guilt. But of course, I hadn't been caught yet. It's a whole different conversation once you're busted.

I fanned some crackers onto the plate next to the slices of Brie and debated if I should add anything else to the tray. I'd already laid out a small bowl of almonds, some grapes, and a dozen of my dad's famous chocolate coconut cookies. I might as well have pulled on a T-shirt proclaiming: *Look at me! I'm trying entirely too hard!* Beth and Britney were my best friends, but I still felt this huge pressure to impress them.

I carried the tray up the stairs. I never used to worry that much about impressing anyone, but hanging out with Brit and Beth was like finding myself on a treadmill that has a problem with the speed control. Sometimes life was going so fast I could hardly keep up, and then without warning it would slow way down and I would almost face-plant onto the belt. But it was never dull. Since they'd pulled me into their world, it felt as if my senses were on high alert. I was hyperaware of everything. I hadn't even known that my life had been blunted and dull before them.

As I walked up to my room I could hear them bickering. Britney and Beth were superclose, but they fought all the time. Britney would get pissed over some perceived slight. Beth would get mad that Britney was being so uptight. They'd vow before lunch they weren't going to hang out ever again and then by sixth period the whole thing would be forgotten. I'd learned to just roll with it. They called each other B, ostensibly because their first names both started with the letter, but in reality it was a way to jokingly call each other *bitch*. In my mind they were almost more like sisters than best friends. They might go at each other, but if someone else went after one of them they would defend each other to the death.

I paused outside my room. Their voices were getting louder.

"Will you give it a rest? I'm not talking about this anymore," Beth said.

"It's not up to you," Britney fired back.

Beth snorted. "Last time I checked, if it's my mind, it *is* up to me."

I pushed the bedroom door open with my foot. Britney's mouth shut with a snap when she saw me. "I've got snacks," I said. I hated how my voice sounded like an overeager nursery school teacher trying to distract the kids from clubbing each other with boxes of crayons.

Beth laughed when she saw the tray. "Think you brought enough food?" I wanted to run back downstairs and just bring up a bag of chips like a normal person, but it was too late. As soon as I put the tray down she leaned in to pick up a cookie. She held it out to Britney as a peace offering. "Here, my darling B, a bit of sweet for the sweet."

Britney's lips pursed like she'd sucked on a lemon. "Do you have any idea what's in them?" She turned to me. "Are they made with butter?"

I hesitated. Knowing my dad, they were loaded with it. His two favorite ingredients were fat and sugar—because of his French heritage, he claimed.

Beth stood up on my bed holding the cookie aloft. "I declare that as these are my birthday cookies, they have no calories and may safely be consumed by all."

Britney chucked one of my pillows at her. "Your birthday isn't until tomorrow."

Beth grinned and dropped to her knees on the bed. "Fine, Miss Play by the Rules, I declare these cookies to be only half the calories due to the proximity of my upcoming, practically today, depending what time zone we are in, birthday."

"I'll stick with fruit," Brit said, taking the smallest, most stunted grape from the bunch. I almost expected her to nibble it in half and put the remainder back on the plate.

Beth shrugged. "More for us." She devoured the cookie in one bite, leaving a sprinkle of crumbs on her lips. She winked and me and licked her mouth. I glanced at Britney as I reached for the cookie plate, wondering if she'd noticed the wink. But Britney wasn't looking at me. Something else had caught her eye.

"Oh my god, what is that?" Most people would be hesitant to whip open someone else's closet, but Britney wasn't the type to let other people's ideas of privacy and boundaries get in her way. She pulled out my blue-and-silver sari. The beading flashed in the light.

"It's what I wore to my cousin's wedding," I explained.

Britney held it up to her face in my mirror. "I have to try this on." She was already peeling off her jeans. When she was down to her panties and bra she looked over at me. "How does this work?"

I handed her the thin, plain skirt and cropped blouse

that went underneath. "Put these on. I'll have to help you with the rest."

She shimmied into the skirt. I started to drape, fold, and tuck the material around Britney.

Beth watched me dressing Britney. "Seems like a dangerous outfit," she said. "One tug and you'd be standing there in basically what your momma gave you." She smiled at me and I flushed like I was the one who'd been standing there mostly naked.

Britney preened in front of the mirror. The fitted short blouse was too tight in the chest, since it had been made for me, but otherwise she looked great. The deep peacock blue made her eyes flash. She kept turning around so she could see herself from all angles.

"Do you have any more of these? Or could you get some?"

I felt a bit uneasy. "I guess."

"We should all show up somewhere wearing these. Can you imagine what people would say?" She pretended to do a belly dance. "Has Zach seen you in this?"

I nodded. "He was my date for my cousin's wedding."

"I bet he couldn't wait to get you out of it. This thing is hot. Jason will flip when he sees me in this." Britney watched herself dance in the mirror. "He won't be able to take his eyes off me."

Beth rolled her eyes at me. "It's not a costume, B."

Brit froze mid-dance, a scowl spreading across her face. "Did I say it was?" She yanked on the fabric to pull the sari off. I winced. My grandma had brought that back for me from Mumbai. I was going to have some explaining to do if Brit ripped the beading. "I was just trying to have some fun, but I forgot things are only okay if they're done your way." She pulled on her jeans. "Or maybe it's that you hate that both Kalah and I have boyfriends instead of always chasing after the latest conquest like you."

"Let's not do this," Beth said.

Britney crossed her arms over her chest. "Of course not. We'll only do what you want to do, Beth."

Beth laughed, but there wasn't any humor in it. "Seriously? You think *I'm* the one who has to have things my way? Right. You'd think the daughter of two fancy psychiatrists would have a little more self-awareness. Apparently not."

Britney's lower lip shook. "That's so not fair." She whirled around to face me. "I'm not like that, am I?"

There didn't seem to be a right answer. "Not all the time," I hedged, making neither of them happy. I looked back and forth between them, wondering what the fight was really about. The only thing I knew for sure was that we weren't talking about the sari anymore.

"I gotta go." Britney grabbed her bag off the floor.

I tried to smooth things over. "Okay. We're still on for tomorrow, though, right? It's going to be amazing." Beth had asked me to make the plans for her birthday night out. I'd put more effort into it than most four-star generals put into an invasion. Britney didn't even bother to answer. She stormed out, her feet thundering down the stairs.

I followed her. "Brit, don't be mad."

She stopped at the door. I was surprised to see she was near tears. "She does whatever she wants and everyone lets her get away with it. If you even try to call her on something, she acts like *you're* the problem. She just takes what she wants and takes and takes and doesn't think once about who might be affected. But you can't just waltz through life, screwing everyone over however you want whenever you feel like it. Sometimes you have to do the right thing, and if she doesn't figure that out on her own, someone is going to teach it to her."

I took a step back. "Beth isn't like that," I said. Beth was impulsive, but she never set out to hurt people.

Britney shook her head like she couldn't believe how stupid I was. She slammed the door behind her.

Whoa. I walked slowly back up the stairs, wondering what the hell had just happened.

Beth was looking through my bookshelf when I got back. She slid a book into place and smiled at me. "That girl needs a proper snack," she said, taking another cookie. "Low blood sugar makes a person whacko."

So apparently Beth wasn't going to confide in me about whatever was going on between the two of them. I shouldn't have been surprised to see her acting like it was no big deal. Beth was comfortable with chaos and didn't get upset easily, no matter what was going on around her. It was one of the million things I admired about her. She never overthought anything. I, on the other hand, had perfected the ability to obsess about everything.

"Is Britney mad that I made your birthday plans?" I asked. It went unsaid that we almost always went where Britney wanted to go. It was just easier.

"I honestly don't care if she's pissed. It's my birthday." Her lips turned up in a smile. "Speaking of birthdays, is that for me?" She pointed at the small box on my desk tied with a red satin bow. As soon as I nodded she grabbed it and shook it. I laughed and grabbed it back from her. I'd known she'd want it right away if she saw it. Patience wasn't on the list of Beth's skills.

"Your birthday isn't until tomorrow," I teased. I held the box behind my back, enjoying how she had to reach around me to try to get her hands on it.

"I should open it now. You never know what could happen between now and tomorrow. War, famine, zombie apocalypse. Think how tragic it would be if I didn't get a chance to see what was inside." She shook her head sadly, but her eyes were shining.

I didn't really need to be convinced. "Okay, you can open it early just in case, but I'll warn you it's not going to do you a lot of good in fending off zombies."

Beth dropped to the floor and crossed her legs. She patted the carpet to invite me to join her.

I was suddenly nervous. "I hope you like it," I said. When I'd found it I had been so sure it was perfect, but now I was second-guessing myself. I'd thought about asking Britney about it—if anyone knew what Beth would like, it was her—but in the end, I wanted it to be something just fully from me.

Beth shook the box again. "I hope it's not breakable," she joked.

"I usually never know what to get people," I babbled, wishing she would unwrap it already. "My brother, Nadir, is like a present-buying savant. Seriously, he always gets the best things. My grandma is convinced in an earlier life he was a psychic. I definitely didn't get that skill."

Beth slowly peeled off the tape and unfolded the thick white paper. I wanted to grab the gift out of her hands and tear it open. I realized I was holding my breath and made myself exhale.

She lifted the lid and looked up at me, her face spreading into a huge smile. "Where did you find these?"

"Online." I didn't mention that I'd spent more time looking for the perfect thing than I had writing my last English paper. "I thought you could wear them on your necklace, or I have a chain you can use. Do you like them?" I could see from her expression that she did, but I wanted to hear her say it.

Beth pulled the two charms out of the box. I'd chosen them because of her favorite book, *Alice in Wonderland*.

Favorite might be an understatement. She was always re-reading her beat-up copy of Lewis Carroll's *Alice* stories. I'd found a small silver pocket watch and a blue enamel teacup that reminded me of what I knew of Wonderland.

"I *love* them. Help me clip them on." She turned and lifted her hair so I could unhook the silver chain from her grandmother that she always wore. I smelled the rosemary mint shampoo that she used. My hands were shaking as I unhooked the delicate clasp and slid the charms onto it. As soon as the necklace was back on, Beth stood and moved toward the mirror to see it. "It's perfect. Tomorrow I'm going to wear my blue cardigan and show them off."

I wanted to jump up and down. I felt a huge sense of victory that I'd picked something she loved.

"Nice pup." Beth flopped on my bed and tossed my stuffed dog in the air, catching him.

I fought the urge to grab Roogs from her and chuck him into the closet and out of sight. "I don't even know why I still have that thing," I said, trying to laugh him off. His worn brown fuzz suddenly looked less well loved and more grungy and pathetic.

Beth held Roogs close to her face. "Aw, he's a cutie. I like him." She kissed him where his nose used to be and I felt a ridiculous flash of jealousy for my own stuffed animal. "You're going to hurt his feelings." Beth made a pout.

I sighed. I'd betrayed my trusty stuffed dog and misjudged completely how Beth would feel about him. There were times when I was so certain that I knew Beth better than I even knew myself, and other times when I felt like I didn't know her at all. We were still so new together. I almost wanted to fast-forward to the time when we would know everything about each other already. I wanted more inside jokes and shared history. Nothing felt better than those moments when we'd look at each other and start laughing because we knew what the other was thinking. "Do you still have any stuffed animals from when you were a kid?" I asked. I didn't remember seeing any in her room.

"Used to. My mom decided one day that it was time for me to grow up and stop acting like a kid. She bagged up a bunch of things while I was at school and chucked them. Even my favorite that I'd had forever, this stuffed giraffe named Max."

The unfairness of it made me suck in a breath.

Beth laughed at my expression. "It's not that bad. I mean, she's right: at some point you have to leave that stuff behind. You can't stay a kid forever. Except my brother, of course, but since he's dead, he traded life for being eternally thought of as young, so he gets a pass."

I never knew what to say when Beth brought up her brother. He'd died six years ago and as far as I could tell her family had been pretty screwed up since then. "It still sucks she threw away your stuff without even asking," I said. "Especially Max."

"What gets me, even though it's totally stupid because

they were stuffed animals, is that I didn't get to say good-bye. What's the term? I didn't have *closure*. I knew I'd get rid of them someday, but I wanted to pass them on or something. It's dumb because not even some Salvation Army kid was going to want my giraffe. Max was well past his sell-by date."

"But Max still deserved better," I said.

Beth stopped tossing Roogs in the air and looked straight at me. "Exactly." I flushed, feeling the snap of our connection. She scootched over to make room for me on the bed. My heart skipped a beat.

I sat down, but my butt was so close to the edge that I slid off the comforter and thumped onto the floor.

Beth looked over the side. "Are you okay?"

"I meant to do that," I said, scrambling back up. If it had been anyone else I would have been mortified, but with her even when I did something stupid it felt okay. Like being safe at home.

I lay down next to her and listened to her talk about field hockey and how she thought I could lead our team all the way to the championships next year. I knew she wanted to pump me up for the idea, but I had a hard time imagining what next year would be like when both she and Britney would be gone. Whenever I even thought about it, it felt like the floor was disappearing out from under me and I was going into free fall.

"You must be excited to play for Ohio State," I said. It

seemed safer to say this than to ask how often I would see her. I wouldn't mind making the seven-hour drive, but she might not want me hanging around a lot once she was in college.

Beth shrugged. "Sure. If it works out."

"Why wouldn't it? You got the scholarship." I didn't look at her face. Our arms were almost touching. If I lifted my pinky finger just slightly it would brush against hers. I wanted to touch her, but even more, I wanted her to reach over to touch me first.

"Yeah, but I'll still need money to cover room and board, and books and—" Her breath blew out in a rush. "And everything else."

"Oh." I hated how my voice came out flat. I hadn't even thought about all the extra costs. It made me feel young and stupid. The fact that her parents weren't going to help went unsaid. "Maybe there's some other kind of grant you could apply for."

"I wish it were that easy." She lifted Roogs's ears. "Never fear, if it doesn't work out I can always go full-time at the diner. It's been my lifelong dream to spend my career asking people if they want a top-off on their coffee or another slice of Maureen's awful pie."

I didn't say anything. Everything I could think of seemed like bullshit. I wanted to have something real to offer her.

"Things are so messed up," she said after a beat. "I used to think I had it all figured out, but I'm not sure anymore.

Sometimes I don't even know what I should do next."

"Dharma," I said without thinking.

"What?"

I flushed. "It's what my grandma would say. *Dharma* means that the universe will work itself out, like cosmic order, if you do the right thing."

"What if you don't know what the right thing is anymore?"

I paused, hearing the echo of Britney's rant. She was so, so wrong about Beth.

"Ask me, maybe I can help," I said.

Beth opened her mouth, but then shut it. I waited. "You ever want to disappear?" Beth said after a while, her words in Roogs's ear, as if she were asking him instead of me.

"Like, put on an invisibility cloak?" I tried to joke. She didn't laugh.

"No, like disappearing. Taking off. Not worrying about anyone else, but just breaking free. Flying away to where no one knows you. Leaving the bullshit behind and starting over."

"I'd miss you if you left," I said. I meant for it to come out lightly, but it didn't.

Beth propped herself up on her elbow. "Come with me."

"What?" I was so shocked that I swallowed the saliva in my mouth the wrong way and started coughing. My own body fluids were turning on me. I got it under control. "You want me to come? Do you—I mean, are we . . ." I tried to form words my brain hadn't even come up with yet to explain what was happening between us. "My parents would never let me." As the words came out I wanted to push them back in. I didn't have permission from my mommy and daddy to run away? Next I'd be asking her if it was okay if I packed Roogs and a night-light. "I mean, they would freak out. And there's your scholarship. . . ."

Beth tapped me on the nose and flopped back down on the bed. The spell was broken.

"Chill, Kalah. I wasn't really asking you to grab your suitcase and bust out the piggy bank so we could hit the road. Just daydreaming out loud, no big deal." Her voice had closed back down. She was back to being Public Beth, Northside High's Favorite Girl. Popular, Pretty, and Impossible to Know. I'd blown it. "You have to learn not to take me seriously," she said.

"But I do take you seriously," I said softly.

Beth rolled over quickly, pinning me down. The heat of her body pressed into mine. Her hair fell to either side of my face, making a tent that contained just the two of us. My heart stuttered in my chest.

Beth stared into my eyes with an intensity that matched everything I felt. She slowly lowered her face until her mouth floated above mine, her breath brushing my lips. She pressed her mouth to mine. My mind went completely blank, everything whiting out as if I'd stared directly into a flash.

I was so consumed by the kiss I didn't even register for a second that it had stopped. By the time my brain caught up, Beth was already standing and pulling on her fleece. I swung my legs over the side of the bed and sat up quickly. I felt light-headed.

It was always like this with her. Hot and cold. Kisses and then confusion. It had been weeks since our first kiss, and despite everything we'd done and what we felt for each other, I still didn't even know what it was that we were doing. Or if she thought we were doing anything. Maybe she was just fooling around. I didn't believe that, though. Beth had a reputation for collecting hearts left and right while never falling in love herself, but things between us were different. I was sure of it.

Maybe Beth was waiting for me to say what I wanted from the relationship. Maybe she thought I was the one who was just playing around. After all, I had a boyfriend. Maybe that was what she'd meant when she said things were messed up.

"You don't have to go," I said. My brain was spinning in all directions. It felt like I'd just gotten off the Tilt-A-Whirl. "We could talk."

"But I do." She grabbed her bag off the floor. "I picked up a shift at the diner tonight," she explained. Beth bent over and scooped Roogs from the floor where he'd fallen. She tossed him to me. I didn't react fast enough and he bounced off my face and into my lap. "See, there are some benefits to keeping him around," Beth said. "It means you'll never be alone." She fished through her bag and pulled out her copy of *Alice in Wonderland.* "Here, you can borrow this. It's like letting you into my head. Now you won't have to miss me when I'm gone." She kissed the tip of my nose and left.

CHAPTER TWO

Friday night I tried on at least sixteen different outfits before I finally decided on what to wear for Beth's birthday. I wanted to look hot but not desperate, sexy but not slutty. What I needed was Britney's closet. She always seemed to find that perfect balance. It was one of her superpowers. Whatever she wore always looked flawless.

Even with all the outfit changes I was still ready long before it was time for Britney and Beth to arrive, but now they were almost thirty minutes late and I was starting to rethink my outfit all over again. I heard a car turn down our street and shot over to the window, but it wasn't them. I tapped the side of the window six times for luck, but the next car wasn't theirs either.

I considered waiting downstairs, but my mom was down there reading. I didn't feel up to tolerating her silent judgment. She would never say anything, but I could tell she wasn't crazy about Brit and Beth. I didn't know if she didn't like that they were seniors, a year above me, or if it was because they were popular, or if she could tell on some level that I was different since we'd started hanging out. Or maybe she was just still protective of me because of everything that had happened at my old school. But that had been years ago, and Beth and Brit were nothing like other girls. She didn't need to be wary of them.

What I couldn't explain to Mom was that it was impossible for me not to be different now. Being let into Brit and Beth's circle had been like discovering a portal to Narnia in the back of the closet. Once you know the world is a magical place, you can't unknow it.

I truly didn't care about popularity—if anything, I'd been avoiding it ever since I transferred to Northside—but I was still flattered when the Bs turned their attention to me. To my surprise, some of their sparkle seemed to rub off on me. I was still myself, but a better, funnier, sharper version. I could feel myself transforming. People noticed me when I was with them. At first I wasn't sure I liked the attention, but then it became addictive.

And that was even before Beth and I got so close. Having Beth in my life was like putting together the border of a puzzle. The whole picture isn't complete, but you get a sense of what it will be, and the confidence that you'll figure out the rest. The first time she kissed me it felt like things clicked, like *we* clicked, two pieces fitting together perfectly.

Still, I didn't know what to make of what was happening between us. To be honest, I wasn't even sure what I wanted it to be. I felt cautious. I'd seen enough people fall head over heels with Beth only to have her spin off in another direction. Commitment wasn't exactly her thing. And I'd never liked a girl before. Even the idea of it made me uneasy. Plus, there was Zach. We'd been together for almost a year, and I couldn't imagine my life without him. Our relationship wasn't electric—more like summer heat, warm and safe. Necessary. The idea of hurting him or losing him made me feel sick. But there was just something about Beth. I couldn't stop thinking about her. Part of me knew I should end it with her, but I couldn't.

Last night I'd decided I couldn't keep the two versions of my life in motion, one public and one private. At first it had felt intimate and intense, keeping the secret of us, but now I was tired of the sneaking and the lies. Too many things were going unspoken, including between the two of us. Beth had given me the chance yesterday to say what I wanted and I'd missed my opportunity. I wouldn't make the same mistake tonight.

Besides Zach, the person it would most probably be hardest on was Britney. I knew she'd be supportive, especially once she saw how good we were together, but it would definitely be weird for her, having her two best friends become a couple. It would change everything in our group, but things had already changed. Britney might feel awkward about it, but it wouldn't be nearly as bad as if Britney found out that we'd kept everything hidden from her.

I bounced on the balls of my feet. Now that I'd decided to tell Beth how I felt, I wanted to do it immediately. The waiting was killing me. I'd wanted to talk to her at school, but I barely saw her in the morning and she'd skipped out at lunch. It was just as well—even I knew school wasn't the place to have a romantic conversation. Maybe Beth would drop Brit off first after dinner and we'd have some time on our own. My stomach spun itself in a circle at the thought.

I picked up Beth's copy of *Alice in Wonderland* and flipped through it, trying to distract myself. My phone buzzed and I dove over the bed to pick it up. I didn't have a chance to say anything before Britney started talking.

"You will never guess who's bailing on tonight." Her voice was sharp.

I felt the bubble of excitement that had been in my chest all day pop. "Wait, what?" I said. "What happened?"

"Who knows? Maybe she's getting laid, or she got a better offer, or she randomly decided to stay home and do nothing. I'm sick of trying to understand that girl. All I know is she canceled."

"But we've been planning this all week," I said, hating how whiny my voice was. "It's her birthday."

Britney sounded suddenly exhausted. "Listen, Kalah, I don't know what you want me to say. You're a sweetie, but you have to get used to the idea that you can't count on Beth."

"That's not true." I shoved a pile of clothing onto the floor and plopped down on the bed. Beth was spontaneous and hard to understand, but not flaky.

Britney sniffed. "Well, excuse me, I'm sure you know better. I've only been her best friend since junior high. It's great that you've got her all figured out in the six months we've been hanging out."

I winced. "That's not what I meant." Upsetting Britney was not going to make this better. "What did Beth say?"

"She didn't say anything. She texted that she's not coming. Just between you and me, I'm done with it. You'd never see me letting her or you down, but Beth feels she's above the rest of us."

I was only half listening to Britney's rant. I wasn't surprised that she sounded so furious. Britney had almost a military precision to everything she did, and god help you if you upset her carefully laid plans. But something was going on between the two of them, well beyond tonight's dinner falling through. Something I couldn't quite put my finger on. I wondered if it could have anything to do with the secret Beth was keeping—the secret about her and me. Maybe Brit could sense that Beth was holding back something important, and it was causing more strain between them. Hopefully, things would get better once it was all out in the open.

"You guys can't be mad at each other," I said, less because I was worried and more because I knew it was what I was expected to say. It was my part in the drama.

"Whatever," Britney said. "Anyway, I thought I better let you know so we both weren't sitting around waiting for her highness."

I could hear the disappointment in her voice. "We could still go," I said. She and I had never hung out alone, but it seemed I should offer.

Britney paused. "Not tonight. To be honest, I'm not feeling that great. Some other time, though, okay?"

"Sure," I said. "Talk soon."

I clicked off the phone with Britney. A shiver of hope ran up my spine. Maybe Beth had ditched Brit but still planned to get together with me. Just the two of us. If she didn't want to see me, wouldn't she have let me know that she was bailing?

Maybe. Maybe not.

I glanced at my screen. There were no alerts.

I chewed the inside of my cheek. Maybe Beth and her mom had had another fight. I fired off a text.

U ok? Want to talk?

I stared at the phone, willing her to text me back right away, but she didn't.

I shouldn't call. If she wanted to reach me she could. She had my number. I bounced the phone in my hand for a beat.

I hit CALL, holding my breath. It rang and rang. When the line clicked, a jolt ran through me, anticipating her voice, but it was just her voice mail picking up.

"You've reached Beth. I'm off believing in the impossible, so leave a message."

When the phone beeped I didn't know what to say. I'd already sent a text. At this rate, I was going to start looking like a stalker. I hung up quickly and flopped back on the bed. My number was going to show up on her screen. Why couldn't I have just left a message like a normal person? I wanted to call back and explain, but that would make me look even more insane.

A few minutes later, my phone rang and I shot straight up, fumbling to find it. I fished through a pile of shirts and tank tops until it was in my hand.

"I'm so glad you called," I said, the words rushing out.

"Of course you are. I'm irresistible."

The hope whooshed out of me. It wasn't Beth; it was my boyfriend, Zach.

"Irresistible, huh? You think pretty highly of yourself," I teased. I pushed away a stab of guilt that I hadn't wanted it to be him on the phone. Pushing away guilt about Zach was a pretty regular thing for me these days. I was practically a pro. Another reason I needed to sort out what was happening with Beth. What I was doing to him was horrible and he didn't deserve it.

"I'd never say something like that about myself," he said. "I'm too humble. That's just what I hear."

I played along. "You hear that from the voices in your head?"

"Nah. It's the hordes of women who follow me around. I tell you, I'm like a one-man boy band. I have to beat them off with a stick. However, despite the legions of women who would gladly sacrifice a kidney to have me merely glance in their direction, I'm happy that you're glad I called."

"I thought you were Beth," I confessed.

Zach let out a groan, like I'd punched him in the nuts. "Wounded! Man down."

"I would never hurt you on purpose," I said, sounding more serious than I'd meant to. But it was true. The problem was that when I was with Zach it also felt right—not the same as with Beth, but there was a part of me that was a fit with Zach. It would be easier if I could split myself in two.

"No worries, I'll be all right. Just a flesh wound," Zach said. "I'm happy I caught you before you headed out. I wanted to hear your voice."

I couldn't bring myself to say it, but it was good to hear his too. Zach would never no-show on me when we had plans. He was rock steady. I felt a fresh stab of guilt, this time for thinking badly of Beth. I couldn't win. "Beth bailed," I explained. "Our plans are canceled."

Zach hesitated. "This is where I'm supposed to say, 'that's terrible,' but to tell you the truth, all I'm thinking is maybe you'll want to save me from a fate worse than death." I heard Zach's sister, Maddy, yell something in the background. "Ow! No hitting," he said.

"Are you getting beat up by an eleven-year-old?" I asked.

"Who knew when someone says 'You hit like a girl' they mean you give a ninja-like ass-kicking? Clearly, what I meant to say is that I would love to invite you to share the joy that is spending Friday night hanging out with me and my little sister, watching movies." There was another mumble in the background. "I'm also instructed to add that she doesn't need a babysitter, no matter what our parents say."

"I suspect your parents think she's babysitting you," I said.

"I'm retracting my invitation if the two of you are going to gang up on me."

"I'll be over in a few minutes. Try and behave for Maddy until I get there."

We hung up and I stood still holding the phone, just waiting for Beth to call. Isn't that the way it always happens? As soon as you make a new plan, the other person finally calls. I watched the clock on my dresser click over two more minutes. Apparently Beth didn't know that rule.

I'd been so sure she would call. I wanted to kick something in frustration. I'd finally worked myself up to talk to her and now it wasn't going to happen.

I guessed I should be grateful that she was sparing me the humiliation.

My eyes popped open far too early for a Saturday. It took me a second to realize what had woken me up. My phone gave another buzz from where I'd dropped it on the floor after getting back from Zach's the night before.

Beth. My chest fluttered with hope. I reminded myself that I was supposed to be annoyed with her for ditching me. I reached down and picked up the phone, mentally crossing my fingers for luck.

The texts were from Zach. My heart hit the ground with a thunk.

Good Morning, Beautiful.

And,

Is it wrong I miss you already?

I sighed and tapped a quick reply. **Yes. But I like you anyway.** My fingers hovered over the keyboard. It felt like I should add something flirtatious, or at least acknowledge that we'd spent hours making out on the sofa after his sister went to bed. But I just couldn't do it. I hit SEND.

Any normal person would be thrilled to get this kind of attention from the guy she was dating. A normal person would text him back how she missed him too and mean it. Of course, it was already clear I'd left normal behind some time ago. And I did miss him; I just missed Beth more. Even texting Zach made me feel like I was cheating on Beth, even though everything I was doing with Beth was cheating on Zach. I couldn't go on like this. It was time to settle things, one way or the other.

I felt a ripple of unease.

I rolled back over and burrowed under the covers. I told myself it didn't mean anything that Beth hadn't been in touch. She wasn't the kind of person who liked to be pinned down. She needed space, that's all. I got that. Beth had enough people wanting things from her—Britney, the team, her family—everyone. I wanted to be that person who wasn't asking more of her. I wanted to give her everything.

I pulled my extra pillow close and inhaled the scent of rosemary and mint still lingering from Beth's shampoo. Even sheets didn't forget her.

I curled around Roogs and hoped he would chase away a sinking fear. Maybe she hadn't blown off Brit and me last night. Maybe she'd just been blowing off me.

CHAPTER THREE

On Monday I stopped at Starbucks on the way to school. Normally, I'd pick up an espresso for Beth and some kind of candy coffee drink for Britney, but I didn't today. I wasn't their waitress.

I'd finally sent Beth another message on Sunday and got nothing back, not even a text telling me she was too busy to talk. Britney hadn't bothered to get in touch either. For all I knew the two of them had spent all weekend together and they didn't even think how I'd still be waiting to hear from them. It wouldn't be the first time they'd treated me less like a friend and more like their pet.

I kicked an empty McDonald's cup across the school parking lot. They could get their own damn coffee.

I felt like an idiot for not seeing this coming. People who I'd thought were my friends had treated me badly before. I'd sworn when I left my old school that I'd never get myself in that situation again, and this time things would be different. Well, they would be. I'd learned my lesson. I wasn't going to let the Bs walk all over me.

I grabbed my stuff out of my locker and went down the D wing so I'd pass Beth's locker on my way to homeroom. I wanted to give her back her copy of *Alice*. I planned to play it cool and icy so the both of them would know I was annoyed. For once they could make it up to me—let them get *me* coffee for a change. And Beth owed me most of all. If I was going to risk everything for her by giving up Zach, she was also going to need to step up.

As I came around the corner, Britney practically tackled me. My chai latte sloshed onto my sweater sleeve.

"There you are." Britney held my arm in a death grip. "I can't believe this is happening."

I almost rolled my eyes in her face. Was she really that ticked that I hadn't brought her coffee? Then I registered that Britney was surrounded by a pack of girls. There was a low-grade hum of excitement, but I couldn't make out what anyone was saying. No one, not even Britney, got this worked up over coffee. "What's going on?" I asked.

Brit stared at me. "Beth's gone," she said.

I pulled my arm back. The tea in my stomach iced over. I looked up and down the hall as if I expected Beth to pop up from behind a garbage can. "What do you mean, gone?"

"I mean she took off. Disappeared. Nobody's seen her since Friday when she left school. Her parents figured she was out partying for her birthday, so they didn't think anything of it, but when she wasn't back by Sunday they started calling around." I squinted, like better focus would help turn Brit's words into something that made sense. She kept talking. "She's used her ATM card and she sent them a text Sunday night saying she's fine but she needs some space." Britney made air quotes around the last three words. "I can't believe she really left." Another senior from our field hockey team rubbed Brit's back, trying to soothe her.

"Did she call you?" I asked.

Britney jumped. "What? No. I told you, she didn't say a word."

"She left without telling *anybody*?" I wanted to ask why she hadn't called me, but I couldn't. Clearly this was Britney's show.

"Apparently." Brit sounded annoyed.

I should have gotten coffee instead of tea. I needed more caffeine to get my brain up to speed. The milk from my chai latte was leaving a sour slick in my mouth. It tasted like rejection.

"Hamstead wants to talk to us," Brit added.

"Me?" I squeaked. Hamstead was our principal. I'd never been called to his office for anything, good or bad. I felt my anxiety ratchet up a notch.

"I told him how Beth canceled on us Friday night. We might have been the last ones to hear from her before she ran off."

"I didn't hear from her. She called you," I reminded her. My chest felt tight. I'd known something was off when she hadn't called me to cancel. Maybe she'd known I would have been able to tell from her voice that she was planning something. Or maybe she didn't want me to say I'd go with her.

I felt everyone clustered around us moving closer, hanging on our every word. I wanted to swing my bag around and clear some space. They were making me feel claustrophobic.

"Just tell Hamstead what you know." Britney steered me down the hall, her shoes clicking with every step. She glanced over her shoulder at the audience that was trailing us. "Don't worry, guys, I'll keep you all posted. I'm sure I'll hear from her soon." She gave a brave smile.

My stomach clenched like a fist. I dropped what was left of my chai into the nearest trash can. "I hope she's okay," I said.

Britney stopped short. "Beth is fine." Her voice was clipped. "Don't be overdramatic." I almost laughed. Britney was the very definition of *drama queen*.

"How do you know?" I wanted her to reassure me. To tell me that this was Beth just being impulsive and not her running away from me. I bit down on my lip to ground myself. It felt like because I had been mad at Beth, the universe was teaching me a lesson.

Britney rolled her eyes. "Please. Beth's been talking about taking off for months. You know that. Part of me isn't even surprised that she did it the second she turned eighteen, when no one could force her to come back. I guess I'm just shocked that she actually had the balls to do it."

My heart stuttered to a stop. "Wait. You don't think she's taken off for good, do you? What about school? What about . . . you know, *everything*? She can't just leave." My voice was getting shrill and people were turning to look. I wanted to grab Britney and shake her, make her promise me that Beth was just trying to make a point. To make me realize how I would miss her if we weren't together. But of course Brit couldn't tell me that. She didn't even know about Beth and me.

"Take it easy. I'm not saying she's gone for good, just that she's talked about it before. She could be back home right now for all we know."

Another possibility occurred to me and I spoke without thinking. "Do you think it had anything to do with what's going on between you two?"

Brit's eyes narrowed. "What do you mean?"

It was too late to backtrack. "I can tell you guys have been fighting about something," I said.

She crossed her arms. "What did Beth tell you?"

"She didn't tell me anything." Which was the whole

problem as far as I was concerned. "All I know is what I heard from you. And what I've seen."

"Well, don't go making things up. That's all I need— people thinking this is my fault. We fight all the time, but it doesn't mean anything. You know that better than anyone." Britney shook her head, looking almost sad. "I don't know what she's trying to pull with this stunt."

My brain wouldn't stop running through worst-case scenarios. "What if she took off because something bad happened?" I was almost pleading.

Brit sighed. "Don't waste your time thinking about her, because she sure as hell isn't thinking about you. After all, she didn't call you, swear you to secrecy, and tell you where she was going, did she?" Britney gave me a pointed look.

Her words hit me like a punch in the gut. Beth had told Britney where she was going. Of course. They *were* best friends. And if Beth had sworn Britney to secrecy, pretending she didn't know anything was exactly what Britney would do. Brit was undeniably loyal like that, and there's nothing she would like more than having a major role to play in the drama. I searched her face for answers.

The hard glint to Brit's eyes suddenly melted to water, as if the fact Beth had left us was fully sinking in and she didn't want to carry the secret alone.

"It'll be okay." I started to comfort her, but Britney was looking right through me. She stepped away from me and practically collapsed into her boyfriend's arms.

Britney buried her face in Jason's shirt. He wrapped his arms around her and looked at me with his eyebrows raised. I mouthed, "Beth." He still looked confused, and slightly alarmed. "You got my text?" Britney mumbled into his chest.

"Yeah, but 'nine-one-one, I'm freaking out,' didn't really tell me much," he said. "You okay, babe?" He rubbed Brit's back while she sniffed loudly.

"Beth's missing," I explained. His eyes widened.

Brit pulled back and looked into Jason's face. There was no sign of her tears. "She's not *missing*. She took off. No one's seen her since Friday morning." She cocked her head and stared at him. "I mean, unless you saw her somewhere? You were gone Friday afternoon too."

"What? Me? I didn't see her. I had a dentist appointment." Jason looked vaguely nervous, like he thought Britney might blame him for masterminding Beth's escape plans. He wasn't totally paranoid; with Britney anything was possible.

Britney shrugged, but didn't break eye contact with him. "I don't know, I just thought there was a chance you two might have bumped into each other."

The bell rang and Jason's head snapped up. "Shit, I have to go. I can't be late again. Ms. Henderson would love to give me a detention and Coach would kill me."

Britney kissed him quickly and smacked him on the ass. "Run along, then. Coach Pitt is right. No one likes a guy they can't count on."

Jason took a few steps away. "You gonna be okay?"

Britney broke into a smile. "I'll be fine. You know me, I always come out on top." She watched him jog down the hall. "I really love him, you know," she said to me. "There isn't much I wouldn't do for him."

"I know," I said. Following Britney's mood swings was like trying to read a book while on a roller coaster.

"Let's go see Hamstead. Get it over with." She hooked her arm through mine.

I rested my head on her shoulder and swallowed hard. Beth was gone. She finally did it. She took off. And she didn't tell me a thing.

I guess Britney could tell how upset I was because she enveloped me in a hug. Being hugged by Britney was like being dropped face-first into a bouquet. I inhaled deeply, trying to push aside all the negative thoughts swirling inside me. I squeezed Brit a bit tighter, grateful she was someone I could count on. I knew I was lucky to have her as a friend.

"Don't be sad. I'm sure Beth is fine. It sucks that she ditched us, but that's who she is. You know what she's like, always chasing after the next new shiny thing." She patted my hair. "With friends you have to accept the good with the bad. Beth is wild and fun, but she's unreliable. Leaving was her choice. Kah-bear, you have to not take the world so seriously. And certainly don't take Beth so seriously."

"Sometimes it is serious," I pointed out, but I could hear the echo of when Beth had told me the same thing.

"You don't have to worry. If something were really wrong, she would have told me. We tell each other everything," Britney said.

I nodded and forced myself to smile. *Not everything,* I thought. *She didn't tell you about me.*

CHAPTER FOUR

There's a special level of hell that is a field hockey scrimmage on a cold wet day. Normally I have no tolerance for people who whine about getting chilly. Today I was ready to quit before I even laced up my shoes.

The season was long over, but since we'd lost the state championship by a single point, we'd all agreed to run extra unofficial practices throughout the spring to make sure next year we kicked ass. Even the seniors stuck around to help. In theory the practices were voluntary, but we all knew Beth and Britney as co-captains were keeping track of who showed up. Unless players were being actively struck by lightning, the field was on fire, or Armageddon was going down, we were on the field on Mondays.

I'd suggested to Britney that we call off practice since Beth was gone, but she'd said keeping up the schedule was important for the team. I couldn't shake the idea that she also wanted Coach to find out that she'd stepped up when Beth flaked out. Britney had never been happy that Beth got co-captain. Brit had been lobbying to be captain for years, while Beth didn't really care, but everyone knew Beth was the better player. Now Britney could finally prove that she was the right woman for the job after all. It wasn't just about talent, it was about dedication.

All day, I'd kept waiting for the world to stop. It seemed like classes should be canceled so that we could wait by the phone, or form search teams, or do something. Instead we all went on with our regular schedules. There were pop quizzes, boring presentations, and more homework assigned. The cafeteria stuck to the same hot lunch menu. The hallways had the same smells. Zach walked me to class like usual, and Britney held court on the senior benches. Life went on like normal, except for the fact that Beth wasn't there.

I'd heard her name all day long, though, in whispers in the halls, echoing off the lockers, on everyone's lips. It was as if she was haunting me.

"Pick it up, Haggerty! That was supposed to be a three at the back formation!" Britney yelled at Stacy. She tapped my stick with hers as she ran by. "Stay close, go right side."

I picked up speed and ran down the field, my muscles

burning with the effort. My feet slid on the wet grass, mud squelching under my turf shoes and splattering up my calves. Britney dodged left to avoid a tackle and sprinted upfield. I knew what she was planning. It was a move she and Beth had perfected, a blind back pass. Beth's absence wasn't throwing off her game at all.

There were all sorts of rumors flying around school about what Beth was doing. The leading theory was that she'd taken off for New York City to live with some ex-boyfriend or to become a model, or possibly both. No one seemed to think it was weird that she'd left. It was like they had been waiting for her to do something like this and were thrilled she'd finally provided some excitement. I was the only one who was shell-shocked.

Every time a new rumor popped up, Britney would oscillate between acting totally mystified and responding with a half smile that hinted she knew more than she was letting on. The only time she lost it was when some varsity jerk made a crack about how Beth had to move on to fresh pastures since she'd already dated every guy on the basketball team and half the cheerleaders too. I was grateful Brit threw a fit about that, so I wouldn't be the only one looking like I wanted to scream.

My mind snapped back to the game when the ball hit my stick, more by luck than any skill. I didn't think. I reacted. I struck the ball with all the pent-up anger I'd had building all day. My shot was hard and fast and it went high, hitting

Amy Chan in the shoulder. She fell to the turf, grabbing her arm. I dropped my stick, shocked at what I'd done.

Britney stopped short and blew her whistle.

"Are you okay?" I asked Amy. She got up slowly, rubbing her shoulder and glaring at me.

"What were you thinking?" Britney yelled. "Are you trying to take her head off?"

I stood there with my mouth open. I didn't know how to explain I hadn't been thinking about the game at all. My shot was illegal. If it had been in a match, I would have gotten a red card for sure.

My lower lip started to shake. I could have really hurt Amy. Everything in my life was fraying apart, and I couldn't stand Brit being mad at me too. She and Zach were all I had left. My eyes started filling with tears.

"Hey, it's okay." Britney lowered her voice as she stepped closer. "You didn't mean it. You just clipped her. She's going to be fine."

"I—I don't know how it happened," I stammered. My jersey was clammy and stuck to my skin, making me shiver.

Britney offered me an out. "Tell you what, why don't you gather up the extra gear and put it away. Call it a day."

Even though a minute ago all I'd wanted was to get out of practice, now I didn't want to be separated from the rest of the team. "I'm sorry. Don't pull me. I want to keep playing."

Brit put her hands on her hips. "Your head isn't in the

game, so the rest of you shouldn't be either."

"I can play," I insisted.

Britney's lips pressed into a line. "Next year you can call the shots, but for now it's still me, and I'm saying you're done." She clapped her hands together. "Keep it moving, everyone. O'Neil, you're taking Richards's spot."

I wanted to argue with her. Technically, I had just as much right to run these practices as she did. I was going to be captain next year. Coach had announced it at our end-of-season banquet. Beth had even put her whistle around my neck like it was a gold medal. But as usual with Britney, it wasn't worth the fight.

Clare O'Neil bounced past me, thrilled with the call-up. My face felt red hot, even in the cold drizzle. I was too embarrassed to demand to stay. It was a stupid mistake. I deserved to be sent off the field. I was one of the best players on the team, maybe the best when Beth wasn't there, but today it was like I'd forgotten even the basics.

"No hard feelings, okay?" Brit gave me a quick squeeze. "I'm doing what I think is right. It's the same call Beth would have made."

I nodded because if I opened my mouth to talk I was pretty sure I'd start crying. I picked up the extra balls and the plastic cones we'd used for drills and dragged them back toward the gym.

As I walked inside, Chester, our school janitor, waved and smiled like she was thrilled to see me. Chester isn't her real name. I'm not sure any of us know what it is. We call her that because she likes to wear her dad's work shirts. He works at an auto repair place and his name, Chester, is embroidered over the pockets. Chester doesn't have it easy at our school. A mentally slow, chubby janitor is easy prey in a high school, but it never stops her from being incredibly positive about everything. I always try to be nice to her. As Beth once said, it seems like the least a person can do is be nice to the people who really deserve it. It's being nice to the questionable ones that's hard.

"You need help?" Chester asked. "I have lots to do, but I don't mind helping." Something about her being so kind made me want to throw myself into her arms and let her tell me everything was going to be fine. Then I could add "freaking out the school janitor" to the list of things I'd screwed up.

"No, thanks. I just need you to let me into the equipment room, if you don't mind."

"Okey-dokey." She pulled her elastic key ring from her belt and let it snap back before walking over to unlock the storage room.

I pulled an old towel off the hook and started to dry the balls off. Having a mindless task to focus on helped me calm my racing thoughts, until I realized I was giving each ball six wipes. When I was stressed I tended to fall into these patterns. I'd have to do everything six times or in a certain order. If I didn't, I'd get more anxious and have to start all over again.

I made myself stop and take a deep breath. My hands were shaking. Chester patted me on the back.

"You sad 'cause your friend is gone?" Her face wrinkled up in concern.

I dropped a ball and picked it back up. "What do you know about Beth?" I said.

Chester blushed and looked away. "I know you're special friends."

I watched her carefully, trying to figure out what she meant, or if she meant anything at all. Had she seen us together? Noticed the spark between the two of us? Sometimes when I walked down the hall with Beth it seemed like everyone must be able to tell that we were falling in love. That neon hearts floated above us and trailed in our wake like bubbles in a cartoon. Of course, maybe all Chester had seen was me mooning over Beth in a delusional love cloud. "Yep, I miss her," I said, my voice catching in my throat. I put the dry ball in the rack.

"Maybe she went down the rabbit hole," Chester said.

I stared at her. Rabbit hole? "Where did you hear that?"

Chester shrugged and pushed her mop and bucket toward the bathroom. "Dunno. Something she said once."

I felt a stab of jealousy. I hated that Beth had shared her love for *Alice* with anyone else. I hated that she'd asked me to disappear with her and instead of just saying yes, I'd given her every reason why I couldn't. If I'd said the right thing maybe she would still be here, or have taken me with her, or at the very least told me where she'd gone.

I shivered as I watched Chester walk away. I was still wet from the rain, and grass was stuck to my calves. With my luck I'd get sick and die before Beth came back, or bothered to send me a text. I tossed the remaining balls into the rack. I didn't care if they were wiped down anymore. I reminded myself that doing something any particular way wasn't making things better, or safer, it was just an obsession. A stupid obsession. It did nothing but waste my time.

The last ball hit the metal rack and knocked a spider onto my arm. The spider skittered across my sleeve.

I stumbled out of the equipment room, shaking my arm and spinning around, trying to get it off me. I whirled into Zach.

"Interpretive dance!" Zach called out. His shoes squeaked on the wood floor as he jerked around, copying my moves.

"There's a spider on me." I whipped around and saw something dark move up my shoulder. "Oh god, don't let it get in my hair."

"Hold still," Zach said. I froze. Zach moved behind me and lightly brushed my back.

"Did you get it?" My heart started to slow down. Zach could always calm me. He's like Valium in a sweatshirt that smells like clean laundry mixed with cedar trees.

Zach showed me his cupped hands. "Got him." He opened his hands slightly so he could peek inside. "Good thing I was here. He looks like a killer."

I shuddered. "Why are you holding him?"

"If I leave him on the floor, he'll get squished." Zach loped over to put his new eight-legged bestie down under the bleachers. He brushed his hands off on his jeans and held them up for me. "Look, no spider cooties."

"Thanks." I shivered again and Zach yanked off his hoodie and wrapped it around me, pulling me into a hug. I let myself melt into him. His hoodie was still warm, like he'd just pulled it out of the dryer. Zach was always warm.

"I went to watch your scrimmage, but Brit said you were in here."

I wondered if she had told him I'd nearly decapitated Amy Chan. Zach wasn't an athlete and couldn't care less how I played, but I still didn't want anyone to know. Field hockey was one of the few things that I knew I did really well. At least, I used to do it well. "I couldn't focus on the game. I keep thinking about Beth."

He wrapped his arms tighter around me. I pressed my lips together, afraid I might spill everything. I needed him to comfort me, even though it was totally unfair.

"It'll turn out okay. She'll come home when she's ready," Zach said.

"So in the meantime I'm not allowed to be sad?" I snapped. No one got it. They didn't know what had really happened: she'd left me. "Everyone needs to stop telling me to chill out."

Zach took a step back at my harsh tone. I winced.

"Sorry," I said. I opened my mouth to try to explain, but I couldn't. Not without crushing him too.

Zach kissed me gently. "It's okay. Of course you're worried. I love that you're such a good friend."

Shame flooded through me. Zach was one of the best people on the planet. The guy saved spiders, for crying out loud. He didn't deserve my lies. I didn't deserve him.

"Hey, come here." Zach pulled me close again. "This sucks. I'm sorry. But I'm sure you'll hear from her soon."

"Thanks," I mumbled. I tilted my face up to kiss him. I meant it to be a quick kiss, but it turned into something else. Hotter. Needier. I pressed against him, wanting his warmth to touch every part of me. I felt Zach respond and Beth's face flashed in my brain. I pulled back quickly. A couple freshmen coming out of the boys' locker room whistled.

"Oops," I said. "I lost track of where we were." *And who we were*, I thought to myself. I hated my body for betraying Beth. For reacting.

"Damn my irresistibility." Zach smiled and threw his arm around me. "C'mon, let's get out of here."

As we walked out of the gym, I felt Chester staring after us. I was too ashamed to meet her eyes.

CHAPTER FIVE

I was packing my lunch the next morning when my dad burst out of the basement, his eyes wide with excite-ment. Or it might have just looked that way due to the fact that his eyebrows were practically gone.

"Is your mom around?" He bounced from foot to foot.

"Dad, did you burn your eyebrows off?" I didn't men-tion *again*. It was implied. I couldn't wait to tell Nadir about it. Dad and his eyebrows were an ongoing family joke.

His hand went to his face. "This? A bit. Nothing much."

Other people have dads who play golf or spend their weekends puttering around the yard. Mine makes robots in our basement. I was genetically doomed to be odd. "Aren't you supposed to be at work?" I asked.

Dad's eyes darted over to the clock on the microwave. "Soon. I woke up this morning with an idea of how to fix my latest project and I decided to tackle it before heading into the lab. I want to show your mom."

"She left for the pharmacy already."

His shoulders drooped a bit, then he straightened. "Do you want to see? I'm calling it Rover." He whipped a robot the size of a Kleenex box from his side and put it on the floor.

"Named after the Mars rover?" I asked. It appeared to be a perfect scale model. In addition to being crazy about robots, my dad was a NASA nut. He'd build his own space shuttle if our neighborhood association wouldn't put up a fuss about the launch pad in the backyard.

"Nope. Watch this." He walked around the granite island and the robot followed him. "Sit," he commanded, and the back end of the robot lowered. "Beg." The robot balanced on its back wheels, its front wheels spinning in the air with a mechanical clicking sound.

"You made a robot dog," I said. Dad walked in a zigzag and the robot followed. "Any particular reason?" I tossed an orange in with my lunch. I wondered what it would be like to have normal parents. The one upside to my dad's robot obsession was that he hadn't noticed the huge dark circles under my eyes that broadcast I'd hardly slept. Around midnight Beth had finally returned one of my thousand texts.

K! Don't worry about me. I'm taking some time off. It's what I need to do.

She didn't say a thing about the two of us. Nothing about missing me. Nothing about when she might come back. Nothing about why she didn't even bother to tell me before she left. I'd immediately hit CALL to try to catch her and hear her voice, but she didn't pick up. I didn't even know what to think.

"No reason. Just wondered if I could." Dad looked down at the robot with pride. "The voice recognition was the hardest bit. We humans take for granted what a complicated process communication turns out to be. It's not just about what's said, but what's heard, and from that, understood."

My heart recognized the truth of what he was saying. Once again it felt like my emotions were in free fall, looking for something solid to grab on to. Beth had been my gravity. Without her around I'd lost my grounding. "I don't take it for granted. I can't figure out what people mean half the time, and in theory I've got better sensors than that thing," I said.

He winked. "I don't know. I did order top-of-the-line sensors. Those are no off-the-shelf RadioShack specials." Dad draped an arm around my shoulders. "Go easy on yourself, kid. Once you get beyond the basic sit, stay, and heel, communication gets complicated. With a robot I can lay out exactly what I mean to say in code and the robot makes sense of it. We're rarely that clear with each other."

I turned his words over in my head. There were times

when I felt so in sync with Beth, as if we were speaking to each other in our own private language. I didn't need to interpret her—it was as if part of me was *connected* to her. But now that connection was severed and communication had stopped and I didn't know why it had happened. It made me doubt I'd ever really understood.

I still wanted to believe there was a chance that we could fix things. But her text hadn't given me much hope. I trusted her with everything, and she didn't even trust me enough to tell me where she was. And she didn't love me enough to say good-bye. I swallowed hard so I wouldn't start crying.

"Well, I suppose we should take off," Dad said.

I looked up. He was holding my lunch bag out in front of him. He shook it slightly. I took it from his hands.

"Thanks."

He smiled. "As much as I'd like to talk robots all morning, if we do we'll both be late." He gave Rover a pat on the head and went to give me a pat too, but I ducked out from under his hand. He blew me a kiss and headed out the door. I glanced at the clock. I needed to get going.

I ran up the stairs and grabbed my bag. Beth's copy of *Alice in Wonderland* fell out. I'd forgotten I still had it.

I flipped through the pages, wondering like a crazy person if it somehow held the key. Maybe there was some kind of message or hidden meaning in the parts she'd underlined. A code of sorts. If I could figure it out, I might be able to make sense of what she'd been thinking when she made the decision to take off. I couldn't escape the idea that if I could just understand *why* she'd left it would make it better.

Last night when I'd been tossing and turning it had occurred to me that it really came down to two options. Either Beth's leaving had nothing to do with me, or she'd left *because* of me. Neither was good.

I tossed the book aside. If I wanted to know what was really going on with Beth, there was only one person who could tell me, and it wasn't Alice. I needed to talk to Britney.

Going to Brit's house is like stepping into an issue of *Elle Decor* magazine. Everything, from the cream-colored Italian leather sofa that's as soft as a baby's butt, to the ice-blue Turkish silk rugs, was absolutely perfect and in place. I suspected dust spontaneously combusted before it was allowed to fall in that house. Even in the fridge things were lined up and color-coordinated. Green Perrier water bottles sat next to a bowl of bright red apples that looked ready for their close-up. You'd think with my compulsion for order I'd love it, but it made me tense. The house even smelled sterile.

"You want anything?" Brit asked. She grabbed a bottle of water for herself. "No, thanks." I was certain I would spill it or leave it somewhere, making a water ring on an inlay table that would turn out to have belonged to Napoleon or the queen of England. "Should we head down to the basement?" I suggested. It was the only part of her house that didn't make me anxious.

The basement was like our personal clubhouse. We rarely hung out at Beth's because of the tension at her place, and while my house was okay, it couldn't compete with Brit's. When her parents built the house the basement was the nanny suite. When Britney grew up, the nanny moved out and Brit took over.

Unlike the rest of the house, the basement looked like an actual home instead of a movie set. Fashion magazines were piled on the floor and bottles of nail polish were scattered on the coffee table. There was an oversized sectional sofa that seemed to hug you when you sat on it, and a pile of unmatched pillows. There was a huge flat-screen TV, a pool table, built-in bookcases filled with every board and video game you could imagine, and even a wet bar with a microwave and fridge. The basement had its own entrance, which meant Jason could sneak over without Brit's parents knowing. The only sign that it wasn't solely Brit's domain was a huge walk-in wine fridge that her dad had installed when he'd been on a wine-as-an-investment kick a few years back. It was like a temperature-controlled vault. Then he'd decided he wasn't interested in wine anymore and started collecting some kind of Old West prints that hung in his office upstairs. Now the only things in the vault were a few cases of wine and Britney's perfectly chilled Diet Coke. Brit's parents didn't care that we hung out down there. It was soundproofed from the main house, so they didn't have to listen to us blasting music or giggling.

"Nah, I don't want to go downstairs." Britney motioned to the stacks of paper she'd lined up on the dining room table. "I already got everything set up here. We need to make a packet for everyone on the student council." She sighed as if she couldn't believe that her role as secretary required actual work.

It was clear to me that when Britney said "we need to do X," what she really meant was that someone other than her needed to do it while she watched. I didn't mind. I sat down at the table and started pulling together the information on next year's elections. Brit leaned against the black granite island and flipped through a *Vogue*.

It felt somewhat weird to be with Britney, just the two of us. Normally Beth was the one that connected everything. Maybe Brit didn't want to go down to the basement because it was a screaming reminder that everything was different since Beth had left.

Even though she was acting like everything was fine, I knew it had to be bothering her that Beth was gone. When I'd told her earlier about Beth's text last night, she'd given me a small hug and said, "See? I told you she's fine," but she clearly hadn't wanted to talk about it. Just like she hadn't wanted to talk about why she hadn't been in school today. "Mental health day," she'd said with a shrug. It was fine if she didn't want to confide in me about her emotions, but I needed to get her to talk.

"How come you aren't running for student council? They're taking applications until the end of the week for next year's slate." Britney popped a cashew into her mouth.

I stapled a stack and set it aside. "I'm not really interested in that kind of stuff."

"Who cares if you're interested? It looks good on college applications. You should volunteer for everything you can now. Next year will be too late." She pointed at me with a perfectly manicured nail. "You can't afford to sit back, unless you have your eye on beauty school . . . or Ohio State." She winked like we were in on the joke together. Britney never missed a chance to make fun of where Beth was going. Britney believed anything below the Ivy League was a waste.

I shifted uncomfortably in my seat. Brit had told everyone that she'd been accepted everywhere she applied, but Beth had told me the truth. Britney hadn't gotten into any of her top schools except Cornell, and she wouldn't have gotten in there except for the fact that her grandfather had donated something like an entire engineering building with a telescope to make it happen.

Before I could respond, Britney's mom bustled in. "Excellent advice. If you'd taken it yourself, then your own applications would have been stronger." She blew a kiss at Britney as if she was joking, but my heart still hurt for my friend. Brit's parents never missed a chance to imply she wasn't quite up to their standards. What else they wanted in a daughter was a mystery to me.

Brit's mom untied the gray-and-green Hermès scarf from her neck and let it drift down onto the counter. She smiled at me, her lips pressed together. I could tell she was trying to remember my name.

"Hi, Dr. Ryerson," I said.

"Kalah came over to help me with a student council project," Britney explained. "I was just telling her she should join."

"Being on student council shows a commitment to service and leadership. Both Britney's dad and I were president when we were in high school." There was a pause where it went unsaid that Britney had only made it to secretary. Never mind that secretary was the position Brit had *chosen* to run for.

Dr. Ryerson was still staring at me. She always did this thing where she kept eye contact for a long time. Maybe it was because she was a psychiatrist and wanted you to feel heard. What it made me feel was that I was under inspection.

"I'm counting on my grades getting me in," I explained. "And maybe field hockey."

"Performance in school isn't enough to make someone a complete candidate. You want to show them a full, well-rounded person. Just because of your heritage, you can't count on getting preferential treatment." Dr. Ryerson noticed an atom-sized piece of lint on her sleeve and flicked it away.

I flushed, unsure of how to respond. I wanted to spit back that the last time I'd checked, I was in fact a full person already, including and regardless of my "heritage." But I was pretty sure there was nothing I could say to change the fact that Britney's mom probably thought of me as "that brown girl."

"Where are you planning to apply?" Dr. Ryerson asked. Britney looked at me behind her mom's back and rolled her eyes.

"I haven't decided," I admitted. "Maybe Ohio State." I felt a band of tension in my chest loosen. It was the first time I'd said out loud what I'd been thinking about ever since Beth got in. I could picture Beth and me on campus, walking through the leaves on our way to a class, holding hands. Of course my whole college fantasy was clearly just a fantasy, since I couldn't even get her to return my calls. I'd tried her again at lunchtime and on my drive to Brit's. Both calls had gone straight to voice mail.

Britney sniffed. "You could do better."

"You'll get a solid education there," Dr. Ryerson said.

I wished the conversation would end. Didn't Britney's mom have something else to do? Didn't her flying monkeys need tending?

"State schools are a great option for some people.

Besides, the Ivy Leagues can't take everyone, and they shouldn't. You can put lipstick on a pig, but it's still a pig."

My jaw fell open but Brit's mom didn't notice. She was eyeing Britney as Brit ate another cashew. She pinched Brit's stomach. "Speaking of pigs, the freshman fifteen will catch up with you soon enough next year. No sense in giving it a head start." Brit dropped her handful of nuts back in the glass bowl. Her mom smiled and patted her back as if she had performed a particularly difficult trick. "Okay, you girls have fun with your project." She waved her fingers at us and swept back out of the room. Brit slumped into a chair.

We sat in silence. It was like Britney's mom had sucked all the air out of the room. She wasn't my mom, but I still wanted to crawl under the table. I tapped my finger in beats of six.

"And people wonder why I'm a bitch," Britney said. "Can't blame the apple for falling close to the tree."

"Everyone can't stand their parents at some point," I offered.

"But parents are supposed to like their kids, right? The difference in my situation is that she can't stand me."

"I'm sure that's not true," I said. At least I wished it weren't true.

"Don't feel bad. I have a lifetime of experience in disappointing my mother. I've got it down to an art by now."

"No way. You are not a disappointment. You're . . ." My

brain scrambled for a way to describe her. ". . . you're Britney."

"I know you're trying to help, and I know everyone thinks I have it all together. But the truth is, I don't. I was so sure I had my life figured out and now it seems like everything is upside down. I'm this huge fraud," Britney said, her voice cracking.

My heart wrenched for her. "No one cares if you got into Harvard or not," I said, though probably plenty of people at school would be all too happy to find out that Britney had failed. It wasn't that she was disliked; it was more that people wanted to bust her perfect exterior to prove she was human like the rest of us. But those people didn't matter. "I'm telling you, it's Harvard's loss."

She didn't meet my eyes. "Duke's and Yale's too. How did you know?" She leaned back, looking up at the ceiling, while I tried to think of how to answer. "Never mind. Beth must have told you. She's the only one I shared it with. After all, if you can't trust your BFF, who can you trust?"

"You can trust us. We love you. Beth only told me because she felt bad and didn't know what to do." I wondered if part of why Britney made fun of Ohio State is that she was jealous. It wasn't as prestigious as Cornell, but it was a good school, and they'd actively recruited Beth. Britney could never stand the idea of someone doing better than her. I wasn't sure if she ever felt she was good enough.

Brit picked at her thumbnail. "I didn't want anyone to know. Sometimes I like my version of reality so much I almost forget the actual truth." She leaned forward. "Don't tell anyone about this."

"I won't."

Britney's face relaxed. "I knew I could count on you." She took the stack of papers from my hand. "Now fess up, why did you really want to come over? You're not looking for a way in on the council, and it certainly wasn't for my mom's company."

I took a deep breath and jumped in. "No one knows Beth better than you." Her face was still. "I'm just trying to understand why she left." When I'd planned this conversation in my head I pictured myself being stoic and logical, but now that it was happening, I wanted to beg her to talk to Beth. To tell Beth that she had to call me, she couldn't just walk away without a word. Even putting aside whatever else was between us, Beth owed me that much as a friend, didn't she? But I didn't say any of that.

Britney looked out the bay window to the manicured yard. "If Beth didn't tell you, then it's not my place to say."

A jolt ran up my spine. I knew it. Britney knew more than she was saying. "You know?"

Her shoulders went up in a halfhearted shrug.

I wanted to hurl the stapler at her in frustration. I forced myself to swallow and calm down. Britney couldn't be pushed. "Okay, fair enough. If she swore you to secrecy,

I get it. I'm not asking you to break any promises to her. You would never break your word to a friend, I know that."

Brit met my gaze. "I would never screw a friend." Her voice was clipped. "And unlike Beth, I *can* keep a secret."

I winced. I'd just made things worse. "I swear, she only told me about your college applications because she wanted to come up with some way to make you feel better. She wanted you to have enough support." That was true.

"You have no idea why Beth does anything. No one does."

Whoa. Apparently we'd both felt burned.

I tried a different tact. "How about if I guess where Beth went. Will you at least tell me if I'm on the right track?" I yanked out the list I'd made in study hall when I should have been cramming for my chem quiz. I'd approached the list the way my dad would. He was a total engineer. He'd taught me every problem can be solved if you work through it systematically.

"People are saying that Beth ran off to Europe, but I'm pretty sure she didn't have a passport. So I don't think she's there," I said.

Britney gave the barest of nods. I felt a rush of relief. One option crossed off the list.

"I don't think she's in town. If she were still here there's no way that could stay a secret. Someone would have seen her by now. It's not like she'd be hiding in someone's basement. She'd have to come out sometime." I realized that my foot was bouncing and made it stop.

"It would be hard," Britney admitted, but she didn't say anything else. I crossed it off my list.

I pressed forward with my theory. "I think she's still in Michigan somewhere. I know everyone likes the idea that she's run off to L.A. or New York, but I don't think she'd go there. She doesn't know anyone in those cities. I can't imagine that she plans to stay away forever. She never talked about wanting to get into modeling or acting."

Britney snorted. "Is that Alicia who keeps telling everyone Beth's going to be a model? Please. Beth is pretty, but she's not model material. Alicia's deranged."

An image of Beth flashed in my head. She wasn't pretty; she was beautiful. I forced myself to stop thinking about her gorgeous eyes and the shape of her hands, and the scent and feel of her hair. I'd end up falling apart right there in Brit's kitchen if I let myself linger on these thoughts.

Of course Brit had taken the idea of Beth modeling as a personal comparison. Brit had done some modeling at our local mall and sometimes mentioned that she'd considered moving to New York and signing with an agency, but she hadn't wanted to leave Jason and all their future plans behind. We knew she was bullshitting, but we never called her on it.

Whatever. The important thing was neither Britney nor I thought Beth was trying to work a runway somewhere. I crossed it off.

I looked down at my sheet of paper. There was one more

option, and I had to ask. I forced myself to look at Brit, who was flicking through pages in her *Vogue* as if skimming for answers there. "Do you think Beth left because she was having some kind of relationship trouble?" I asked, trying to stay vague.

Britney's head snapped up from the magazine. "What do you mean?" I didn't answer. Her lips twitched. "Everyone knows Beth doesn't do relationships. She hates the mere idea of commitment."

I forced my voice to sound casual. "I don't know; it just seemed like lately she was different. Like maybe she was falling in love."

"Oh, she was in love all right," Brit said. "Head over heels is my guess."

My heart soared. I felt as if I could float away. I had to fight the urge to beg her to go on. If Brit could tell Beth loved me, then what we had was real, and whatever was happening now was some kind of horrible mistake, a misunderstanding that we would sort out.

"Of course, the person Beth's in love with is herself."

My heart crashed to the floor and shattered.

"Look, I know people want to believe she ran off with some secret boyfriend, but I guarantee you, if there was a secret someone it was just another conquest. Beth played with people's hearts because she wanted to know other people could love her. It was never about her loving anyone back."

Her words knocked the air right out of my lungs.

Britney reached over and squeezed my hand. "It says tons about you that you're so worried about Beth. You're a good friend."

I managed a weak smile.

Britney put her finger to her lips to motion for me to be quiet. She peeked out of the kitchen to make sure we were alone and crossed to the fridge. She opened the freezer and pulled out a chocolate bar. "It's my mom's secret stash, and I think we deserve it." She broke off two squares of the fancy Belgian dark chocolate and tossed one to me. "We've got each other. We'll get through this year with or without Beth."

"I miss her." My voice caught. Suddenly I wanted to tell Britney about Beth and me. I wanted to pour out the whole ugly, beautiful mess. How I'd been so sure we'd been falling for each other. How we hid it from everyone, which at first seemed almost exciting, but then started to feel wrong. How I'd lied to Zach and to Brit too, but I'd been so certain that it was going to work, and now I didn't know anything.

"I know you love Beth," Brit said. My heart lurched, but I realized she didn't mean it that way. She hadn't guessed the truth. I wasn't sure if I was glad or sorry. She nibbled her chocolate. "People always love Beth, but she's not what she seems."

This whole conversation was making me sick. "What do you mean?"

"Well, for example, I know you think we both loved you from the start, but the truth is, she didn't want you as our friend," Brit said. "I had to talk her into letting you hang out with us."

I could tell she expected me to be shocked, but I wasn't. Britney often had her own version of the truth, but she wasn't lying about this.

CHAPTER SIX

I'd always been aware of Beth and Brit. You couldn't go to our school and not know who they were. Even though we weren't friends before this year, I knew them better than most because we were on the team together. Membership has its privileges.

I've always been good at sports. My parents have no idea where my athletic ability came from, since they are tied for the Least Coordinated Person in the Universe title. My brother never played sports either, but for some reason, if it involves running and a ball I'm good at it. I'd played soccer since I was little, but as a sophomore, when I transferred to Northside from the private school where I used to go, I tried out for the field hockey team on a lark. Given what happened at my old school, I was ready for a change with everything.

As soon as I held the stick it felt natural and right. I made the team as a varsity starter.

Beth and Britney were the stars of the team. They were hypercompetitive, not just with other teams, but also with each other. Where they went, the rest of the team followed. If either of them ever yelled "good play" at you, it was better than hearing it from Coach. It was like suddenly having the sun come out and focus on you.

They almost didn't seem like real people, more like celebrities. They existed on another level compared to the rest of us mortals. I would smile at them in the halls and they would yell out my name if I made a great play on the field, but I was also pretty sure they didn't care at all who I was, at least off the field, which was why when Britney invited me to go out for frozen yogurt after a game this fall, I was so shocked.

I looked around the locker room, surprised that Brit was talking to me. "You mean, like everyone's going?" I asked.

Brit was only half-dressed. Her bra was fancier than the dress I'd worn to prom last year and probably cost twice as much. "No, not everyone. Just us." She motioned toward Beth, who was sitting on the bench, stuffing her gear into her bag.

Beth looked up and nodded. I noticed some of my team-mates glancing over at us. I could almost see the thought bubbles above their heads: "Why are they asking her?" I was wondering the same thing. If you lined up the three of us, it wouldn't be hard to pick out which one was not like the others.

As proud as I was to be chosen and as much as I wanted to go, I was also almost afraid. It had been two years since I'd left Windsor Prep and left my mess of a life there behind, but I was wary of girls still. Wary of friends. Aside from Zach, I wasn't interested in even risking getting too close to anyone. Besides, Beth and Brit were way out of my league.

Then I saw Melissa, who was sort of the leader of our junior crowd, watching closely. Melissa and I had been butting heads ever since I became our starting sweeper, a position she thought should have been hers. Melissa was popular and the fact that I didn't kiss her ass was also a problem. I could tell she thought it was some kind of huge mistake that Brit was inviting me instead of her.

"Yeah, sure. That would be great," I said. I looked over at Melissa and smiled. Take that.

Brit drove and Beth rode shotgun, with me in the back. Brit had the windows down with the music up, and one hand on the wheel. The way she drove made me fairly certain that these might be my last few minutes on earth, but at that moment, laughing and joking with the two of them, I didn't even care. I wanted to take a picture, or stream it to the world so there would be a record that it was happening, that it was real.

We got our fro-yo and loaded it with toppings, and grabbed a table at the back. Beth gave us an update on her latest hookup. Britney teased her for being a heartbreaker and started singing *a Taylor Swift song in a funny voice. Beth used Brit's spoon to steal a bite of my ice cream out of the dish. Before I even knew what I was doing I reached over, grabbed her hand with her cone in it, and took a huge lick of her ice cream. As soon as I'd done it, I let go of her, horrified, but Beth burst out laughing.*

I remember thinking I would do anything to make her laugh like that again.

After that I was one of them. They pulled me into their jokes and conversations, appeared by my locker and made it clear I should stop by theirs. And when practice was over it was assumed I'd go wherever they were going. I spent less and less time with the people I used to hang with and devoted myself to Beth and Brit. I still made time for Zach, of course, but aside from him and them, no one else mattered. The dynamic duo had become a trio.

I hadn't had a real best friend since eighth grade, when my friend Ella had moved to Minnesota with her parents. Freshman year at my old school there had been all this drama with my other so-called friends and I didn't have any interest in repeating it once I transferred. I hadn't felt like I needed close friends at Northside since I had Zach, but once I had Beth and Brit in my life I realized how much I'd missed having girlfriends.

I knew it wasn't an equal partnership. We all hung out, but of course there were times they still got together without me. I wasn't included in every conversation. I was clearly the apprentice and they were the masters. They decided where we went and when, and what we did when we got there.

It was also clear to me that everyone who had started being extra-nice to me since I became a part of their group was waiting for me to fall. Melissa most of all. She was supersweet to me now, but it was as fake as a bucket of artificial sweetener. Every so often I would catch her watching the three of us, looking like she wanted to feed me to a pack of wolves.

Beth used to joke about how she'd protect me if Melissa so much as tried to steal the basket of goodies I was bringing to Grandma's house. But now Beth had left me alone in the woods.

I stapled the last of the student council packages together, staring down at them as if basic office tasks took 100 percent of my attention. I could feel Britney watching me closely.

"I didn't mean to hurt your feelings," she said. "I just thought you should know. Don't get me wrong, Beth loves you now." She smiled as if she thought this would make it better. "I chose you because I knew you and I were alike. Beth is awesome, but sometimes she's so . . . scattered. It's great to have fun, but sometimes you need the other person to be reliable. I knew you'd be the kind of friend I could count on."

I pushed down the desire to blurt that Beth could count on me too.

"All I wanted to say is don't take Beth, or the fact she only sent you one lame text, personally. That's just how she is. After her brother died, she sort of shut down with other people. She'll laugh with everyone and sleep with everyone, but she doesn't let anyone too close. I'm the only person she'd really reach out to in a time like this." Brit gave me a meaningful glance. "She has trust issues, to say the least."

I stacked the piles of paper, tapping them so they lined up perfectly. The clean edges relaxed me. "You didn't hurt my feelings," I said.

Britney's eyebrows drew together in concern. "I know you have a crush on Beth." Adrenaline flooded my system and I opened my mouth to explain, but she waved off whatever I was about to say. "Don't deny it. Everyone gets a crush on Beth. It's apparently impossible to not fall for her charms." She smiled and shook her head like she found it adorable, but her voice sounded annoyed. Even with Beth gone, I felt like they were still somehow fighting in front of me. "Look, I'm only bringing all this up because I don't want you to feel like Beth singled you out for rejection. She didn't want anyone to know she was leaving, but in fairness did she ever really tell you anything?"

"Actually, I knew she didn't want me to hang out with you guys at first," I said. "She told me that."

Britney's pitying look broadcast that she didn't believe me and thought I was lying to save face.

"I asked her once why you guys picked me. Beth told me she didn't, that it was all you. She said you guys fought about it before you invited me."

Britney blinked. "Oh." She busied herself with organizing the already organized things on the counter, lining up the bowl of cashews with the edge of her magazine. Apparently my OCD was catching. "Well, that doesn't change my point. I wanted you to know that you can count on me. And that I trust you back. Beth let us both down by taking off like this, but we have each other. No matter what happens, you're my Kah-bear."

I smiled at her. "I know." And I knew she meant it.

But I didn't tell her the rest of what Beth told me that day.

I wanted Beth to say she was joking. When I asked, I'd been hoping she would tell me she'd seen something special in me, something that made her want to be near me the way I wanted to be near her. But now I was discovering it wasn't that at all.

"It wasn't anything to do with you," Beth said. She stopped her bike and it slid a bit on the sand that had blown across the cement. We'd been riding on the path that ran along the bay. It was the first time we'd hung out without Brit. Now I almost wished we'd invited her along. Beth pushed her hair out of her eyes. "You seem so . . ."

I held my breath, waiting to hear how she would define me.

"You seemed so good." She saw my expression. "I don't mean like a goody-goody. I mean . . . you're this fresh, honest, nondamaged person. I didn't want you to get sucked into our messed-up dynamic."

"I'm not that innocent," I promised. "I'm actually pretty screwed up."

Beth tilted her chin. "You're screwed up in all the right ways." She turned her handlebars so her front tire tapped mine. "Trust me, I would have been doing you a favor if I'd kept you away from us."

"And now?"

She turned back to the wind and the seagulls. "I guess now I'm hoping you'll be my way out."

Before I could respond, she pushed off and pedaled away. She looked back over her shoulder. "First you have to catch me!"

I watched her for a second and jumped back on my bike. Her hair blew behind her, just slightly beyond my reach.

CHAPTER SEVEN

As I pulled into the school parking lot the next morn-ing, I saw Zach waiting for me with a weird expression on his face.

"I called you like three times in the last fifteen minutes," he said as soon I opened the door.

I hoisted my bag from the passenger seat. "I was driving. You know I can't pick up the phone when I'm in the car. If my parents ever found out, they'd revoke my car privileges and skin me alive to make a giant Kalah puppet that would go on the lecture circuit talking about driver safety."

Zach didn't laugh. He grabbed my elbow and squeezed it gently. "I need to talk to you about something."

He knew. He knew about Beth and me.

It was as if I'd suddenly swallowed a thousand-pound lead weight. I hitched my bag up on my shoulder. "Okay," I managed. "What's up?"

"The police are here." Zach yanked his head to the side and I noticed a cop car parked in the no-parking space right in front of the school. "They're taking Jason to the station to ask him some questions."

"Questions about what?"

"About Beth."

My brain scrambled trying to figure out what he was saying. It was like he was suddenly talking in pig Latin. "What does Jason have to do with Beth?"

"Someone saw Jason and Beth together before she left."

I pushed down a wave of annoyance. "So? They're friends. He's been dating her best friend for two years."

Zach gave me a look. "Not together like hanging out. Together like, you know, *together*."

My skin prickled. "Wait. Someone is saying Beth and Jason were screwing around?"

Zach flushed. There were times when he acted like he was in the 1800s and some things could not be said aloud in case we all got a case of the vapors. "Some freshman saw them out in Lighthouse Park having a fight. Beth was crying and yanked away from him, but Jason pulled her back and then they were kissing. Full-on making out. Then they got into Jason's car and took off. This was on Friday afternoon."

"No way." But my mind flashed an image of Beth bending

back as Jason kissed her, his hands winding into her hair, her mouth tasting like cinnamon gum. I started tapping my foot in rapid beats to stop my heart from racing. I stopped when I saw Zach glance down.

We watched as Jason walked out of the school with Officer Siegel, our official school liaison officer. She gave the yearly talk on how we should all avoid drugs, and let her know if we knew anyone was planning to go all video game crazed and shoot the school up. Every so often she wandered the halls like a sheriff in an old Western movie, minus the white hat and jangling spurs.

Jason wasn't wearing handcuffs, but he looked scared. His shoulders were up around his ears. He saw me standing in the parking lot and he stopped. Officer Siegel followed his gaze. I had an urge to drop to the ground behind my car so she wouldn't see me. I didn't want to be connected to any of this. She took Jason's elbow and guided him toward her car. People were standing by the front door, staring and whispering.

The reality of what was happening hit me like a door being slammed in my face. *God, Brit must be freaking out.* "They can't really think he did something to Beth, can they?" I watched the cop car pull out of the lot, the tires grumbling through the gravel. "Beth texted me. She's fine. She just wanted to get away. Why are the cops involved?"

Zach shrugged. "He was the last person to see Beth *and* they were fighting. I think it makes people wonder if their fight had something to do with her leaving. Or maybe the cops know something about Beth that we don't."

My brain screeched to a hard stop. "No." Panic nibbled on the edge of my thoughts. It's my nature to assume the worst, but she had to have taken off on her own. She'd used her ATM card. She'd talked to Britney. She'd texted me. She had to be okay.

I wanted to believe she'd come back when she was ready. But if the cops were questioning Jason . . .

I swallowed hard. I felt like I might throw up.

Zach rubbed my back in slow circles. His hand was the only thing keeping me from flying apart in a million jagged pieces. "I don't think anyone believes Jason did anything bad to Beth. Her parents just want some answers."

I pulled on my sleeves so they covered my hands. Zach kept talking. "Maybe they were fighting about if they should tell Britney about the two of them. Maybe Beth wanted to and he didn't, or the other way around." Zach tugged me closer. "I'd run off before I'd tell Brit I was messing around with her boyfriend."

"Beth was not *messing around* with Jason," I snapped. "Why is everyone believing some stupid freshman?" But even as I said it, I realized how much it would explain. Beth and Brit had been on edge for weeks. Beth had always kept me at arm's length, never pushing me to drop Zach. And if Brit suspected anything at all, that explained her bitterness when we'd talked yesterday, and why she'd asked Jason on

Monday if he'd seen or heard from Beth. And more than all of that, it explained why Beth hadn't bothered to answer my calls.

I was falling for her, and she was fucking Jason. Beautiful.

I wanted to believe that what Beth and I had was real. But if she felt what I felt, or anything even close, there was no way she'd be hooking up with someone else.

Except, who was I to talk? How could I be mad at her when I'd done the same thing? My relationship with Zach was proof that it was possible. Confusing, but possible.

I should have told her that I love her and made her tell me what she felt, whether or not it was the answer I wanted to hear. I'd thought I could float in the middle, not committing to her, not letting go of Zach. I'd thought I could keep my heart safe until I knew what I wanted, but now I was stuck in this horrible place, wondering where I stood.

"I didn't mean anything against Beth," Zach said. He tucked my hair behind my ear. "All I meant is it's possible Beth and Jason fell for each other. You can't always control who you fall in love with. They wouldn't have set out to hurt Britney. It might have just happened."

I closed my eyes. Zach had no idea. I doubted he'd be as understanding if I told him the reason I wanted to insist Beth and Jason weren't hooking up was because she and I were. He wouldn't be so likely to pontificate about not being able to control who you fall for then.

The bell rang. Zach hugged me and I held on tight. He felt like the one thing that still made sense in my life. Something I could count on. I'd been so stupid to risk everything with him.

"Hey." Zach pulled back so he could see my face. I didn't want to look at him. I just wanted to burrow into his chest. "I'm sorry about all of this." He kissed me gently. "I wanted to tell you before you heard it from someone else. I know everything about this sucks for you." He took my bag and steered me inside. "I'm guessing everyone's going to be talking about it."

I wished I could run back to my car and drive home. I wanted to be in my room with the door locked and the blinds down. I felt as if there was too much space around me. I wanted to make the world small and safe and in my control. My skin felt clammy and I couldn't get a deep breath.

"You okay?" Zach's face was too close to mine.

"Not really." I tapped my index finger to my thumb in beats of six until I started to feel my breath even out. I knew I shouldn't give in to the tapping. I hadn't seen a therapist in two years, but I hadn't forgotten what she'd told me: giving in to the compulsions only makes them worse. That I needed to let the anxiety wash over me and remind myself that I'd be fine. Except it didn't feel like the anxiety would wash over me; it felt like it would wash me away.

Zach stopped in front of my locker. "Look, maybe now that the truth is out Beth will come home."

One of the things that I love about Zach is that he always believes in the bright side of things. He's like a bundle of silver linings tied up with a rainbow, carried by cute puppies riding on unicorns. "You're going to be late for class," I told him.

He curled his lip and spoke in one of his character voices. "Darling, you're worth it. Of all the dames and all the gin joints, I'm glad you walked into mine."

"What's happening to your lip?" I asked. It sort of looked like his mouth had epilepsy.

"It's my Bogart impression. *Casablanca.* I'm still working on it." He bent low and offered me his arm. "May I escort you to class?" He saw me hesitate. "C'mon. It's not going to be that bad."

I wanted to believe him. But maybe it was going to be worse.

CHAPTER EIGHT

As soon as my first class was over I bolted to Britney's locker. I had to find her. Not only because I was the best friend she had left, and she must need me, but also because I wanted to see her reaction to everything. If Brit called bullshit, then there was a chance none of it was true. And if it was true, she was going to be devastated. We'd either beat the rumors back together or get each other through this betrayal.

As I wove my way down the halls I could hear people buzzing about the news. Their voices chased me like a hive of angry bees. I wanted to stuff my fingers into my ears so I couldn't hear anything.

I rounded the corner, but Britney wasn't there. I

clenched my teeth together and forced myself to nod to people as they walked past, pretending everything was fine. I paced back and forth in front of her locker. The bell rang. I waited another few seconds, even though I knew she wouldn't show.

I slipped into World History class. Our teacher, Mr. Brandt, raised his eyebrow at me as I dropped into my seat. Maybe he could see I was upset, because he mercifully didn't say anything or ask me for a note. He just continued talking about the English Reformation.

Melissa turned to look at me, her eyes wide with questions. I stared at her blankly until she turned back around. From the seat behind me, Zach slid his foot forward so it was next to mine. His touch made my heart slow slightly. I focused on my breathing, feeling my chest rise and lower. I'd catch Brit later. If I was freaking out, she must be nearly apoplectic, whether the rumors were true or not. Even if she believed Jason was innocent, I knew she'd be furious about the gossip. She did not tolerate dents in her carefully controlled image. Even if outwardly she was rolling her eyes at the ridiculousness of the claim, she had probably already figured out a plan to get the rumor-starting freshman's head on a pole.

Britney and Jason had been together almost two years. They were more than just the future prom king and queen, more than a high school match of two pretty, popular people.

Brit really loved him. She was the type to be over-the-top with affection. She was always hugging people and talking about how she loved this or that, but it was different with Jason. You could see it in her eyes. The way she leaned into him, as if she knew he would hold her. Brit had their whole lives planned out, and it always seemed like Jason wanted to be with her forever too. They were solid. They were real.

My chest hurt, like there was a deep bruise. I raised my hand. "Can I have a hall pass?" Mr. Brandt looked at me. "Please. I'm not feeling well." I swallowed hard.

Mr. Brandt tore a pass off his pad and scribbled his name at the bottom before handing it over. I could feel Zach and Melissa and everyone else's eyes following me as I ducked out of the room. Now Melissa would have something new to chatter about with her friends. And Zach would have one more reason to worry.

Britney had AP Physics this period. I slipped down the hall and walked slowly past the lab and peeked in the narrow window in the door. My adrenaline spiked when I saw Brit. In that instant I realized part of me was afraid that she might have taken off too.

I backed up and leaned against the wall in relief. She was there. It would be okay. I had no idea how she would fix things, but the one thing I knew about Brit was that if something wasn't going the way she thought it should, she did something about it.

I peeked back in the window and tried to catch her attention, but her gaze never moved. She looked almost like a mannequin. She sat totally still in her seat, her hands in her lap as she stared blankly ahead.

The guy next to her noticed me. I pointed at Brit. He looked at her, and then back at me. I wanted to fling open the door and scream at him not to be so stupid. After a beat he leaned over and tapped Brit and she turned slowly to face him, like she was moving through mud. He jutted his chin over to the door and Britney finally saw me.

I could tell, even at this distance, that her jaw was clenched. She raised her hand and I heard her muffled voice asking for a pass. I moved back from the door so the teacher wouldn't see me when Brit opened it.

Brit came out and grabbed me by the wrist. She was walking like the blood in her veins had turned to brittle glass. I opened my mouth, but she cut me off before I said a word.

"Not here," she said.

After the bathroom door swung shut behind us, Brit pushed on the stall doors to make sure we were alone, and sank onto the heater that ran along the wall.

My heart was breaking all over again to see her like this.

Britney made a small sound, almost like a whimper. "Everything is spinning out of control," she said softly.

I looked down and noticed her hands were shaking. I touched her shoulder. "It's going to be okay," I said.

"You have no idea." She stared down at her lap, shaking her head as if I were arguing with her.

"I'm here for you. Whatever you need." I wanted to tell her that Beth had betrayed me too, but I couldn't. Brit had lost her best friend and her boyfriend in an instant. That trumped my loss. I didn't want her to think I was competing with her about who had it worse.

Brit's head snapped up. Her eyes looked almost crazed. "I—" Before she could say more, the bathroom door swung open and Melissa came in. The air seemed to go out of Britney.

"Sorry to bust in on you guys. Is everything all right?" Melissa was all innocence, but I didn't believe it for a second. "I came to make sure you were okay. You left class in such a rush. I told Mr. Brandt I thought you might be really sick."

"I'm fine." I spit out the words and willed Melissa to leave.

Brit ignored her completely. "I've got to get back to class." She gave me a quick hug. "I really appreciate you coming to find me. We'll talk later, okay?"

She didn't wait for me to answer and instead slipped out of the bathroom, walking past Melissa without a second look.

"Wow. I heard about Beth and Jason, but I didn't want to believe it," Melissa said. I wanted to smack her.

"Don't say another word." I leaned into her face. "Don't

act like you care. You have no idea what you're talking about, so keep your fucking mouth shut."

Melissa backed up quickly, hitting one of the sinks. I was glad I'd gotten that smug look off her face. I pushed past her. I didn't even have it in me to cry.

CHAPTER NINE

I spent two periods lying on the cot in the nurse's office staring up at the ceiling. It felt like the world was spinning too fast and I couldn't keep my balance. At lunch the nurse declared that since I wasn't running a fever maybe I should try to make it through the rest of the day. I went down to the cafeteria, but when I didn't see Britney, I ducked back out. I stood in the hallway, uncertain where I should go. I needed something to do or I might snap.

I'd promised Zach I would make a banner for the show his improv-slash–a cappella group, the Fleshtones, was planning. When Beth disappeared, Zach had told me not to worry about making it, but I was already winning the Worst Girlfriend of the Year award. I could at least keep one of the promises I'd made to him and create a simple sign.

I knocked on the art room door. Ms. Schneider let me in and left me alone while she went to the teacher's lounge for her own lunch. The Fleshtones wanted something they could hang over the doorway to the cafeteria where everyone would see it. I'd offered to design one in Photoshop and print it off, but I felt like getting my hands dirty. I knew they'd be excited to get a giant retro hand-painted banner instead.

I pulled a long sheet of paper from the roll and draped it over the table that I'd already covered with newspaper. I used a wooden yardstick to block in the words for the banner so everything would be centered and neat. This was a thousand times better than sitting in the lunchroom where everyone could see me.

I pulled some poster paints out of the cabinet. The chalky smell was relaxing. I wasn't a great artist, but if I drew something you could tell what it was supposed to be. In junior high I'd wanted to be a comic book artist. I drew my own series starring the Amazing Amanda: part woman, part jungle cat. I felt the world needed some female super-heroes who had more going for them than giant breasts. I'd created a whole backstory that was pretty much a rip-off of the X-Men. I was into mutants at the time, maybe because everyone in junior high kinda feels like one.

Once I got into sports I spent less time making art, but I didn't give it up altogether. A few months ago I'd done a sketch for Beth, a small Alice in Wonderland dwarfed by a giant Cheshire cat. It hadn't been much more than a doodle, but Beth loved it. She'd taped it up in her locker. I used to get a rush every time I saw it hanging there. For all I knew, it still was. Why would she bother taking it with her? It was clear I wasn't nearly as important to her as I'd thought I'd been.

I pushed thoughts of Beth out of my head. I sketched three cartoon faces leaning in toward an old-fashioned radio microphone on the right-hand side of the banner. It looked pretty great.

I painted in the letters I'd written across the top: See the Fleshtones LIVE. I dipped the brush in a bright red to use on the time and date below, when a door slammed open in the hall and I dropped the brush, splattering the banner with paint.

It was ruined. I closed my eyes. There went the last forty minutes of my life, wasted.

"Don't you freaking touch me!" someone yelled in the hall.

I felt my stomach drop. It was Brit. I'd know that voice anywhere. I took a step forward and saw her and Jason reflected in the big mirror on the opposite wall.

"I knew it." Brit crossed her arms. "I knew something was going on, but I had no idea it had gone that far. And with *her!*"

"It's not what you think. People have it all wrong. Listen, I'm an idiot," Jason said.

"It's more than that. You made an idiot out of me. All day long, people staring, feeling sorry for me. Thinking they know what it's like to be me. Poor, pathetic Brit. How could she not have known? It's humiliating. Do you have any idea what I'd do for you? What I've *done*?" Britney's voice was high and shrill.

"I wanted to talk to you, to tell you, but I didn't know how."

His words were like a kick to the gut. There was no way to protect myself from the blow. He was confessing.

I wanted to run, but I couldn't. The door to the art room was wide open. I couldn't leave without going right past them. I was stuck.

"What were you going to tell me? That I was an idiot for thinking that you loved me?" Britney's face was red. Jason looked shell-shocked. "Were you going to wait until you got to Syracuse? Or was your plan to keep me in the dark forever?"

"I only applied to Syracuse because you're going to Cornell. I didn't even send them an acceptance yet." Jason ran his hands over his head. "That was your dream that we'd be close next year, not mine. But you didn't ask me what I wanted."

Britney shoved him and he hit the wall. "Don't you dare make this my fault."

Jason held up his arms in surrender. "I'm not saying it's your fault. I'm the jerk here. I should have talked to you when my feelings changed. It was already happening, way before there was anyone else. I didn't want to admit it. I didn't want you to be upset. Things are complicated, but it's not what you think." He took a step forward. "I'm a coward, okay? And no matter what, I still care about you. I never wanted to hurt you, Brit."

Britney slapped him hard across the face, and both Jason and I gasped at the same time.

"Don't say that. Don't stand there saying that like you *pity* me. Like it's some second-place consolation prize for the girl who didn't win. I always win. And you have no idea what you're up against. Did you think I was going to let you and Beth just ride off into the sunset? It's not happening. Do you get it?"

"Listen—"

"We were supposed to be together forever. There is no happy-ever-after for you without me. Beth is not coming back for you." Britney stamped her foot. She looked ready to throw herself down on the ground and have a full-on tantrum. I almost wanted her to, for both of us. I was too numb to scream.

Jason shook his head slightly. "Baby, this is not about Beth. I don't know where she is, I swear. Our problems have nothing to do with her. Please just hear what I'm trying to tell you. I knew you wouldn't be reasonable about—"

"*I* decide what's reasonable," Brit interrupted, jabbing Jason in the chest. "*I'm* the one who breaks up with people.

People don't break up with me."

"You can break up with me if you want," Jason said, almost hopefully.

Britney looked defeated, like all the fight had leaked out of her. "It's too late. I could have fixed it, but now I can't. Everyone knows what happened. They know you dumped me. That you chose her. I wasn't good enough."

I wanted to race out of the room and throw my arms around my friend to protect her from these feelings, and from having to listen to any more of his excuses.

"That's not it at all. It wasn't about you." Jason touched her arm. "Brit, you're amazing."

She yanked her arm away. Her mascara was streaking in black lines under her eyes. I realized I was holding my breath. I'd never seen Britney cry like this before, a full-on ugly cry. "Don't be an idiot. It was always about me."

"Brit—"

"Forget it. You had your chance. There's no making this better. It's all gone to shit, and it's all your fault." Brit spun around and took off down the hall. Jason buried his head in his hands.

I was shaking with anger. I wanted to go out into the hall and punch him. I wanted to kick him so hard his nuts came out his nose. I wanted to hurt him for hurting Britney, for hurting me, for stealing Beth.

Maybe I had no right to, but I still felt like Beth belonged to me.

CHAPTER TEN

As soon as Jason left the hall I scooped up the paints, shoved them back in the cupboard, and dumped the brushes in the sink to soak. Ms. Schneider was going to be pissed that I hadn't cleaned up properly, but this was an emergency.

I jogged down the hall and spotted Chester up on a ladder changing a lightbulb in front of the office. Her eyes popped when she saw me, almost like a cartoon character.

"Lordy, are you okay?" Her face was flooded with concern.

For a split second I wondered how she knew my life was falling apart, until I glanced down. I looked like an extra from the movie *Carrie*. I had red paint splattered all over my shirt, and my hands were caked with it.

"Paint," I explained. "I need to find Britney. Did you see her go by?"

Chester nodded. "Yep. She didn't look too good either. I offered her a cookie. I have cookies in my lunch. Chocolate chip."

I fought the urge to shake the ladder. "Where did she go?"

Chester seemed disappointed I wasn't interested in her cookies either. "She left."

I didn't wait another second, just bolted out the front door. I half expected someone to stop me.

My eyes raked over the rows of cars in the student lot until I spotted Brit's champagne-colored Jeep Cherokee still parked in the front. I could see her hunched over, crying, inside.

I ran up and tapped on the passenger window. Britney hit the automatic locks and I climbed inside. It felt weird to sit in the front. This was where Beth sat. I tried to avoid touching anything, paranoid I'd leave a smear of paint on the butter-soft leather. Britney was crying hard, her sobs catching in her throat as she tried to get her breath. I reached for the tissues in the side door and passed them over to her.

"I'm so sorry," I said.

We sat in silence while she pulled herself together. "Did you know? Did Beth tell you? Was everyone laughing about it? About me?"

"No. I swear to god." I felt a flutter of panic that she wouldn't believe me.

Brit stared at my eyes like she was trying to see into my soul. Finally she leaned back in her seat and rubbed her temples.

"I knew," she said. "Or at least, on some level, I suspected. But I never really thought it could be true."

I had no idea what to say.

"Beth was my best friend." She sounded exhausted.

"Don't say it like that. Like it's past tense and you guys will never be friends again. What she did was horrid, but you don't throw away a friend you've had since elementary school for a guy. Even Jason."

Brit looked at me like I was insane. "Oh, it's past tense all right. There's no way we're ever going to be friends again."

"Let's find her. Go to her and sit down and demand to hear the truth so you guys can hash this out." I was mad at Beth, and sick about what she'd done, but I still wanted to see her. I could be the peacemaker between the two of them. I'd done it before and I was sure I could do it again. I could somehow fix this mess.

Brit gripped the steering wheel like she wanted to choke it. She looked at me. "Would you actually hang out with her? After she did this to me?"

I wanted to say no. I wanted to be the kind of person who stood up for myself and for my friends, who would say that if Beth treated me or Brit this badly then I didn't need her in my life. But my gut told me the truth. I wanted to see her again, and if she made even a mild apology for leaving me out in the cold, I would probably take her back. I would do almost anything for one more chance with her. I wasn't proud of that fact, but I had to at least be honest with myself. I couldn't be that honest with Britney. "Let's talk to her and hear what she has to say."

"She's got nothing to say." Brit leaned her head back. "The truth is even if I wanted to go and hash it out with her, I couldn't. I don't know where she is."

My heart sank. "I thought—"

Brit shrugged. "I heard from her at first. Then she dropped off the planet when I confronted her straight-out about Jason."

"Oh." I felt deflated. It had been stupid to get excited about the idea of seeing her, even for a second.

Brit sighed. "Beth's got it pretty good." She gestured to the school. "She's left all this behind. Started over in a new place where no one knows her. It's all a big adventure. New people. New friends. She's probably going to get a job and her own apartment. No parents nagging her. No tests. No expectations on her all the time."

"But she's all alone," I said.

"At least if you're alone, no one screws you over. It sounds better than my life." Brit sniffed. She looked ready to cry again.

"You want to go back to your place? Maybe get some movies? Let's get out of here." My parents would be livid that I'd cut school, but I'd deal with that problem later.

Brit didn't answer and for a second I wondered if I'd even made the suggestion out loud. "No. Thanks, though. I want to be alone for a bit." She reached over and squeezed my hand. "I'm lucky I have you as a friend. I won't forget that."

"I don't think it's good for you to be by yourself right now," I said.

Brit sighed. "Maybe not, but that's what I want."

It was a dismissal. I opened the car door and slid out. "Are you sure?"

She was crying again. No loud sobs this time, just tears running down her face.

"Take care, Kah-bear."

I watched her SUV pull out of the parking lot and knew that things would never be the same.

CHAPTER ELEVEN

I had the treadmill in the basement cranked up high.
Maybe if it went fast enough I could run away from everything happening in my life.

The rumor mill had taken off as the afternoon went on. Beth disappearing was one thing, but now there was sex and scandal mixed in. People were practically giddy with the idea that Beth had betrayed Brit. Stories about Jason and Beth were exploding like fireworks, each one flashier than the last.

Some of them had to be lies. There was one report that Jason and Beth had been seen up at the sand dunes making out on the last night of spring break. I knew without any doubt that one wasn't true because I'd been with Beth that night. Beth was pretty amazing, but even she couldn't be in two places at once.

There were others that I couldn't prove were false, but they didn't feel right to me, like shoes that don't quite fit. Something about the stories was off. Or maybe I just still wanted to believe that Jason and Beth weren't the star-crossed lovers everyone kept trying to make them out to be.

I pressed the speed button up another notch. My breath was ragged from my pace, but I kept pushing myself, liking the sharp sting as my feet slammed down on the belt. I had my music up so loud I didn't hear my mom calling my name. When she touched the back of my shoulder I jumped and missed a step. I started to stumble, but my mom hit the emergency button that shut off the belt before I fell. I pulled the buds out of my ears, panting.

Mom held up the phone. "Call for you." Her mouth pressed into a thin line. I started to get that uneasy feeling that I was in trouble. She pressed the phone into my hand.

"Hello?"

"Kalah? This is Dr. Ryerson. Have you seen Britney?" Her voice was frayed. I could feel the waves of panic coming through the receiver. "Have you talked to her since school?"

"Um, no." My mom was staring at me while I talked. She still had on her pharmacist lab coat. I turned so I couldn't see her looking at me.

"Did something happen at school today? Something to upset Britney?" Dr. Ryerson asked.

"I'm not sure. . . ." I hedged. My mom grabbed my hand and that's when I realized that I was tapping my fingers on the treadmill. My skin felt itchy from the inside, like I was breaking into hives.

If Brit hadn't told her mom about Jason and Beth, I wasn't sure that I should. Brit would be pissed if she knew I was talking about her. I couldn't betray her—I was the last person left she could count on. She trusted me. I bit down on my lip.

"Listen to me. Britney's missing." Dr. Ryerson's voice went up sharply.

My heart jerked in my chest.

Brit's dad got on the phone. "Kalah, is it? It's Dr. Matson. It's very important, do you have any idea where Britney might have gone?"

"No," I said honestly. My mom was still holding tight to my hand to keep me from tapping. I wanted to explain to her that I had to tap. That stopping meant something bad could happen, that I was barely holding the universe together.

"But you know something," he said.

Both of Britney's parents are psychiatrists. They also appeared to be at least part psychic—that, or playing around in other people's brains all day made them sniff a lie out before it was past your lips.

"Britney and Jason had a fight," I admitted.

Dr. Matson let out a whoosh of air. "What about?"

My throat squeezed shut, as if Britney was pinching my

airway closed to keep me from saying anything.

I felt like Alice in the illustration from Beth's book, when she drank from a bottle labeled *Drink Me* and shrank down, and everything suddenly towered over her.

"Kalah. What was the fight about?" Brit's dad demanded. Something in his voice scared me into telling him.

"They're breaking up," I said. "Jason cheated on her. Brit was devastated and really mad. She left school early, right after lunchtime. I don't know where she was going. I offered to go with her, but she just wanted some time to think." The words flew out of me. My mom patted my back like I was a baby spitting up and she wanted me to be sure to get it all out.

"If you hear anything from her, if she calls or texts you or stops by, you need to call us right away, do you understand?" His voice was harsh.

I nodded before I realized he couldn't see me. "Okay," I whispered. I opened my mouth to say I was sorry, but he'd already hung up. I stared at the phone as if I expected it to spring to life and do something, but it was just a phone. I turned to my mom. "Britney didn't come home for dinner. Her parents are freaking out."

"I know. They're concerned about her."

I waited for her to tell me that everything was going to be okay, but she didn't. "I should take a shower," I mumbled. The air on my sweaty skin gave me shivers.

"I wonder if you should talk to Dr. Sherman." Mom

tried to sound casual, but I knew there was nothing casual about the suggestion.

"I don't need to see anyone," I said. I clenched my hands to make sure they wouldn't start fluttering around. I didn't need therapy. I needed my friends to come back.

"You've got a lot on your plate these days," Mom said. "It's normal to find it upsetting."

"I'm fine," I insisted. I could tell she was trying to decide if she wanted to push it. "All right, I'm not fine, but I'm okay. I'm dealing."

"I wish I could save you from feeling anxious," Mom said. I knew she felt guilty. There's a genetic component to OCD anxiety, and even though I didn't have it nearly as bad as my grandma, I could tell my mom still felt responsible. Genetics can be a real bitch. Personally, I was more upset that I'd gotten my dad's giant flipper feet, but saying so probably wouldn't help.

"I think being seventeen means I have to be anxious. It's part of the job description," I said, trying to make things lighter.

Mom didn't smile. "Maybe all this is a good reminder that it's important to spend time with your other friends. Not just being all wrapped up in Britney and Beth."

My jaw clenched. "I like Beth and Brit." I didn't mention that my "other friends" weren't real friends at all, just people I hung out with. If I told her that, she'd be even more convinced I needed some kind of help.

Mom held up her hands. "I like them too, but they're intense."

"You don't even know them," I protested.

"It isn't that I don't like them . . ."

"But?" I crossed my arms, creating a barrier between us.

"There are some people who collect more than their fair share of trouble. I'm not saying it's their fault, but they do. It's my job as your mom to want to keep you out of it."

Too late. When it came to Beth and Brit, I was already in deep.

Beth stole a bottle of her dad's bourbon and we took it out to Lighthouse Park.

"Will you get in trouble for taking his booze?" I grabbed a few more pieces of driftwood and stuffed them in the fire pit. I rubbed my hands on my jeans trying to get them warm, but my fingers felt stiff and clumsy from the cold.

Beth had her turtleneck sweater pulled up over her chin. "This?" She waved the bottle. "My dad goes through so much he hardly knows what he has anymore. He won't miss it."

I touched the match to the dry beach grass under the sticks and blew on it. I tried to buffer the small fire from the wind with my body. I didn't want to fail after I'd bragged I could do it.

"Look at you—you're a regular Girl Scout."

I couldn't tell if Beth was impressed or making fun of me, but either way, the attention made me glow. "A few years ago my dad got it in his head that we were going to become campers,"

I said. "We bought all the gear and took a daylong class on how to forage, build a shelter, escape from bears, that kind of thing." The fire started to grow and I added some larger sticks. My fingers loosened up in the heat.

"So, do you guys go camping every summer?" Beth held her hands out to warm them.

"Nope. We only made it three days before my brother quit and my parents remembered that they're basically allergic to everything that lives outdoors." I shrugged and pointed at the now roaring campfire. "At least I got some use out of those classes."

Beth passed me the bottle after taking a swig. "Handy skill to have. I'm totally going to keep you around if there's a zombie apocalypse."

I felt absurdly proud. I didn't know what it said about me that I wanted a brain-eating undead end-of-the-world event to happen just so Beth could find me useful and want me around.

Spending time with Beth was random. There never seemed to be any sort of plan; she would just show up at my house and ask if I wanted to go somewhere. If I invited her to do something, she would either say she was busy or invite Britney to join us. Time with her alone was on her terms or not at all.

I took a sip of the bourbon and tried not to spit it right back out. It was like liquid smoke, burning as it went down. I'd had beer at a few parties, but bourbon was so different it didn't seem possible that they could both be in the alcohol family.

"Thanks for coming with me. I had to get out of the house. My mom is in a fighting mood." Beth tossed a stick in the blaze.

I could tell it was too damp to burn well, but didn't stop her.

"Did you guys always have trouble getting along?"

"No. Yes." She laughed. "How's that for exact? We never got along as well as I did with my dad. I was a daddy's girl. My brother was a total momma's boy. I think she resents me because she lost her half of the deal."

The smoke from the fire was making my eyes water. I wanted to say something that would make it better, but I didn't have any idea what that would be.

"I know she wishes I'd been the one to die instead of Lucas."

Whatever I'd been about to say turned to ash in my mouth. My heart winced.

"I can't blame her. You never met Lucas, but he was an amazing kid. He had this giggle that made you laugh, even at his stupid knock-knock jokes. And he was mischievous but insanely cuddly. The thing is that he died when he was really young, right? So he never had a chance to screw up. He never snuck out of the house or brought home a C in math. He never stole liquor from my parents or put a dent in the car. He's frozen at sort of this perfect stage, whereas I just keep on disappointing my parents over and over. I don't think I'm that bad, but I'll never be as good as he was, or as good as she imagines he would have been. We're sorta doomed."

I wanted to reach over and hug Beth, fold her into my arms and keep her safe from anyone trying to hurt her. I shifted on the log, trying to figure out if it would be okay or just weird. She wasn't the superhuggy kind of friend like

Brit. Beth hardly ever touched me.

"Things are so bad I told my mom I thought our family should see someone. She told me there wasn't anything wrong with her."

"I saw a psychiatrist for a while," I said. The bourbon was burning a hole in the center of my chest. It was like the Iron Man power pack. I took another sip to buy some time. I didn't know why I'd admitted that.

Beth nudged me with her elbow. "You don't have to look like you're confessing to murder. It's no big deal."

"I get anxious," I explained, just in case she was imagining something worse. Or something less. The tip of my shoe made a pattern in the sand. "I worry about stuff. Like if someone is late, I start thinking about how they might have been in an accident, and then I picture it. How the car would look with all the glass broken and the air bag slowly deflating. And I start thinking about that person being hurt or even dead. I know it's stupid because the person is only a few minutes late and now I'm all worked up. So I started doing stuff to feel better."

"What kind of stuff?"

I flushed, and I hoped Beth couldn't see how embarrassed I was. "Weird stuff. Like tapping a set number of times, or needing things in my room to be arranged a certain way or else it feels like I'm putting people at risk. I have to do it right or something bad will happen."

"Wow."

"Yeah. I don't do it anymore." I realized I was holding a stick so tightly that it was going to break. I forced myself to loosen my grip and be honest. "I still do it sometimes if I'm really stressed, but at least now I know I'm doing it. Knowing you're crazy is half the battle, right?"

"You're not crazy. Well, no crazier than the rest of us." Beth took the bottle from me and took a drink. "We've already established I'm screwed up. And Brit's whole family is seriously fucked."

"I guess we're all messed up a bit," I said.

"All the best people are."

I took the bottle back and took another drink so I'd have something to distract me from wanting to touch her.

Beth leaned toward me. "You've got sand on you." She ran the pad of her thumb along my lip. I felt grains of sand slide off under her touch. It felt like a match being lit. My breath was coming faster. Beth leaned in closer, pausing just a few inches from my face. "Okay?" she asked, her voice soft.

I nodded, not entirely sure what she was asking. Not knowing what I wanted to happen, or maybe knowing, but unwilling to admit it.

Beth's mouth touched mine. Her lips soft and then pressing. She cupped her hand behind my head, her fingers weaving into my hair. The sound of waves hitting the beach thumped like a heartbeat, filling me, connecting us.

She pulled back and let out a long breath. "I shouldn't have done that."

My heart was in overdrive. "I'm glad you did."

She took the bottle back from me and took a sip. "Well, this is going to complicate things."

"I like complicated things," I said, sounding braver and surer than I felt. I had no idea what was happening, I just knew I wanted her to kiss me like that again.

She tapped the bottle to her forehead in a salute. "Then we'll just have to be careful. Brit. Zach. Et cetera. How many times do I have to do this to keep us safe?" she teased.

"Six times."

Beth beamed. "Six is my favorite number! Why, sometimes I've believed as many as six impossible things before breakfast," she crowed.

The bourbon was making my lips tingle. If I started laughing I wouldn't be able to stop. "What?"

Beth rolled her eyes. "How do you not know that? It's from Alice in Wonderland."

"I never read it."

"Serious?" Beth leaned back in shock and fell off the log, her legs in the air. I pulled her back up, giggling. I glanced down at our hands, our fingers laced together. "It's my favorite book of all time."

Beth tapped her head with the bottle six times. "There, now we're good!"

I nodded. Technically, since she'd done it once before, that was seven times. Not that it mattered. As she leaned in to kiss me I tasted the sand and bourbon on her lips, and realized I'd never felt safer.

CHAPTER TWELVE

As soon as I came downstairs the next morning, I sensed something was wrong. The tension in the air was like a fog filling up the house. I paused in the doorway of the kitchen. My parents stopped their whispering. I stepped forward and reached for the paper on the counter between them.

There was a giant photo of Brit splashed across the front page. It was her senior photo, the one that looked like it belonged in a modeling portfolio. My dad took the paper out of my hands before I could read it. Mom picked up her tea mug and put it back down without taking a drink.

"We need to talk with you," my dad said.

"Brit didn't come home last night," I said, guessing what

he was going to say. If she had, the paper wouldn't have bothered to run her photo. I was worried about her, but I wanted to ask why Britney being gone for a few hours merited a front-page story. Beth had been gone six days and no one had even put up a flyer.

"They found a note," Dad said.

"Did it say where she was going?" If she'd figured out where Beth was and had gone to confront her, I wanted to go there too.

"Honey, I'm so sorry, but it was a suicide note."

I blinked, trying to make sense of what Mom had said. It felt like someone had hit me in the head with a bat. My ears had a strange ringing sound to them.

"Brit would never kill herself." I hoped by saying it aloud I could make it true. I knew Brit had been upset yesterday, but had she been *that* upset?

I pictured how distressed she had looked in the car and tried to remember exactly what she'd said. Had she been hinting, asking for help, and I'd been so consumed about Beth that I'd missed it?

I sat down hard on a kitchen stool. She'd tried to tell me and I hadn't heard it. I swallowed hard to keep the vomit down.

"They found her car out at Lighthouse Park. She left her purse and phone on the beach with the note," my dad explained. "The police found it last night."

"We saw that in a movie." My mind spun around trying to remember what it had been called. We used to have these movie marathons in Brit's basement, one film blurring into another. Popcorn and diet soda and Beth's feet in my lap. "The guy left all his stuff and just walked out into the water." The music had swelled as he kept moving forward until the water went over his head. "Brit loves that kind of drama. But you can't drown that way, can you? She's probably just trying to make a point about how much Jason hurt her. She wants to scare him."

"Sweetheart, she never came back for her car or her things. Her note was clear about her intentions." Dad squeezed my hand. "I know you wish this weren't true, and I wish it too, but the facts tell us different. The police believe Britney killed herself by jumping from the Point."

I waited for both of them to yell they were joking even though I knew they would never make a joke out of something like this. I caught sight of the headline under Britney's picture in the paper. LOCAL TEEN PRESUMED DEAD. It came to me in a flash that when Beth heard this news she would rush back immediately. I felt sick and ashamed for even having had the thought. My eyes were burning.

"We're both going to be here for you, whatever you need. I'm going to call into work and stay home with you today," Mom said. She put her arm around me and squeezed.

"They canceled school?" Once I said it I realized how

stupid that sounded. Britney might be the unofficial queen of the senior class, but they wouldn't close school down just because she was gone.

"I thought you might need some time," Mom explained. "I know this is a shock."

"No. I want to go to classes. I want to see Zach." I wanted things to be like they had been, even if not a single thing felt familiar anymore. Maybe if I acted normal this would all magically turn out to be some kind of giant mistake.

My parents exchanged glances. My mom looked unhappy with my plan.

"Sometimes distraction can be the best thing," my dad said, taking my side. "And the school is bringing in an additional counselor too, in case kids want to talk."

"I don't know. . . ." Mom's earrings swayed as she shook her head.

"I think we can trust Kalah to know what's best for her," Dad said. "If she wants to go, then that's what we're going to support her doing." He patted my shoulder. "Why don't you take your time and go in a bit late this morning? I'll let the school know. If you change your mind about staying all day, it's no problem. We're going to take our lead from you."

I got to school at the end of first period, and as I walked through the halls, everyone moved back a step or two, leaving a space around me. I couldn't really blame them; I wouldn't know what to say to me either. One of my best friends had run off, and the other had killed herself. I would have avoided myself too if it were possible.

Zach was waiting for me by my locker, like he'd promised when I'd texted. His hair was sticking up in the back and it looked like he hadn't slept. When he spotted me, his eyes softened. I both wanted to throw myself into his arms and to spin around and hide in the girls' bathroom. I already felt like brittle ice, crisscrossed with cracks, on the verge of shattering. I knew Zach. He would want to talk about how I was feeling. He would wrap his arms around me and I could burrow into that warm spot between his neck and shoulder and cry. If I let that happen, I didn't know if I could stop. It was taking every ounce of strength I had to hold it together.

Zach pushed off from the locker and walked toward me, his arms spreading to pull me in. I backed up quickly and rammed into the water fountain. My bag fell from my shoulder and spilled out onto the floor. I dropped to my knees and started gathering everything back up. My hands were shaking. Zach reached down, wanting to pull me up.

"It's okay, Kalah. Just leave it."

"I can't have them stepping on everything," I said. I pulled the copy of *Alice in Wonderland* to my chest as if it were a rare relic I'd saved from a horde of wild savages. I shoved everything else back into my bag.

"You're wrinkling up your papers," Zach said. He

reached for my bag, but I pulled it away.

"I like them wrinkled," I snarled. Zach stared at me and I couldn't meet his eyes. He dropped down next to me and put a steady hand on my arm.

"I'm so sorry," Zach said. His eyes were filled with the pain I felt. "I know how upset you must be."

"You don't know," I said, but I leaned into the warmth of his touch. "No one knows. No one understands. You don't even like Brit that much." I willed my eyes not to cry. "You always resented how much time I spent with her and Beth. I know you did."

Zach didn't get angry. He looked impossibly sad, like a puppy that had been kicked. He touched my hand softly. "Sometimes I wish we spent more time together, and I'm not as close to Beth or Britney as you are, but they're important to you so that makes them important to me," he said. "Whatever happens, you're not alone."

But I was alone. Beth was gone and Brit was dead. I forced myself to repeat the thought. Britney was dead.

"I still can't believe it." Zach shook his head. "Britney never seemed like someone who would do that. Especially not over a guy."

"It wasn't about Jason. It was about Beth, and everyone knowing." I whispered. I didn't want to say it too loudly. Saying it at all, even to Zach, felt like a betrayal of the dead. "Brit knew people wanted to knock her off her pedestal.

People wanted to see her fail. I'm pretty sure that's what she couldn't face."

Zach's forehead wrinkled in confusion. "Everyone loves Britney."

I shook my head. He didn't get it. Brit was popular and people liked her, but they also envied her. And envy could be dark. It could be dangerous. Apparently, it could kill.

Beth and Brit were best friends, but envy had corroded their friendship. Brit envied Beth's ease with everyone, her ability to take things as they came and not stress about being good enough for anyone other than herself. I knew that, but Beth must have envied Brit too. Maybe the way Brit's family was so engaged with her, how money was never an issue. How Brit always had a plan and knew what she wanted. And I guess she'd envied what Brit had with Jason. Envied it so much, she chose to destroy it. Even though that also meant destroying me.

Beth would be sick when she heard what had happened. No matter how tense things got between her and Brit, no matter what she was doing behind Brit's back, I know she loved Brit too. She'd be devastated by what Brit had done, and probably racked with guilt over her role in it. Maybe that's why Brit had done it. She felt destroyed, so she wanted to destroy Beth too.

I wanted to vomit.

"Ms. Richards?" I jumped, surprised to hear my name. It

was Ms. Eisberg, my English teacher. She passed me a small slip of yellow paper. I took it cautiously, as if it might burn my fingers. "You're wanted down in the guidance office," she said. "Nothing to worry about. Just come to class when you're done, if you feel up to it."

I nodded and watched as she ducked into the classroom. I glanced down at the hall pass, hoping it might disappear.

"I'll walk you," Zach said. He pulled me to my feet and led me down the hall. "My class is on the way to Ms. Harding's."

Ms. Harding was our school counselor. She was okay, except for the trying too hard. You could tell she really wanted us to like her, to stop by just to chat. She would sometimes stand outside her door with a bowl of Hershey's Kisses and wish each of us a "sweet day" as we rushed past. Someone should have told her that desperation repels. She probably had been waiting a long time for this kind of tragedy. I didn't want to see her.

"You should go. You don't need to get in trouble for being late." I pressed my hand to Zach's chest and felt the regular thumping of his heart. I wanted my own heart to feel that steady. "I'm sorry I'm being so . . ." I tried to find the words.

"No sorry required." Zach put a warm hand on either side of my face and kissed me. For a second everything felt like it would be okay. He pulled back and I spotted a small spot of shaving cream by his ear that he must have missed, and it made him seem vulnerable and safe at the same time.

How had I ever risked everything with Zach? He kissed me again, gently on the forehead this time. "I'll find you later," he promised.

I nodded and watched him lope down the hall. I turned toward the guidance office and ran almost directly into Jason as he was coming out. He looked terrible. His eyes were red and swollen and his clothing was rumpled. His skin was ashen. He was usually completely pulled together, a perfect accessory to Brit, but today he was a mess. He grabbed both of my arms above the elbow.

"You know I loved Brit, don't you?" He pleaded, his fingers digging into my flesh.

I tensed under his grip. Jason glanced down like he hadn't been aware he was touching me. He let go and ran his hands over his short hair. He looked like a junkie coming down from something.

"She killed herself," Jason said. It didn't sound like the words seemed real to him. I knew the feeling. I'd been so mad at him yesterday, but now it felt like he was the only person who understood the enormity of what was happening. What was lost.

"It's not your fault," I said. I meant it. As much as I hated how Jason had hurt Brit, I couldn't blame him for falling for Beth. If Brit's death was anyone's fault, it was mine. As the only friend she'd had left, I should have seen it coming. I should have been the one to stop her.

Jason choked out a laugh. "Don't be so sure. They

showed me the note. It's clear. She said this is all my fault. That I ruined her life. That she had no choice but to end it."

I sucked in a breath. That sounded like Brit. Vindictive to the end. Of course she wouldn't go down without taking a few people with her.

"I never meant to hurt her. I didn't know how to tell her about everything, but I was *going* to. I never wanted her to find out that way. I wasn't trying to be cruel."

"Does Beth know yet?" I asked. I hadn't been able to bring myself to text her, and I already knew she wouldn't answer if I called. How do you tell someone this type of news in a text?

Jason closed his eyes. "I don't know. I have no idea where Beth is or why she took off."

"You have to know," I insisted.

Jason shook his head. He looked down at his feet. "It was never Beth. I sort of let Britney think that because I was too much of a coward to tell her the truth."

The ice surrounding my heart cracked and melted away. I wanted to cry again, this time from relief. The rumors were untrue. Beth had never been involved. "Who was it?" I said. "You *were* cheating."

"Sara Green."

Sara. My mind raced through the student body trying to place her. She was a sophomore. Quiet and studious, the opposite of Brit. I was pretty sure she was in the band. Brit never would have seen her as possible competition. She probably never noticed her at all. Someone like Sara was beneath Brit's notice.

Sara was attractive, though. She even looked a little like Beth, at least coloring-wise. I could see how if someone had spotted her with Jason and wasn't looking too closely, they could easily think she was Beth. That would explain some of the rumors.

It was clear Jason didn't mix the two of them up. The way his voice softened when he said Sara's name told me everything. It hadn't been a hookup. Jason was in love.

"Don't tell anyone about Sara, okay?" Jason said. "I don't want her dragged into all of this. I was trying to keep her out of it. Things between us just happened, and Sara felt horrible about it. Neither of us wanted to hurt Brit. We cut things off until I found a way to tell Brit, but then Beth took off and all the rumors started. I never meant to get Beth mixed up in everything either." Jason swallowed. "All of this is my fault, not Sara's. She was always afraid Brit would find out."

"Guess she doesn't have to be afraid anymore," I said. Jason flinched. I hadn't meant for it to come out so harshly, but it's hard to be gentle when your friend is dead.

Sara was smart to have been afraid of Brit. If Brit had discovered Sara was messing around with Jason, she would have taken her apart. There would only have been a Sara-sized smear on the ground with broken bits of her clarinet left to mark the spot.

A wave of nausea came over me. Now Brit would never know that Beth hadn't betrayed her. If only Beth hadn't disappeared, none of this would be happening. We'd both be taking Brit out for fro-yo and pedicures, and blasting breakup songs and singing along in Brit's Jeep, helping her get over Jason for good. Beth would get a Jason voodoo doll and we would have burned it on Brit's barbeque grill while drinking beer Beth stole from her dad. With her two best friends by her side, Brit would have powered through this. Instead, we'd both failed her, and now Brit was gone.

"I won't tell anyone about Sara," I said to Jason. "Though, of course, when Beth comes back, the truth will come out." I couldn't blame Sara for not wanting to be connected to this mess. The whole thing was like a black tar pit, dragging anyone who got close into the muck. "Did Brit say anything about Beth in her note?"

Jason shrugged. "I don't know. I haven't been allowed to see the whole thing. The police still have it."

"The police?" I looked past Jason and saw Officer Siegel in Ms. Harding's office. Of course. I swallowed. "I guess they want to talk to me too."

"It'll be okay," Jason said.

But it wasn't okay. I didn't want to talk to anyone, much less the cops. I had to get out of here.

I slumped against the wall. Jason moved quickly to my side.

"Easy," he said, tucking his arm under my elbow to keep me up.

"I can't talk to them now," I said. "I can't do this. I'm not ready. I want to go home." I knew I might break into tears at any moment.

"Do you want me to drive you?" Jason asked.

That was the last thing I wanted. I needed to be myself. I needed time to think and cry and grieve. I stood up straight. "No. I can do it. Thank you. And thanks for telling me the truth about you and Beth."

Jason gave me an awkward hug. "We're going to get through this," he said.

I was glad he was sure, because I wasn't.

CHAPTER THIRTEEN

As soon as I stepped outside the school doors I stopped short. The harsh white sun bounced off the windshields of the parked cars and stabbed me through the eyes.

I bolted down the front steps toward the parking lot, but with the sun in my eyes I missed the last step and stumbled. I pitched forward, my bag hitting the cement, but just before I wiped out someone caught me by the arm and pulled me up.

"Whoa," he said.

My heart was pounding in my chest. "Thanks," I said. I reached over to pick up my bag.

"You a student here?" he asked.

I glanced at him. He was entirely too young and

attractive to be someone's dad. His hair looked messy in a deliberately styled way, and he was wearing enough cologne to take down a horse. "The office is just inside," I told him.

"I'm not looking for the office. I'm hoping to talk to some students. I'm Derek Iriven. Do you mind if I ask you a few questions?" He flashed a smile so white it could star in a toothpaste ad.

"I'm sorry, I have to go." I took a few steps toward the parking lot.

"Did you know the dead girl? Britney Matson?"

His words hit like a shot to the chest. I turned to face him. "What?"

He gestured with the hand holding his phone. "I'm curious if you knew Britney Matson, the girl who killed herself. I'm a writer. I'm doing a piece on her and teen suicide. I'm hoping to get some reaction quotes from other students."

When I didn't say anything he stepped closer, holding his phone between us. I realized he was recording our conversation.

"It's your chance to be famous," he said with a wink.

"I don't want to be famous." I turned away, but he walked behind me as I wove toward the back of the lot, where I had parked my car. "Please go away."

"Did you know Britney? Have any stories you can share? Something to help readers feel like they know her?"

"I have nothing to say to you," I spat out.

Instead of leaving me alone, he seemed encouraged by

my reaction. "I understand she was pretty popular. I know how those girls acted when I was in school." He made a face like he'd tasted something foul. "Now's your chance to tell the world what she was really like. Maybe she killed herself because she realized she'd made so many other people's lives miserable. Maybe she was nothing more than an airheaded, lip-glossed bully."

I knocked the phone out of his hand, and it hit the asphalt with a loud crack.

"Hey! What did you do that for?"

"Leave me alone," I said. "Leave Britney alone. You have no idea what you're talking about."

"Bitch," I heard him mumble as I yanked open the car door and fell inside. I slammed the door behind me and started the engine.

"You cracked my screen," he yelled. I cranked up the radio and gave him the finger. He jumped to the side as I started to pull out. Maybe he thought I was going to run him down. *Good.*

I peeled out of the parking lot, tires squealing. I made it two blocks before my hands started shaking. I pulled over into a Wendy's to park before I crashed.

A hysterical giggle-sob rose up in my throat. If I crashed it would make us pretty much three for three: one runaway, one suicide, and one accident. Our group would become one of those urban legends that other kids talk about in hushed voices over summer campfires.

I jammed the car into park, opened the car door, and leaned out. I thought I might vomit, but nothing came up. I spat, trying to clear the sour taste from my mouth. A few crumpled napkins blew past, the smiling logo on them tumbling over and over. When I was sure I wasn't going to be sick, I closed the door and leaned back in the seat.

Jason wasn't messing around with Beth. I repeated it to myself over and over—six times, six more times, and six times again. By the sixth set of six, it was starting to sink in.

Jason hadn't been messing around with Beth, but Brit had been certain he was. She'd died believing that her best friend and her boyfriend had both betrayed her, and everyone knew and was laughing at her. That would have been hard for anyone to take, but for Brit, it was unbearable. I wished I could tell her that despite her perfect image and polished appearance, the ways she was imperfect had only made me love her more.

Brit had said that on some level, she'd known all along. I wondered what Beth knew. If it was possible Beth had left because she was afraid of what Britney might do.

But that made no sense. Beth wouldn't have been afraid of Britney's wrath, because she *wasn't* messing around with Jason. All she'd have had to do was tell Britney the truth: that it wasn't her. Beth was probably as clueless as I'd been as to why Brit had been acting so short-tempered with her lately. The timing of Beth skipping town was just a horrible coincidence.

I felt a spike of anger in my chest. Minutes ago I'd felt bad for Jason, but my empathy was evaporating quickly. Jason and Sara were at least partly to blame. Of course, he couldn't have predicted that Britney would have done this—but if Jason hadn't cheated, Brit wouldn't be dead.

Then again, if Beth hadn't vanished, she could have maybe stopped this too.

My anger deflated. It was my fault as well. If Beth and I hadn't been sneaking around, Brit wouldn't have had good reason to suspect that Beth was hiding something. Beth *was* keeping secrets from her. But it wasn't the same secret Brit feared.

I pulled out my phone and called Beth again. It rang and rang, but no one picked up. When it finally clicked to voice mail, I held my breath, wanting to at least hear her voice on the recording, but it wasn't her.

"The mailbox for this number is full. Please try again later." I jabbed the phone off.

This wasn't the kind of news I could leave in a text, but I was running out of choices.

B, please call me. It's urgent. It's about Brit. Please, please, please call.

I hit SEND and waited, hoping that she would call me right back, and trying not to read anything into the fact that she didn't.

CHAPTER FOURTEEN

As soon as Nadir started to talk, I knew our parents had asked him to call me. My brother is a computer genius, kicks ass at chess, and can touch his tongue to the tip of his nose, but he absolutely sucks at lying.

"Hey, Kay-Kay. I wanted to ask about what we should get Grandma for her birthday." Nadir's voice boomed through the phone line in my room. He only called me Kay-Kay when he either wanted something or had broken something of mine. "I thought we might go in on it together," he suggested.

"Grandma's birthday isn't until June," I pointed out.

"Yeah, but it's a big birthday for her. We should get something special."

"What birthday is it?" I pushed.

Nadir paused. Even over the phone I could sense him scrambling to come up with something. "I don't know, but at her age aren't they all important?"

I snorted. "That's the best you've got? You're supposed to be the smart one."

"Fine, brat. Mom and Dad wanted me to call to see how you're doing. I was trying to be stealth-like. Heavy on the subterfuge."

I flopped onto the bed. "When you report in you can tell them I was never the wiser. No reason for them to be disappointed in both their kids."

"Hey, it's not your fault you're all deformed and smell funny."

I laughed and squeezed my stuffed dog, Roogs. If my brother was teasing and insulting me then at least part of the world still made sense.

"Seriously, how are you?" Nadir said.

"Did Mom and Dad tell you everything?" I asked.

"Yeah. It sucks." Nadir always had a way with words.

"I didn't help Britney," I said, my voice low. "I knew she was upset and I didn't do anything. I feel like it's my fault."

"Did she tell you she was planning to kill herself?" Nadir asked.

"No. I mean, not directly, like that. She talked about how her life was ruined and how she felt betrayed by Beth." A tear ran down my face, and I used one of Roogs's ears to wipe it away. I was surprised I was still capable of crying.

I'd done so much of it lately it felt like I should have already dried up.

"You totally should have picked up on that. What with your PhD in psychology, and years of working in the field, I can't believe you didn't see it coming." Nadir made a tsk-ing sound.

"I'm serious, Nadir."

"I'm serious too. You were her friend, but that doesn't make saving her, or anyone else for that matter, your job. What about her other friend, Beth? Where's she gone? Why didn't *she* save her? They've known each other since birth or something."

At least one of those was a good question. "No one knows where Beth is. I've called her like a thousand times and she never picks up. I sent her a text after Brit died, telling her we had to talk, that it was an emergency, and still nothing."

"That sucks too," he said.

Even though that was exactly what I thought, I felt the absurd need to defend Beth. "She doesn't suck; she's just checked out. I'm sure she'd call back if she realized what had happened."

Nadir wasn't having it. "I don't care what her excuse is. She's hurting my sister."

"What if she can't call for some reason?" I whispered into the phone.

"What kind of reason?"

I wound Roogs's tail around my finger. "I don't know. Maybe she was abducted or something."

"What I'm about to say is going to piss you off, but hear me out first."

No good conversation starts with that opener. "I'm listening," I said.

"You have a tendency for drama."

"I do not," I fired back.

"You said not even two seconds ago that you were going to listen. I knew I should have asked for it in writing."

I took a deep breath. "Sorry. Go on."

"All I'm saying is that you lean toward the dramatic. You're a one-woman worst-case scenario show. In my programming class when we're trying to figure out a bug with the software, our teacher always tells us, 'When you hear hoofbeats, look for horses, not zebras.'"

I paused, waiting to hear if he was going to spout any other wisdom. "And your point is?"

"The point is, don't make a conspiracy theory out of thin air. If it looks like she ran away, most likely she ran away. People do that. It happens. It doesn't mean kidnappers or aliens or murderers are involved. Mom said Beth's parents aren't even all that worried. They expected this. If they're not concerned, why should you be?"

"Because I love her," I said.

Nadir was quiet. I could feel the silence stretching between us.

"Oh, Kay-Kay." His voice was heavy. "I'm sorry."

The sadness swelled in my throat, making it almost impossible to speak. "Why are you sorry?"

"Getting your heart stepped on is never easy."

"What do I do?"

"If you start turning to me for romantic advice, you're in deep shit. What I can tell you, from painful personal experience, is that if you love someone and they don't love you back, you have to walk away. Love isn't something you can talk the other person into."

I sighed. I hate when he's right. I knew I had to let go of Beth, but I didn't want to. "Maybe she does suck," I mumbled.

I did blame Beth. Not for Brit's death, but for leaving us both. She should have been here. She should have called me. She owed me that much, even if she didn't love me. Now that Britney was gone, it wasn't right that Beth was leaving me alone to deal with it.

"Look, Kalah, it might seem easy to blame yourself for what Brit did, but you can't do that. And you can't make Beth feel what you want her to feel. People make their own choices. If you want to blame yourself for something, then feel bad about breaking my Xbox, not this."

I rolled my eyes. "Jesus, you're still upset about that? I was *eight*." The pressure on my chest felt lighter. Nadir would have told me if he thought I'd wronged Brit.

"Do you know how many lawns I mowed to earn the

money for that?" Nadir sounded indignant.

I scoffed. "You never mowed lawns. With your allergies it's a wonder you don't combust as soon as you go outside. Mom and Dad bought it for Christmas." I pulled my blanket up over me. I felt like I might actually be able to sleep tonight.

"The point is, I *would* have mowed lawns to buy it. I loved it and you broke it."

"Does it make it better if I tell you I'll feel bad about it for the rest of my life?" I yawned.

"A bit. You sound beat; I'll let you go. I've got to study anyway. I'm going to tell Mom and Dad you're okay. Do your best to be normal, or what passes as normal for you, so you don't make a liar out of me."

"I'll talk to you later." I curled around Roogs. "Hey," I called out before he hung up. "Thanks for calling."

"Anytime, Kay-Kay. You know you're my favorite sister."

"I'm your only sister."

"True." Nadir's voice softened. "Take care."

We hung up. I felt exhausted. My brain, which had been racing for days, seemed to have finally worn itself out.

I clicked off the light and typed one more text.

Britney died. Please come back. I didn't want to tell you like this. Sorry.

It went without saying that I wouldn't have had to tell her that way if she'd left me any other options.

I closed my eyes and fell asleep.

CHAPTER FIFTEEN

I'd only been to see Ms. Harding, the guidance coun-
selor, once before, to talk about my possible college plans. I
suspected she knew, though, about my history with mental
health professionals. It seemed the kind of thing that would
make your permanent record. Maybe a red dot on the file,
indicating the potential for trouble and emotional liability.
I'd managed to avoid the meeting with her yesterday, but
this morning there was a note waiting for me in homeroom.
I wasn't going to be able to dodge it forever.

I slipped down the hall toward the guidance office, feeling people's eyes crawling all over me like insects. Jason
hadn't come into school today. I couldn't blame him. There'd
been three news reporters and two television cameras in

the parking lot this morning. At least Hamstead had barred them from entering the school.

When I came around the corner I saw her. Sara stood by her locker, surrounded by her fellow band members, nodding at something one of them was saying. I felt a hot rush of anger. Why should she get to be surrounded by friends when, because of her, one of my two best friends was dead? I wanted to shove her against the wall and spit in her face.

Sara must have felt my rage pulsing toward her, because she turned. When she saw me, her mouth dropped open and she quickly looked away. I thought about marching over and confronting her, screaming in her face, despite my promise to Jason. My anger was like a creature inside me, scratching and howling to be set free. If I let it out, I wasn't sure what might happen.

I closed my eyes so I couldn't see her anymore. When I opened them a few seconds later, she and her friends were gone. I realized the note telling me to go to Ms. Harding's office was clutched tight in my hand, the black ink smeared on my skin. I tossed the paper in the trash.

Ms. Harding's office was decorated to look like it was in her house instead of part of the school. She'd gotten rid of the industrial metal desk and replaced it with a wooden table. There was a cheap Oriental rug on the floor, but you could still see the linoleum tile around the edges of the room. The shelves were filled with books and knickknacks.

Ms. Harding gestured for me to take a seat. I dropped

into the nearest chair, trying to ignore Officer Siegel's intense gaze. She was unapologetically watching my every move, like she was assigning a meaning to everything I did. I wondered if I should ask to have a lawyer in the room, or if that would make me look guilty of something. Granted, I was guilty of a lot.

"How are you doing?" Ms. Harding asked, her eyebrows scrunched together in concern. Officer Siegel was leaning against the bookcase with her arms crossed. I didn't want to look at her because she made me nervous, but I also didn't want it to look like I was trying to avoid her, so I kept shooting glances over at her and smiling. Except my mouth wouldn't cooperate and make a normal smile. I probably looked like a twitchy clown.

"I'm doing okay." I gave Officer Siegel another one of my killer clown smiles. "I mean, considering." I reminded myself that this wasn't a formal investigation. Not realizing your friend is suicidal isn't a crime. It made me a crappy friend, but it wasn't like Officer Siegel was going to read me my rights, march me out of there, and toss me into prison.

"If you need to talk at any time, feel free to come straight here. I've cleared it with your teachers that you don't require any kind of pass." Ms. Harding reached into a folder on her desk and pulled out a brochure, which she slid across the table at me. "This is the contact information for the local crisis center, in case you feel upset outside of school hours."

I must have looked worse than I thought if she was

worried I might not make it through the night without having someone to talk me off the ledge. "I don't have any thoughts of that," I reassured her.

"Of suicide?" Officer Siegel asked. Both Ms. Harding and I winced at her directness. "Did you know Britney was thinking of ending her life?"

"No." I could feel the sweat pooling at the base of my back. Maybe I should have known about Brit, but I hadn't. I'd been too focused on Beth.

Officer Siegel nodded, like she'd known that all along. "What was your reaction to the rumors going around that day? Were you surprised to hear why she and Jason were breaking up?"

"I didn't really know much about it." I glanced over at Ms. Harding to avoid Officer Siegel's eyes. "Brit was really private about some stuff." I wasn't sure why I'd lied, but I didn't know how to take it back once I'd said it. Keeping Brit's secrets just seemed like the right thing to do.

Officer Siegel rubbed her chin. "That's odd that you didn't know. From what I've heard, everyone at school was talking about it. How Britney believed Beth was sleeping with Jason."

"I don't listen to rumors." I hated how my voice came out sounding prissy.

"Not even when they're about your best friends?" Officer Siegel smiled and I hated her. "She and Beth are your best friends, aren't they? Beth must be really upset about Britney's death."

It felt like the room had gotten about twenty degrees hotter. I shifted in my seat. "I don't know what she thinks. Beth isn't around."

"Has she been in touch with you?" Officer Siegel pressed.

"No," I admitted. "Just one text a few days after she left. Saying she needed some time off."

"Huh. That's odd too, isn't it?"

"What's odd?" Ms. Harding asked.

Officer Siegel cocked her head like she wanted to see the situation from a new perspective and spoke to me as if Ms. Harding wasn't even in the room. "It seems odd that Beth hasn't been in touch, or told you where she went. It seems odd that Britney didn't tell you her suspicions about Jason and Beth when she was so upset that she felt driven to suicide." She chuckled, but it sounded forced. "Heck, when I was your age my friends and I never shut up. We'd talk for hours. My dad used to say that the phone was connected to my head. It seemed like there wasn't a single thing I didn't know about their lives. I guess friendships are different now, huh?"

I shrugged, refusing to take the bait. "I guess." I couldn't even imagine Officer Siegel in high school. She looked like she'd been born in that uniform and holster.

"Beth and Britney were a year ahead of you, is that right?" She waited for me to nod, even though we both understood she already knew the answer. "When I was in high school you practically had to pay a senior to hang out with someone younger. Course, that didn't keep some from hanging around, like groupies."

My back stiffened. Were cops allowed to keep sticking your face in it? "I wasn't their groupie. We were friends." Even to my ears, the claim sounded pathetic, like I was really trying to convince myself.

"*Were?* Aren't you still friends with Beth? Or did something happen between you two? Maybe a reason she left her two besties behind?"

If she was trying to upset me, it was working. "Of course Beth is still my friend. I just meant we were all friends. I don't know why Beth left. She used to talk about it all the time. Her home life wasn't great."

Officer Siegel nodded. "Sure."

I pressed my lips together. There wasn't any point in arguing with her about it. She was going to twist anything I said.

"If it makes you feel any better, I haven't heard from Beth either," Officer Siegel said. "I've left her a bunch of voice mails, but it seems she has her phone off. She sent a handful of texts those first few days after she left, telling people she didn't want to be contacted, but since then, nothing. Her parents asked the phone company to track her phone, but she'd taken the SIM card out. There's not much else her parents can do since she's eighteen. If she wants to disappear, she can." Officer Siegel inspected her nails as if the conversation was starting to bore her.

"Do you think she's okay?" I asked.

"Do you?"

I wanted to throw something at her face. "I don't know. I told you I haven't been in touch with her."

Officer Siegel brushed her hands on her pants. "Well, I don't know how she's doing exactly, but she's used her ATM card a few times, so she can't be doing all bad. She logged into a couple of her online accounts from a library in Cadillac. She also registered for a night in a hotel, just outside of Charlevoix. She paid cash. I drove up and talked to the clerk, but he doesn't really remember her very well. She didn't look distressed to him." The officer paused. "He couldn't remember if she had anyone with her. Of course, if there was another person, he or she might have been waiting outside. Maybe the person who gave her all that money."

I jolted. "What money?"

Officer Siegel seemed to be watching for my reaction. "She didn't mention that either? The day after Beth left, she deposited almost ten thousand dollars into her bank account. Technically, it was nine thousand, nine hundred fifty. Just about the same amount, minus a few hundred, that Britney had withdrawn from her education savings account. How's that for a coincidence? Course, it's almost all gone by now."

I stared at her, blinking. Was she trying to tell me Beth had stolen from Britney? That Brit had paid Beth to leave? "I don't know anything about that," I said.

"Guess Beth and Britney both had a few secrets, huh?"

"I guess." I realized I was tapping sixes with my foot. Officer Siegel was watching.

"Anxiety?" she asked.

"Just a habit." I clenched my hands together to make sure my fingers didn't start tapping, but I could feel the pressure inside starting to rise. I wanted out of there.

"How would you describe your last interaction with Britney?" Officer Siegel asked, switching gears.

I looked over at Ms. Harding for help. "I don't know what you want me to say."

Ms. Harding looked a bit nervous. "If you're planning to ask these kind of questions, maybe I should contact Kalah's parents."

Officer Siegel raised her hand to her chest as if shocked. "I didn't mean for this to come across like some kind of interrogation. I guess I can't help myself—habit of the job. There's no formal investigation. Britney's death has been declared a suicide. I'm just trying to get a better handle on why."

"I don't know anything," I said.

"No guesses at all?"

My tongue felt dry. "Things weren't always as easy as they seemed for Brit. There was a lot of pressure from her family to be perfect. She went out of her way to seem flawless, but of course she was only human. But anything less than the appearance of perfection always felt like a huge failure to her." I felt a little bad about shifting blame to Brit's parents, but it was clear I had to tell Officer Siegel something if I wanted the questions to stop. "I'm sure all the rumors were devastating to her. She didn't always want to talk about things, though. Not even with her closest friends."

"So with all that Beth and Britney were keeping from you, did you keep secrets from them too?"

I twitched. "People are allowed to have secrets," I said. A trickle of sweat ran down my chest and into my bra. Maybe I shouldn't have agreed to talk without a lawyer, but there was no way I could ask for one now.

Officer Siegel pushed off from the wall and moved toward the door. "Of course. Everyone has a secret or two. I didn't mean to upset you further. I'm sure all of this has been really difficult. I'm just making sure we have all the information we need. I wouldn't want to overlook anything."

I wanted to shove her the rest of the way out the door. "I understand," I said.

Officer Siegel paused. "Of course, you know what they say about secrets. They never stay buried for long."

"That's enough!" Ms. Harding had finally found her voice. She gave the officer a glare as if she'd only just realized a line had been crossed.

Officer Siegel held her hands up like she didn't mean any offense, but I could swear she smirked at me as she left.

CHAPTER SIXTEEN

A week later, Britney's parents had decided they wanted "closure" and would go ahead with a funeral, regardless of the fact that Brit's body had not been found. Word spread quickly around school that Doctors Matson and Ryerson had hired party planners to arrange the memorial service. Technically, they were "event" planners, and the funeral was certainly shaping up to be an event, but still. The idea of it set my teeth on edge despite Zach's gentle reminder that everyone mourns in their own way. They'd lost their daughter, their only child. However they wanted to say good-bye was up to them.

At least Brit's parents' way of coping was better than how Beth was dealing with things. She hadn't answered a single text. I assumed by now that she'd abandoned her phone, but unless her new residence was under a rock, it was hard to imagine she hadn't at least seen the news reports.

Not that I was coping any better. I'd sleepwalked through the days. I was there, but not present. Unlike the clusters of girls who kept bursting into tears in the hallways, I'd walked around school with a poker face. It wasn't that I was in control of my emotions; it was that I felt half-dead.

The church was decorated with fluffy white tulle bows on each pew, like at a wedding. Maybe Brit's parents figured since she'd never get to take a walk down the aisle, this would have to be the next best thing. There was a huge framed picture of her at the front of the church and a giant display of white roses with a single bloodred rose in the center.

The casket hadn't arrived yet, but I knew it would be closed, since there was no corpse to show. The reporters had said it was likely that Brit's body had been swept out by the tides and might never be found. But one of her strappy Manolos had been discovered washed up on the beach. Apparently Brit had dressed up for the occasion. That was like her. She would have wanted to look good to the end.

I wasn't sure why Brit's parents were bothering with a casket at all. Maybe the party planners had told them no memorial service was complete without one. Might as well have a birthday party without a cake. I wondered what they were going to do with the empty casket when it was over.

Keep it in their garage until Britney was found? Or were they going to bury it?

Brit had already been dead for nine days, but still nothing about this felt real to me.

I kept thinking of all the firsts there would be without her: the first summer, the first birthday, the first Christmas. I wondered if I would ever stop slamming into the realization that she was gone.

I turned and glanced behind me for what felt like the thousandth time in the past ten minutes, looking for Beth. Even though she'd never replied to my texts, I was certain that she would show up. She wouldn't miss her best friend's memorial service, even if the two of them had been on the outs. Even if she was avoiding me. No matter where she was, I was sure she would come back today.

I closed my eyes and told myself that if I kept them closed and counted to sixty, when I opened them Beth would be there. But she wasn't.

My parents were seated across the aisle. They'd wanted me to sit next to them, but I preferred to be with Zach. I held on to his hand like it was the only thing keeping me tethered to the earth. Nadir had offered to come home, but I'd told him not to. I had to do this without my big brother.

I heard the doors at the back of the church being shut, and felt my hope shut down too. Beth really wasn't coming. The realization sat in my stomach like an ice-cold boulder. I let out a slow breath.

"You okay?" Zach whispered. His thumb rubbed over my knuckles.

I nodded and squeezed his hand, and as if that were the cue, "Over the Rainbow" started playing over the church's sound system. Showtime. I barely managed to avoid rolling my eyes. Brit would not be impressed by the music selection.

The minister led the way down the aisle. Brit's coffin followed on the shoulders of six solemn pallbearers. I recognized her cousin Ryan in front. Brit had told me Ryan once tried to feel her up when she fell asleep on his mom's couch after Thanksgiving. She'd called him Randy Ryan the Creeper Cousin.

Jason was bearing the coffin at the rear. I'd heard that he'd called Brit's parents and begged to be included. He looked horrible—eyes red, face full of pain—and I worried he might not make it through the service. Brit would have been glad for that, at least. I could picture her watching with her arms crossed over her chest, thinking he deserved to suffer.

The coffin was a highly polished dark wood. As it glided past I had the absurd urge to reach out and touch it, to prove to myself that what was happening was real. Maybe that's why her parents had gotten it. It pulled everything into sharp relief. You can't pretend someone isn't dead once they bring out a coffin.

I bit my lip to keep myself from crying. Britney was

larger than life. The idea that she was just gone seemed impossible. I let my head rest on Zach's shoulder.

Brit's parents walked right behind the casket. Her dad kept looking around almost stunned, like he couldn't figure out what we were all doing there. Her mom was more composed. She looked like those photos you see of Jackie Kennedy at the president's funeral, poised and elegant. But Dr. Ryerson's eyes were blank and empty. She was like a shell of a person.

A girl from my history class casually lifted her phone and took a picture of the casket. I looked away.

Tons of people had shown up from school. Even now that she was dead, people still wanted to be part of whatever Brit was doing. Or maybe that wasn't fair. Maybe they were sad and shocked and genuinely felt like they had lost something. I didn't know what other people were feeling. I just knew I was jealous they could feel at all.

Brit's suicide was all anyone had been talking about all week. Like any other disaster, people wanted to share where they had been when they'd heard and how they'd first reacted. They all had stories about her—how she'd once told them how much she liked their sweater, or borrowed a pencil from them for a test, or stood behind them in line once for fro-yo. That time she'd charmed a teacher out of giving the whole class a pop quiz, an amazing play she'd made in field hockey, a boring party she'd turned into the best event of the year. Every time I turned around Melissa was crying about how she'd talked to Britney just hours before it all happened. She acted like she and Brit had been the closest of friends. That Brit had poured her heart out to Melissa in the bathroom. She'd told the same story to all the cable news cameras too. I'd been avoiding the reporters at all costs.

The yearbook crowd was talking about the page they would dedicate to her and the student council was trying to get a local twenty-four-hour suicide help line started. I'd even heard that some senior had Brit's name tattooed on his arm so he could always remember how fragile life could be. I guess he didn't realize Brit hated tattoos. "Future regrets," she'd called them.

I tried to focus as the minister started the service. I suppose there really isn't anything good to say when someone has killed herself, but it felt like he'd Googled "what to say when a young person dies" and was reading a generic script. He talked about how she was a "bright light that burned out too quickly" and how we could "take comfort that she is in the bosom of our Lord." None of it had anything to do with Brit. When he got to the part about how some people are so kind that God can't wait to call them home to heaven, someone in the crowd actually snorted. They covered it up a split second later with a cough, but everyone still heard it. Zach put his arm around me and pulled me closer.

I imagined Brit standing off to the side, evaluating her own funeral. She would think roses were too common; she would have preferred something more exotic. She would have spotted from across the sanctuary that Randy Ryan the Creeper Cousin was wearing brown socks with his black suit and shoes. She'd know at a glance if the coffin was real mahogany or just a veneer. She'd sniff at the choice of recorded music over having live musicians. If Britney had known this would be her funeral when she was walking into the lake, she would have turned right around and walked back out.

The minister paused and called Jason up to speak. Jason dragged his feet to the pulpit as if he were on his way to the gallows. He gripped the sides of the lectern, and I could see his Adam's apple bobbing as he swallowed. There was an awkward stretch of silence. I wondered if he'd be able to speak.

"I've tried to figure out what to say at least a dozen times," he started. "I don't know how to find the words to express what's in my heart. Brit's a challenging person to describe, to give justice to. I know I let her down in the past, and I don't want to do that now. I want to say the right thing." Jason's voice cracked and he looked down to pull himself together.

"Most of you know I wasn't always the best boyfriend, but I did love her. Britney was difficult. Sometimes she had a temper. If she didn't like you, she was really bad about hiding it. She wasn't patient with people when things didn't go her way. She picked out all the cashews in the mixed nuts container and would leave everyone else the plain peanuts. She could look you in the eye and lie if she felt she needed to." Jason's lip twitched into a smile. "If you didn't watch her like a hawk, she would cheat at Monopoly. She used to steal hundreds out of the bank."

Brit's mom shifted. I could see this wasn't the eulogy she had counted on. But whether she liked it or not, that was the real Britney. She deserved to be remembered as she was.

"Brit was also the kind of person we all invited to our parties because she lit up a room. She made it a party. When she laughed, we all felt like laughing. She was a great athlete with a competitive spirit, and she could organize anything and anybody. She had a fierce sense of loyalty, and if you were part of her circle there was nothing she wouldn't do for you. No lengths she wouldn't go to for a friend. I'm not perfect and neither is anyone in this room. Brit wasn't perfect either, but she should have had a chance to keep trying to be. She deserved a life." Jason choked back a sob.

"None of this feels real. If there's anyone that I would have described as invincible, it would have been Brit. I don't know what to say, but for me, there will always be something missing because she isn't here. I don't know what would have happened between Brit and me in the future. Heck, I don't know if any of us will stay in touch when this school year ends, but even if we never came across each other again, I am certain that the world is incomplete because she isn't in it. She will always be the first girl I loved. The first girl who loved me back. And I was so lucky we had that." Jason started crying.

I didn't even realize I was crying too until Zach passed me a pack of Kleenex. He pulled one from the package and gently blotted my face as if I were a small child.

The minister reached over to guide Jason back to his seat, but he was still gripping the sides of the podium like he had more he wanted to say. In the end, the minister had to tug on Jason's suit jacket before he let go.

Jason stumbled back to his pew. I noticed he wasn't sitting with Sara, and I wondered if they were still together. I wondered if she'd dared to come.

The minister looked at me and nodded. There was a split second when I thought I wasn't going to be able to stand, but then my legs went on autopilot and I walked to the front. Brit's parents had asked me to read something for the funeral. I'd picked a poem we'd learned in English class.

I cleared my throat and looked out over the congregation. I knew people were waiting to see if I'd fall apart like Jason. Strangely, now that I was standing in front of everyone, I felt calm. I'd been paranoid that my anxiety would kick in and I'd be tapping away on the pulpit, but my breath actually came smoothly.

I searched the crowd for Beth once more, but no matter how badly I wanted her there, she refused to materialize.

My eyes fell on Zach. He smiled and I realized I wasn't completely alone.

"'Remember,'" I said. "A poem by Christina Rossetti.

"Remember me when I am gone away.
Gone far away into the silent land;
When you can no more hold me by the hand,
Nor I half turn to go yet turning stay.
Remember me when no more day by day
You tell me of our future that you plann'd:
Only remember me; you understand
It will be late to counsel then or pray.
Yet if you should forget me for a while
And afterwards remember, do not grieve:
For if the darkness and corruption leave
A vestige of the thoughts that once I had,
Better by far you should forget and smile
Than that you should remember and be sad."

When I finished, Brit's dad was crying full force and I could tell Brit's mom was barely holding it together. For her, falling apart would have made everything worse. All she had left were appearances.

From the pulpit I saw teary eyes all over the church. Emotion moved like a wave through the crowd. Brit would have loved to see it.

That's the problem with being dead. You miss everything.

My dad nodded when I glanced at him, and I knew I'd accomplished what I wanted for Britney, as best I could do without Beth.

"Curiouser and curiouser," I whispered to myself, but the microphone picked up the words and carried them out over the sanctuary. I snapped my mouth shut. I didn't wait for the minister to reach for me; I scurried back to my seat.

"What was the last bit?" Zach whispered as I sat down, his words warm on my neck.

"Just something Beth might have said," I explained. "Sort of an inside joke."

Zach reached over and took my hand again. Now that my part was over I wanted to slip off my uncomfortable shoes and curl up on the pew next to him and go to sleep. For the past few days, Zach had been my safe place. I would smell the woodsy soap he used and feel the soft worn cotton of his jeans and have the sense that I could breathe again. He was my own personal life support system. I didn't like him to be beyond my touch.

I felt impossibly tired. The minister said a few more things and the music started again. I winced; the volume was up too loud. Someone should have told the party planners it was a funeral, not a nightclub. At this volume I half expected a mirrored disco ball to drop from the ceiling.

Brit's parents led the way out. When I turned I could see a hearse parked right outside the front doors.

"Is that it?" I asked Zach.

Zach shrugged. "I think so. There's usually something at the graveside, but since they don't have anything to bury, there's no point." Zach was a pro at funerals since he'd lost two grandparents, so he could be counted on to know what to expect. Before today, the only funeral I'd been to was when Nadir buried his hamster, Thor, in the backyard when I was ten.

Zach glanced down at his program. "There's a reception at the country club. That starts in half an hour."

My shoulders slumped. "Why throw an after-party for a funeral? The last thing I feel like doing is eating egg salad sandwiches and making small talk over cake."

"Do you want to skip it?"

I wanted to. I longed to make a run for the door and have Zach take me somewhere else. Somewhere where I could pretend none of this was happening. But I knew it was impossible. "I can't," I admitted. I owed it to Brit to be there. One of her best friends should make the effort.

Besides, Brit had made plenty of effort for me. She'd plucked me out of a pile of no ones, welcomed me into her fold, and been a true friend. She'd led me to Beth. Beth had given me a glimpse of who I could be. What I wanted right now didn't matter. I needed to be there.

"Okay," Zach said. "I'll stick with you the whole time. You just have to be strong a little longer. I know you can do it."

I hoped he was right.

"Hey, sweetie." My parents had crossed the aisle to join us. My mom hugged me and my dad patted my back. I could tell my mom had been crying. "Your poem was beautiful," she said.

"Do you want us to take you home?" Dad offered.

All week, my parents had been hovering over me. Checking to make sure I was okay. Afraid I was going to fall apart. If I went home with them now, they would follow me around the house, driving me crazy. "We're going to go to the reception for a bit," I said.

"Okay," Dad said. "We'll see you there."

Zach placed his palm on my lower back as we filed out of the pew and followed the crowd into the parking lot. Outside it was bright and sunny. I squinted and turned away from the group of journalists and cameramen across the street, taking pictures and filming as the hearse pulled away.

As we walked up to Zach's car, I saw something stuck in the passenger-side window. A playing card. I picked it up and flipped it over. It was the Queen of Hearts. I whipped around, searching the parking lot.

"Jeez, someone's trash is blowing all around." Zach bent and picked up a few more cards, along with an empty take-out container and Pepsi bottle. He held out his hand to take the card from me, but I held on to it. The Queen of Hearts was one of Beth's favorite characters. Was it just trash, or was it a message from Beth? Zach jogged over to the trash can to throw the rest of the junk away.

A woman walked over to me and it took me a second to realize it was Officer Siegel. I hadn't recognized her out of uniform. She was wearing a plain black suit that made her look more like a lawyer than a cop. Or a giant crow.

I backed up a step closer to Zach's car. I didn't want her touching me, even by accident. I slid the card into my pocket so she couldn't see it.

"That line, what you said after the poem, it was from *Alice in Wonderland*, wasn't it?" Officer Siegel asked.

I looked over, surprised. She laughed. "Did you think the only things I know are how to take fingerprints and tap phones? I assure you I've read more than Sherlock Holmes."

I didn't answer.

Officer Siegel leaned against the car parked next to Zach's. "So, Beth didn't come today," she said.

"Nope." The bright sunshine poked out from a cloud and blinded me for a second. I held my hand up to my eyes.

"Sad, don't you think? She and Britney had been friends since they were kids."

I tried to act casual. "Maybe she didn't hear about it in time."

"Maybe she didn't feel she should come." Officer Siegel pulled on a pair of sunglasses, which made it even harder to read her expression.

The wind blew my hair into my eyes, and I pushed it

away. Zach walked up and gave a bit of a start when he realized who Officer Siegel was. "I don't know what you want me to say," I said to her. I kept my voice cool and calm, channeling Britney. She'd never let someone like Siegel push her around.

Officer Siegel held up her hands. "All I'm trying to do is understand what's happened."

"That's all I want too," I said. Zach put his arm around me and I stood a bit straighter, pulling strength from him.

Officer Siegel shrugged. "You might think so, but it's my experience that when people are hiding things, it's because they don't want the whole truth to come out."

"I'm not hiding anything." My face flushed, leaving both of us knowing it was a lie.

CHAPTER SEVENTEEN

The polite distance that the reporters knew to keep outside the funeral apparently didn't apply to the reception. As soon as we arrived at the country club, a group of people bore down on me, shouting questions and shoving microphones in my face.

I shielded myself with my hand as Zach wrapped his arm around my waist and maneuvered us through the crowd. "No comment," he said firmly as they called out question after question about where I thought Beth had gone to, and if I blamed her or Jason more for Britney's death. Apparently they'd gotten ahold of the suicide note. Brit's suicide made an even better story when there was a beautiful, missing best friend to blame it on.

Let Beth come back and set the story straight herself. I wasn't going to defend her.

Zach pulled me forward and finally we were at the entrance of the reception hall, where someone waved us in before closing the door, leaving the journalists outside.

I stood blinking in the foyer.

"Are you okay?" Zach looked freaked out himself. "They're just trying to come up with a story. Don't let them upset you."

I nodded, still not trusting myself to speak. It had been like being chased by bees, each of them darting in to sting. I noticed a group of sophomore girls standing in the corner of the foyer whispering and watching us. The excitement over a possible scandal came off of them in waves. I breathed in to a count of six and told myself to remain calm. They wanted a reaction, something they could talk about with the journalists outside to get themselves some camera time. I wished I had Brit's talent for shutting people up with a single dismissive glance.

Zach ran his hands through his hair to pull himself together and led me into the reception room. I stood in the back while he went to get the two of us something to drink.

I pulled the Queen of Hearts out of my pocked and flipped the card between my fingers like a magician. If only I had some actual magical ability, I'd wave my wand and make Beth and Brit come back, and everyone and everything else disappear. But there wasn't a magical bone in my body. Brit was dead, Beth was gone, and I was stuck in the magician's box with my heart sawed in half.

I watched Brit's parents at the front of the room looking shell-shocked. They shook hands and accepted hugs and condolences from the long line of people filing past them to pay their respects.

I had no idea what to say to them. *Sorry your daughter killed herself? Sorry I didn't say anything even though I knew stuff was seriously messed up? I loved Brit but at the same time I'm so mad at her for doing this?* Their perfectly ordered world had just blown up in their faces. They didn't need to deal with my grief on top of it.

The sound of Beth's name pulled my attention to the conversation of some girls at a table nearby. "I heard it was blackmail," one of them said. "She was involved in some really heavy stuff with, like, a married guy and this major drug trafficking thing. That's why she didn't come to the funeral. There's basically a price on her head."

"Don't be stupid." The other girl lowered her voice. "She didn't come to the funeral because it's her fault Britney's dead. Beth was screwing Jason. Everyone knows that."

"No, I know, but I heard there's drugs and blackmail in it too. That's how she bankrolled her escape. You know her family's dirt poor and her dad spends any money they have on booze."

I closed my eyes and silently willed them to shut the fuck up.

"So I guess this means Jason's single now?" Another girl said. She let out a high-pitched giggle. I wished I had the energy to strangle them all.

Zach returned with a glass of sparkling water for me. "Come here," he said, pulling me toward the small upholstered bench against the wall.

"There isn't room," I protested even as I sank down to join him.

Zach positioned his legs so I could lean into him, my back resting against his chest. He wrapped both arms around me, put his face into the back of my neck, and inhaled.

We sat in silence together. Our heartbeats fell into sync. "You're going to be okay," he said.

"I hope so," I whispered.

Zach kissed the top of my head.

I tried not to look over, a few feet away, to where Jason stood, surrounded by a group of friends. My jaw clenched. How nice for him to be comforted and treated like he was some kind of victim in all of this. Things seemed to be turning out just fine for him. He could be with Sara or whoever else he wanted now and not have to worry about Brit. Jason saw me and made his way over.

"Do you guys want to join us? We have a table over there," he said, motioning to the far side of the room.

"I don't really feel like making this into a social event," I snapped.

Jason flinched and I felt flooded with shame. Despite

my mean thoughts, I knew this wasn't easy for him either. I wondered what questions the reporters had asked him on the way in. Even avoiding the media reports and trying not to listen to hallway gossip, I knew he'd been dubbed "The High School Heartbreaker" by one of the twenty-four-hour news channels, which were all dragging his reputation through the mud. It didn't seem to be changing how people at Northside saw him, but I could only imagine what it would be like for him, already being known for this when he started college next year.

My feelings about Jason were complicated. I felt badly for him, I knew he was hurting. At the same time I hated him, and I hoped he got the comeuppance Brit had intended.

"Sorry," I mumbled. "I'm just not ready to talk to people."

"We'll stay here for now," Zach said.

Jason shoved his hands in his pockets. "I understand. If you change your mind you know where to find us." I watched him walk away.

"Can I tell you a secret?" I sat up so I could turn to face Zach. "You can't tell anyone." I didn't want to be the only one who knew anymore.

Zach nodded, his face serious.

"Jason was cheating, but it wasn't with Beth. He's hooking up with Sara Green."

Zach's eyebrows shot up. "Whoa." He shook his head slowly. "That's seriously fucked up."

It was a relief, finally telling someone. I nestled into

Zach's chest, pulling his arm around me.

"So why isn't Beth here, then?" Zach said. I stiffened slightly when he said her name. "You'd think she'd want to be at her best friend's funeral. And to clear her own name."

I shrugged so I wouldn't have to open my mouth. I had no idea what might spill out.

Zach's arms tightened around me. "For the record, I think Beth was stupid to leave you behind."

I had the crazy urge to tell him everything. About how Beth and I were more than friends. How her touch made me feel electric and alive and how her kisses were intoxicating. Being with her was almost like being drunk. I felt dizzy in her presence and then when we were apart, it felt almost like something that had happened to someone else. I wanted to tell him how her leaving me hurt, but what almost hurt more was the feeling that I must not have known her at all. The anger I was left with. And how sick and sorry I was about the whole thing.

"You know, you can always count on me to be here," Zach said.

"I know," I said. "You're one of the good guys."

I pulled away from Zach. As much as I wanted to crawl into his arms and not come out, this wasn't the time or place. "I'm going to say hi to Brit's parents and then we can go."

"You want me to come with you?"

"No. It's okay. I'll be back soon." I walked around the edge of the reception hall. I spotted a cluster of our field hockey teammates hugging and crying, with Melissa at the center of the huddle. I knew I should join them. They would surround me in an instant and do whatever they could to make me feel better. We might not be close friends, but they were my teammates. I stood there trying to force my feet forward, but I couldn't do it. I wasn't ready to feel better. I didn't deserve it. And all I had left was the pain.

At the front of the hall, Britney's dad tapped on a microphone. It let out a squeal that made everyone wince and stop talking. Dr. Matson cleared his throat.

"We want to thank everyone for coming today," he said, his voice cracking. "As you can imagine, this has been the most difficult week of our lives. There are no words to describe the pain of losing a child. Britney was an amazing young woman filled with promise and beauty, and we will regret every day that she won't have the opportunity to live up to all that potential." Brit's dad put his arm around her mom. "We wanted to do something that would allow us to mourn Britney in a positive way, in a way that ensures her memory will live forever."

Brit's mom leaned forward to speak into the mic. "We are proud to announce the establishment of the Britney Matson Foundation. The foundation will be dedicated to expanding counseling services in low-income high schools so that teenagers everywhere will always have someone ready and able to listen." Dr. Ryerson pulled a loose drape off of a framed poster that said THE BRITNEY MATSON

FOUNDATION in thick red script.

There was polite applause and Brit's parents posed next to the framed poster for a photograph. I knew they were trying to do a nice thing, but they'd done it all wrong. If they wanted to honor and remember Brit, they should have chosen something that mattered to her. If Brit were going to have a foundation, she would want it to support female athletes, or aspiring fashionistas, or even shelters for homeless cats. But instead they had chosen something important to them and their careers. They hadn't even put Brit's photo on the poster.

It was just like Brit had told me when she was alive: her parents were always putting what they wanted above her. Now she was dead and they were still doing it.

The room was feeling too warm for me. I needed some air.

I dodged down the hall past the coatroom. Everywhere I turned there seemed to be more people. I couldn't go outside in case the journalists were still there, waiting to tear the flesh off me, strip by strip. I tried a random door and found an empty reception room with chairs stacked against the wall and giant windows that looked out over the bay. It was a nicer room than the one the party was in. But I guessed that a water view would have been in poor taste, given how Brit had died.

I watched the waves march in. When I closed my eyes I could imagine Brit's body floating faceup, bumping along the shoreline, her mouth slightly open, her eyes blank. A second later, the image morphed and it was Beth's corpse I saw, her hair mixed with seaweed, her stare unforgiving. I shook both images out of my head.

I sat down on the floor, half hiding in the thick dark blue velvet curtains, in case anyone peeked in. It reminded me of the blanket forts Nadir and I used to build as kids. Cozy. Safe. Eventually I'd have to go back into the party and find Zach, but I needed a few minutes of silence here first.

I pulled out my phone and stared at the screen. I must have checked it a zillion times in the past few weeks. I'd done everything I could think of to make Beth reach out to me— I'd made all sorts of deals with fate—but other than that one text a few days after she left, she'd stayed silent. That meant either she couldn't call me, or she was choosing not to.

A tear ran down my cheek and I wiped it away. All I wanted was to know that she was okay.

No, that wasn't true. I wanted to go back to the moment when she offered to take me with her, and this time I wouldn't say no. But that wasn't going to happen.

I kept acting like she owed me an answer, but the truth was she didn't owe me anything. It was time to face the fact that whatever I felt, she clearly didn't feel the same. Sometimes, as Nadir tried to tell me, no message is a message. I thought of one of the lines that Beth had underlined in her copy of *Alice*: "If everybody minded their own business, the world would go round a great deal faster than it does."

It was time to let go. If Brit were still alive, that's what she would have told me. Beth would come back only if and when she felt like it.

I pulled the Queen of Hearts card back out of my pocket. It had come to a point where I was finding trash in parking lots and deciding that it was supposed to be some kind of message. Talk about seeing things that weren't there. At this rate I was going to end up wandering around in a tinfoil hat, trying to receive messages from the beyond.

I pulled up my email and typed a quick message.

> **Beth—**
> **Sorry if I've been a nag. I hope things with you are good and that you find everything you want in life. Take care.**
> **Kalah**

I read it over once, making sure there weren't any extra guilt strings, and hit SEND.

With the swooshing sound of the mail flying off, my chest loosened. I stood. I would go back and find Zach, and we'd get out of here. It was time I stopped wishing things were different. Britney was dead. Beth wasn't coming back. I'd been left on my own, but I didn't have to stay in place. I could choose to move forward.

I tore the Queen of Hearts in half and dropped the pieces in the trash as I walked out of the room.

CHAPTER EIGHTEEN

The cafeteria table where the three of us had always sat was empty. It wasn't draped in half-dead flowers, molding teddy bears, and notes, like one of those roadside memorials, but no one wanted to sit there either. People avoided it like it was haunted or infected with bad luck. Or like they still knew they couldn't sit there without an invitation from Beth or Brit. Its emptiness stood out as I scanned the busy room.

A few of my teammates sat together at a table near the soda machines. Amy Chan waved to me and pointed to an empty seat next to her. I held up my history textbook and shrugged. I wasn't really going to study, but the thought of being around anyone besides Zach made me want to crawl out of my skin, and Zach didn't have lunch this period. I could feel the entire group watching me as I walked across the room toward Brit's old table.

Yesterday, Melissa and Amy had approached me in the halls to suggest we resume our Monday field hockey practices, "like Brit would have wanted." As next year's captain, running the practices should fall to me, but I couldn't imagine playing on that field without Beth or Brit. "Be my guest," I'd told them. I knew Melissa felt she should have been tapped as a co-captain anyway. As far as I was concerned, she could have it.

I plopped down at the table and opened my book to a random page. I could pretend to read so people would leave me alone, but I wasn't taking in the words. They just swam in front of my eyes. Ever since Brit's death, studying had proven impossible.

I knew everyone thought it was weird I sat by myself. It wasn't just Amy—a bunch of people had tried to let me know I was welcome at their table. Just because Beth and Brit were gone didn't mean I'd lost the status their approval had given me. But I couldn't fathom listening to people talk about their plans for prom, the test in biology, or whatever inane stuff was going on. For most other people, normal life had continued, but I wasn't ready to join in. It was easier to be alone.

I'd promised Zach we would go out tonight, though. He said I could pick anything I wanted to do, but he wanted to go out. He kept telling me that it wasn't a betrayal of Brit to have some fun. I'd agreed to at least try.

I pulled out my lunch bag and a folded piece of paper fell out. It was a Far Side cartoon my dad had downloaded and printed off for me. He'd scribbled at the bottom, *Love you!* The Tupperware contained my mom's famous mango quinoa salad. She knew it was one my favorites. Both of my parents kept going out of their way to be extra-nice to me while trying to act like they weren't doing anything different. There was a constant undercurrent of "Please be okay" that ran through every interaction I had with them. Pretending to be normal was exhausting.

I stabbed a cucumber slice and made myself chew it. Nothing tasted right since Brit's death. The food actually felt wrong in my mouth—foreign, like chewing Styrofoam peanuts—and it was hard to swallow. A few times I'd spit things back out into a napkin because there was no way to get them down. I knew my mom was getting worried. If I got any thinner she would make me see our family doctor or go back to Dr. Sherman. I didn't want that. I forced down two more bites of salad.

A memory came to me in a flash. Brit had loved this salad too. She'd even asked for the recipe once. We laughed about it because she never cooked, but she insisted someday she would start. Now she never would.

I put the fork down. My life was a minefield of memories of Brit and Beth, and I never knew when one would pop out of nowhere and blow up in my face. I took a long, slow breath, in and out, trying to calm myself.

My fingers ran over the scarf I'd tied around my neck. It was Brit's. Her parents had given it to me after the funeral. If I held it up to my nose, I could smell a faint hint of Brit's perfume. I knew the scent would eventually fade, but for now it was nice. It made me feel less alone.

A tray plopped down on the table, startling me out of my thoughts. It was Sara.

"Mind if I join you?" She sat without waiting for an answer. "I'm Sara." She jammed her hair behind her ears, her movements jerky and awkward.

I blinked, shocked that someone had broken the bubble of space around me. It was clear I wanted to be by myself. "I know who you are," I said.

Sara flushed. I looked down at my book and hoped she'd take the hint to leave.

"I, um, just wanted to say I'm sorry. About everything that's happened." Sara folded and refolded the paper napkin on her tray.

I felt the fog I'd been in start to clear. It was replaced by sharp, clear anger. "I'm not really the one you should be apologizing to," I said. "That person's dead. And isn't it a little late for you to be making amends?" I knew I sounded bitchy, but I wanted her out of my face.

Sara's hands were shaking slightly as she played with her fork. "I just, I see how Jason's suffering, and I know this must be really hard for you too. I thought I should say something."

"And since you've been comforting Brit's boyfriend, you thought maybe you'd sit down at her table too?" I said. "If you're looking for someone to forgive you, you'd better look somewhere else."

Sara jumped up, her chair squealing on the floor. Her mouth quivered and her eyes were filling with tears. "I'm sorry. I just wanted to help."

"You've helped plenty already," I spat out.

Sara bolted, tripping and knocking over a trash can on her way out. Food and wadded-up napkins fell out onto the floor. A bunch of dickhead junior guys let out a cheer.

"She was trying to be nice," Jason said. He loomed over me, his face hard.

For a split second, his anger scared me, then I stood so I could look him in the eye. "If she wanted to be nice, she shouldn't have fucked my best friend's boyfriend," I hissed.

Jason jerked his head around to see if anyone had heard me. "We're not talking about this here."

"Why? Ashamed?" I cocked my head. "Why do you care if everyone knows you're already nailing someone else?"

Jason took me by the elbow and tried to steer me toward the door. I yanked my arm back. Jason flinched. "Would you please come with me?" he asked.

I crossed my arms and followed him out of the cafeteria. I wanted to hear what he'd have to say for himself. We stepped around the corner so we could have some privacy.

"Look, I know you're mad at me, and I get it," he said. "You're not the only one who blames me. I've been blaming myself plenty too. But at the end of the day, this was Brit's decision. I'd give anything to change what happened, but Britney's gone."

"So that's it? We just forget she was ever here?"

Jason rubbed his eyes. "No, of course not, but people can't grieve forever."

My mouth fell open. "Forever? It's been, like, two weeks."

Jason looked down. I hoped that look on his face was shame.

"If moving on is the right thing to do, why aren't you telling people about you and Sara? Why are you letting everyone still think you were hooking up with Beth? Does it make it better for you to let the whole world think that Brit's best friend also betrayed her, when really it was only you?"

Jason's eyes were filled with misery. "I know I should tell the truth, but Brit is dead anyway, so the truth isn't going to help her. Beth isn't here to be hurt, but Sara is."

"I don't care about Sara," I said.

"But I do. I love her. I didn't mean to fall in love with her, and I sure as hell never meant to hurt Brit, but it happened."

I did not want to feel sorry for him. "Well, I loved Beth and Brit, but that doesn't mean it's enough," I said. I spun around and walked away.

If Britney knew how Jason was acting, she would be sick that she'd killed herself over him. It was still hard to believe that it had really happened. I wondered if Brit had believed it herself, if she'd truly understood that what she was doing would be so final. Or if, right until the end, some part of her believed that someone would stop her, someone would save her, or somehow it would all turn out to be a terrible dream.

I pictured her standing on the cliff above the water, curling her toes over the edge of the rock, preparing to jump. I imagined her turning her head when she heard a noise, and seeing Jason rushing toward her, shouting for her to stop, apologies falling from his lips. I imagined the sad, relieved smile that would have crossed her face as the wind whipped through her hair and dried her tears.

Then I imagined Jason looking at Brit but thinking of Sara, and realizing how much he had to lose. I pictured his face curling up in a snarl as, instead of saving Britney, he shoved her hard, pushing her over the edge of the cliff, listening as she screamed before her body hit the water and her head smashed into the rocks below.

I saw him standing there in shock, realizing what he'd just done. Then, pulling himself together as he realized too that she'd helped him get away with it. Britney would have already written the suicide note. No one would have to know what he'd done.

I squeezed my eyes shut. This daydream was crazy. Jason may have broken Brit's heart, but that didn't make him a monster. Just because I could imagine something was true didn't make it true. Still, my stomach felt as if I'd filled it with lead. Was the idea that Jason may have killed Brit any harder to accept than the idea that Brit had killed herself?

I leaned against the wall. I didn't want to go back in the cafeteria. It wasn't like I was going to be able to eat anything more anyway.

My phone buzzed in my pocket. It was Zach, probably, wanting to know the plan for tonight.

I'd vote for a movie. At least then I wouldn't have to talk. I glanced at the notice on my screen. There was a strange buzzing in my ears. After all this time.

Beth.

CHAPTER NINETEEN

Hi K—

Surprise! Bet you thought you were never going to hear from me. I'm sorry I've been so out of touch. I promise I'll explain everything soon. You'll have to trust me that I can't right now. It's complicated.

How are you holding up? Thanks for telling me about Britney. I heard the funeral was beautiful and standing room only. How is everyone at school taking it?

I don't want to use my old email and stuff (long story) and texting is complicated (even longer story!) so write me back at this address okay?

Beth

I stared at the email, trying to rearrange the words and letters into some sort of new pattern that would make more sense.

That was all she had to say? I shoved the phone back into my pocket.

Maybe I wouldn't answer for a couple of days. Let her see what it feels like to be ignored. Let her wonder if something happened and her message didn't get through and then realize that it did, but the other person couldn't even be bothered to respond.

I chewed the inside of my cheek. There was no way I'd wait. I might like the idea of teaching Beth a lesson, but I wanted to talk to her more than I wanted to be in the right. I couldn't even lie to myself.

I was going to have to lie to someone, though.

"No, don't cancel on me," Zach said. "Please."

"I'm just not up for it tonight. Maybe next week," I said.

"We could do something low-key, like a movie," he said. "I really think it would be good for you to get out."

I knew he was trying to be supportive, but I was irritated. I wanted to go home so I could reread Beth's message in private and think about how to answer. I wanted to be alone. "I'm really tired. I haven't been sleeping well. I need to go to bed early tonight."

Zach sighed. "Kalah, I know how hard this is for you, but you have to at least try. It might feel like your life is over, but it isn't. Come out with me. Do some of the things you used to do. Live. Brit would want you to be happy."

That showed how little Zach understood Brit. She would love it if the rest of us never moved on.

But this wasn't about Brit. It was about Beth. "I can't go out and act like everything is fine," I said.

"You'd be out with me. You don't have to act," Zach said, taking my hand.

How could I tell him I'd been acting for so long I didn't even know who I really was anymore? "I'm sorry. I can't do it."

Zach's mouth pressed into a tight line. "Fine."

"Don't be mad," I said.

Zach shrugged like he was fine, but the tension in his shoulders told the truth. "I'm not mad." He grabbed his bag off the floor and walked away.

Now both of us were lying.

I shut the door to my locker and headed down the hall. As I passed by the art room, my memory flashed on the last time I'd seen Britney in school, fighting in this hallway with Jason. The hair on the back of my neck went up, and for one crazy moment, I thought I could feel the presence of Britney's ghost, standing there just beyond where I could see.

I peeked into the room. There was no floating specter, no ghost version of Britney.

I let out the breath I'd been holding. I was actually

disappointed. Part of me had been hoping Britney would be there, my own personal ghostly advisor, like from one of the books she used to read. Dead, but not gone.

Brit would have known how to handle the email from Beth. She would know exactly what to say.

"Brit, I need you," I said softly. I didn't expect her to answer, but I was still sorry she didn't.

> Beth,
>
> I was really glad to get your email. I'm sorry things are so messed up for you. I hope you know you can talk to me about anything, and if you don't want to talk about everything that's okay.
>
> But you also have to know things have been difficult for me too.
>
> You should have been at Brit's funeral.
>
> I miss you.
>
> Kalah

I deleted the "I miss you" and then added it back in a thousand times. I didn't want to come across as clingy, but I also wanted her to know how I felt. I was mad, but at the same time every atom in my body ached for her. There was an inescapable gravity still pulling me to her.

I'd barely sent the message when there was a ping indicating I had one in return. She must have been waiting for me to respond.

I know I let you down. I'm sorry.

B

It's not just me. You let Brit down.

K

Let's switch to chat. I'll send you an invite. I want
to explain and I can't call.

B

I sat in front of the computer, waiting. My emotions kept
shooting from one extreme to another—excited, nervous,
relieved, furious. I wanted to jump up and down because
she'd finally reached out and at the same time I wanted to
shake her and demand she tell me how she could leave me.

The chat window opened with a beep and I leaned forward.

You're right. I should have been at Brit's funeral. I
owed her that. Brit's words scrolled across the screen. She
deserved so much better. It shouldn't have ended like that for
her. How is everyone taking it?

People are still sort of shocked, I wrote.

Me too.

It's been weird watching everyone at school react to it like
it's their own tragedy. I guess they're allowed to be shocked
and sad, but also . . . they didn't know Brit like we did. They
didn't lose one of their closest friends. You know?

I know, she wrote. **How's the team reacting?**

Same. Everyone wants to do something for Brit next year, maybe put a patch with her initials on our jerseys.

Then you guys would win State for sure.

I pushed aside some annoyance. I didn't care about field hockey right now. **Why didn't you respond to my messages?** I held my breath, waiting to see what she would say. I wanted her to have a good reason, something that would make her silence seem okay.

I'm sorry, K. It's hard to explain. I wanted to start all over. I thought it would be easier if I just cut off all contact. Things with Brit and me were really complicated. Obviously.

My foot was tapping and I forced myself to stop. **What about things between us?** I typed.

Not complicated at all, she responded.

I wanted that to mean good things, but I worried it could go either way. **I will always be here for you,** I told her.

I thought you might be pissed. Because of the thing with Jason. How is he? Is he sick about what he did to Britney? I bet everyone hates him. And me, of course.

I guessed she didn't want to talk about us. **I was angry at first. Since I hadn't heard from you, I thought it might really be true. Maybe I should have known better, but everyone was so convinced. I hate that Brit died thinking that you betrayed her. I wish she could have known the truth.**

I waited for Beth to answer, but there was no response. **I'm sorry, I'm not blaming you,** I wrote. **It's just been really** hard. But of course you would never have done that to Brit. I considered adding that I knew she wouldn't have done that to me either, but then she started typing.

Who was Jason with?

A sophomore named Sara Green. There was no response, so I kept going. **People don't know yet, but he told me the day after. She looks a bit like you, so I guess that's how the rumors started.**

Still nothing. **I wish you'd come back and set the record straight,** I wrote.

It's a little late for that now.

I swallowed against my disappointment. That wasn't the response I'd wanted.

WTF. Sara? Are you kidding me? Beth wrote. **I can't believe Brit killed herself over nothing. She should have stayed and just crushed Sara. No way would he have picked her over Brit in the end.** I stared at the screen. That was kind of a weird reaction.

Jason still hasn't told anyone else, I wrote. **He's letting everyone still think it was you because he wants to protect Sara.**

Wait. He's still dating her? After Brit died?! I could practically see Beth's outrage pulsing through the screen.

He says he really loves her.

NO FUCKING WAY, Beth wrote.

I know. And I hate that he did this to Brit. But also I feel kinda bad for him sometimes.

Why? He deserves to be shot. Or castrated. Or both. Whose side are you on?

I should have known Beth would react that way. **I just meant that sometimes love can get confusing.** I shut my eyes, afraid to see what she'd say.

I've never been that confused, I saw when I opened them.

I paused. Once again, her words could mean anything.

Besides, look at you and Zach. No confusion there, Beth typed.

That was a low blow. But she had a right to be angry about him and me. And at least we were finally talking about this. **Is that why you left?** I wrote.

Honestly, Kalah, I don't even know what you mean. For the record, sometimes it's not about you.

I felt two inches tall. **When are you coming home?**

Never. I can't.

You can, I insisted.

You have no idea what I'm dealing with, Beth wrote. **It was a mistake to contact you. Just forget me.**

I wanted to reach through the screen and throw myself against her and beg her to take it back. She couldn't disappear on me again now. Not when I'd finally just gotten her back. **Please don't say that. Hearing from you means everything.**

There was no response.

I lost Brit. I don't know if I can handle losing you too. If

you can't come back, fine, but promise me you'll be in touch again.

Beth still didn't reply. My foot tapped like mad below the desk. **Please don't do this to me,** I begged. I didn't care if I sounded desperate. I *was* desperate.

I watched the curser pulsing like a heartbeat.

Okay. I'll be in touch, Beth wrote. Before I could say *thank you,* she had already signed off.

CHAPTER TWENTY

I stood back a few feet while Chester turned the com-bination on Britney's locker. It opened with a pop.

"There you go," she said, giving me a smile that looked more like a grimace before she left me to my task.

My hand rested on the locker door. It felt momentous pulling it open, like opening King Tut's tomb. Hopefully neither Chester or I would end up cursed. Maybe I would make sense of Britney's death by the artifacts she'd left behind.

It was eerie in the empty hallway, entirely too quiet. The office had given me permission to skip gym class to clean out Brit's stuff. Principal Hamstead didn't want there to be a crowd around when I did it. Someone might take pictures and try to sell them to the media. Anything from Brit's life was practically a holy relic. The week of the funeral I'd turned on the TV and seen Melissa reverently holding Brit's hockey stick while she was interviewed. I'd turned it off before I kicked the screen.

The school would have had Chester clean out the locker, but Brit's parents didn't want that. Dr. Ryerson had called and told me how they couldn't stand the idea of a stranger "pawing" through Brit's things. I couldn't tell her I didn't want to do it, that it still felt too raw. This was yet another reminder that Britney was gone.

Beth was gone again too, apparently. Four days had passed since our Friday-afternoon emails and chat. I'd had no new messages from her all weekend. I was wearing my phone battery down from constant checking. I'd even had Zach send me an email Monday morning, in case my phone wasn't getting messages right. The phone worked fine. I'd given up.

I swung the door open. A sour-sweet smell wafted out of the locker. Something had rotted. I spotted Brit's lunch bag up on the shelf. I grabbed it between two pinched fingers and tossed it directly into the trash can I'd dragged over, without even risking a look inside.

The knowledge that Brit's body must be rotting now too hit me with a thud. I imagined her skin, soft and bloated from almost three weeks in the water. Her flesh loosening from the bones. I backed up, gagging. I bent over and put my hands on my knees, sucking in clean air. I shoved the image out of my head. When I was sure I had control, I approached the locker again, breathing through my mouth to avoid any hint of the smell.

I took Britney's sweater off the hook, folded it up carefully, and put it in the box the office had provided. She had a pair of ballet flats at the bottom of the locker. I slipped my foot out of my shoe and tried one on. They fit Cinderella perfect. I kicked it off and put the flats in the box along with her textbooks. Wearing the shoe made me feel uncomfortable, like I might be next.

Brit had papered the inside of her locker with pictures of her friends and glossy pages from magazines. There were photos of her and Jason, one of the entire field hockey team covered in mud after a game, and one of her and me and Beth. It was at the mall. Christmastime. The three of us perched on Santa's lap. Beth was laughing so hard that her face was blurred. Brit had a perfect model smile, and I was grasping a nearby giant stuffed penguin to keep from falling off the lap. I peeled the picture off the metal door and stared at it.

I wanted to reach inside the photo and warn the earlier me that trouble was coming. I should have savored every amazing moment we had before everything went bad, and hugged it close. I hadn't appreciated every second of my time with them because I didn't know then that there were only so many seconds left.

I'd thought we had endless time together. The me in the

picture wasn't able to even imagine this moment, standing in front of my dead friend's locker, wishing my missing friend would call.

I carefully pulled the tape off the rest of the pictures and tucked them into the box, but I kept the Christmas photo for myself. Brit's parents wouldn't miss it. I grabbed another stack of things from the locker. The sooner it was done, the better.

"I know you won't believe me, but it will get easier."

I spun around, dropping the notebook I was holding. Officer Siegel stood right behind me.

"Sorry. I didn't mean to sneak up on you." She stepped even closer and lifted a picture out of the box. It was a photo-booth strip of Jason and Brit mugging for the camera, crossed eyes, goofy smiles. In the last frame they were kissing. Brit had crossed a giant red X through Jason's face. The pen had torn through the paper. She must have done it after she knew. "She had her whole life ahead of her," Officer Siegel remarked.

I took the picture from her hand and threw it out, like I should have done in the first place. Jason's mangled face stared up at me from the trash. "Yep."

"How are you doing?"

Did she expect me to think she cared? "Fine." I tossed a stack of calculus handouts into the trash.

"Do you still have the number that Ms. Harding gave you?" she pressed.

"Do I look like I need a crisis center?"

Officer Siegel shrugged. "Sometimes when one person does the impossible, it doesn't seem that impossible to people around them anymore."

"You're too late," I said. Officer Siegel's left eyebrow went up. "We already got the talk from Ms. Harding last week," I explained. "Suicide can happen in clusters. We should talk to someone if we find ourselves feeling depressed, or tell someone else if we hear one of our friends talking about it." I parroted Harding's speech in a flat voice.

"Good advice."

I made a noncommittal noise and went back to the locker. I reached in to make sure there was nothing pushed to the back of the top shelf.

"I heard you didn't go to yesterday's field hockey practice."

Did Officer Siegel think I needed another mom? "I'm not feeling like it these days." The truth was, I didn't feel like I would ever want to play again.

"You're the captain. I bet they count on you."

"Our season is over. The practices are voluntary."

"Have you heard from Beth? She might have some advice on how to get through this."

The lie came out before I could think why I was saying it. "No." I hadn't told my parents or Zach about the messages. I wasn't about to make Officer Siegel my only confidante.

"I wanted to tell you I'm sorry we got off on the wrong foot," she said. I fought the urge to snort. Wrong foot? She'd basically called me a loser groupie. "If you need someone to talk to, I'm around," she offered.

"Sure," I said. "I should finish this. I'm supposed to get back to class."

Officer Siegel looked like she wanted to say something else, but instead she walked away.

I picked up Brit's notebook that had fallen on the floor, shoving the loose papers back in. I froze when I saw Beth's handwriting.

> B—
>
> I need to talk to you. It's about Jason. I'll come over an hour early tonight so we can talk before we pick up K. Don't freak. It's going to be okay.
>
> B

I turned the note over. Beth had scribbled it on the back of a Donut Dreams receipt. The date at the top was her birthday, the day she disappeared.

I flipped it over to read it again. It certainly didn't sound like Beth was planning to skip town that night when she wrote it. What had happened to change her mind in the hours between when she'd scribbled these words to Brit, and when she'd bailed on our plans and left? And if Beth somehow knew about Sara and Jason, why did she act so surprised when I'd told her? And why hadn't she found a way to tell Brit herself? Brit had said they were in touch, at least at first. Her angry words from our last conversation came back to me: "She dropped off the planet when I confronted her straight-out about Jason." But it made no sense that Beth would choose that moment to disappear on Brit.

Unless . . . no. I didn't believe it could have anything to do with Beth taking Brit's money. Whatever Officer Siegel had been trying to hint when she'd told me about that, she was wrong. That wasn't Beth.

Something was off, but I couldn't quite put my finger on it. I was missing a big piece of the puzzle.

I pulled out my phone and sent a quick message.

Cleaning out Brit's locker. Heartbreaking. Would love to talk.

The bell would ring soon. I checked once more to make sure I had everything. Brit's locker was empty, with just a faint hint of rot. I shut the door with a clang and hefted the box of Brit's things to take them down to the office.

I slept with my phone near my pillow so the instant it vibrated I woke up. I fished through the covers to grab it. The clock on my nightstand showed it was almost midnight. The bright light of the phone's screen made me blink. *Beth.*

You still awake? Chat?

Did you get my message? I typed. I rubbed my face, trying to wake up more fully.

Why were you going through Britney's stuff?

Did she really think privacy was one of Brit's big

concerns now? Her parents asked me to clean it out. Not fun.

How are her parents?

I don't know. Probably not good.

I bet they're sorry they were always so hard on her.

I didn't want to talk to Beth about Brit's parents. I wanted to talk about her and Brit. I found a note in B's locker from you. Saying you needed to talk about Jason. But I thought you didn't know about him and S?

I didn't, but I knew something with J was off. I was going to meet up with B, but decided I didn't need the drama after all. My birthday was a big blur. I had so much stuff going on. I was like the White Rabbit: late for my important date at the tea party. Ha!

I pulled the covers up to keep warm. Beth had an answer to everything. I bit my lip. No guts, no glory. You could have told me you were leaving.

Sorry. This was something I had to do on my own.

Tell me where you are, I typed. Let me come see you. I won't tell anyone.

You shouldn't be up so late, you'll turn into a pumpkin! Get some sleep. Talk to you soon.

Beth, wait.

I stared at the screen until it turned itself off, plunging me back into darkness.

I scrolled through our conversations again, looking for something I'd missed, trying to pin down what was off. But it wasn't a Nancy Drew mystery; there was no secret code.

Just the clear message that I wasn't wanted.

It was like Beth had decided to act like we'd never been together, or like she'd forgotten what we'd meant to each other. But nothing about that made sense.

Unless the person writing me wasn't Beth.

And if it wasn't Beth, there was only one person I could think of who could pretend to be her this convincingly.

Britney.

I scanned through the chats over and over. I felt uneasy, like when you hear a noise late at night when you're supposed to be alone in the house. The idea that Brit might have faked her own death and was now reaching out to me as Beth was absolutely insane. But so was the idea that Beth was ignoring our entire past. And, after all, they'd never found Brit's body. Maybe, just maybe, my friend wasn't really dead.

Wanting it so badly didn't make it true.

I paused, rereading the line about the White Rabbit being late for the tea party. It had been a few weeks since I'd read that part of the book, but I was suddenly certain that wasn't right. I grabbed Beth's copy of *Alice* from under my bed and flipped through it madly.

I found the section and skimmed through it. I dropped the book. The White Rabbit hadn't been on his way to the tea party. He'd been late for his job to announce the Queen of Hearts.

No way Beth wouldn't know that. No way.

CHAPTER TWENTY-ONE

Zach came up behind me at my locker. He slid his hand under the hem of my shirt and around my waist. His palm was callused from building theater sets. It made a whispering sound as it slid across the skin of my belly. My flesh rose up in goose bumps. He pulled me gently back against him and kissed me just below my ear.

"Hey, Zach," I said. I leaned back into him, grateful for how solid he felt.

"I brought you something."

I turned so we were facing. He held up a paper bag. Parts of it were transparent from grease. My stomach rumbled. "Honey's?" My nose was already twitching. I reached for it. Zach held it out of my reach for a second, then handed it over. I bit into the donut. "Oh God, these are the best," I said, spraying crumbs.

"Best donuts for the best girl." He leaned in and kissed me.

I kissed him back.

"Mmm, you smell like sugar," Zach said. "Instead of perfume you should just sprinkle some donut behind your ears." His eyes sparkled. "Maybe down your shirt too."

I put my hand on his chest and pushed him lightly, but I couldn't help smiling. "I'll keep that idea in mind."

Zach hoisted his backpack. "Walk you to homeroom?"

"Sure." I brushed the last crumbs from my face and we headed down A wing, holding hands. For the first time in weeks, I felt like I could breathe normally. It still hurt like hell that Beth had left, and I had to accept that she probably had abandoned me forever. But the small flicker of hope that maybe Brit was still alive had brought part of me back to life again too.

Late last night, lying awake in the dark, it had seemed almost obvious. Britney had pretended to kill herself in the heat of the moment, to teach Jason a lesson and go off to cool down. But she missed me, just as I missed her, so she'd reached out to me, pretending to be Beth. She couldn't reach out as herself, of course, since everyone thought she was dead. But once I let on that I'd figured it out, I would help her see that she could come back. She was probably scared that she'd get in huge trouble—faking a suicide might even be illegal—but I knew everyone would welcome her back like a queen.

Zach draped his arm over my shoulder. I wished I could tell him the incredible news, but I knew it would sound crazy to him. Instead of believing me, he'd tell me I had to start getting some decent sleep or I was going to snap. I'd convince Britney to come home first, and then I'd tell Zach.

"Kalah!" Ms. Harding was leaning out of her office door and waving like she was trying to flag down a plane. "Can I see you, please?"

I glanced at Zach. "You want me to wait?" he asked.

"No. It's okay." My stomach tightened around the donut as I saw the look on Ms. Harding's face. Deep lines were etched in her forehead. Whatever she wanted to talk about, it wasn't something good.

"Text me, okay?" Zach squeezed my hand and took off before the bell.

I dragged my feet. I could see Officer Siegel standing in Ms. Harding's office. Centipedes of nerves ran down my back. I swallowed hard.

"Kalah, come have a seat." Ms. Harding motioned me toward a chair. She shut the door behind her and a wave of claustrophobia buried me. I wanted to open the window so I could breathe.

"Is everything okay?" I kept my eyes on Ms. Harding. My toes curled up and released and curled up again inside my shoes. Ms. Harding and Officer Siegel were exchanging looks. I wished they would just tell me whatever they had to say.

When I was a kid I needed allergy shots, and I used to close my eyes while waiting for the jab of the needle. The waiting was always the worst. Nadir was the one who taught me to keep my eyes open.

"There's been some news," Ms. Harding said. "I thought it would be best if you heard it from us. However, I'm going to have to ask you to keep it quiet for now." She pressed her lips together.

I nodded.

Ms. Harding swallowed. "I'm not sure how to say this—"

"We've found a body," Officer Siegel said. "We believe it's Britney."

There was a strange ringing in my ears. It felt like I'd run right into a cement wall. I blinked a few times, trying to clear the fog in my head. "But . . . how?" I said. I'd been so convinced Brit wasn't dead.

"A fishing boat found the body when it came to the surface," Officer Siegel said.

I felt light-headed and ice-cold, as if I were floating in a half-frozen lake.

Officer Siegel moved so she was directly in front of me. "This will give us some answers, maybe put some questions to rest."

"Can I see her?" I asked.

Ms. Harding shook her head. "Oh, sweetheart, I don't think that's a good idea. She's been in the water a long time. You should remember her the way she'd want to be remembered."

I clenched my fists, squeezing until my nails bit into my palms. My hands almost didn't feel connected to the rest of me. I pushed away the ugly image that threatened to surface. Britney's body bobbing on the waves. Fish eating her eyes.

My lungs couldn't pull in enough air. Black spots started to crowd my vision and the roar in my ears grew louder.

"Okay, put your head between your knees." Officer Siegel's hand was on my shoulder pushing my head forward. I started to push back when I realized she was right, I was about to pass out.

"Are you sure it's her?" My voice came out sort of whispery. "How do you know it's Brit?"

"We're very close to certain," Officer Siegel said.

I lifted my head. "But not *certain* certain?"

She frowned. "Her face was . . . damaged, so it's a bit difficult to make a positive visual identification." She lowered her voice. "Her body likely smashed against the rocks and it looks like a boat hit her with its propeller. Not to mention she's been in the water for quite some time."

My stomach hitched as I pictured a boat motor slicing through Britney's face. More black spots blurred my vision and the room tilted. My lungs felt like they were filling with icy water. I was drowning. I swallowed hard to keep from throwing up on my own shoes.

"We're still sure it was her. The body type was a match and she was wearing Britney's clothing and sapphire ring."

Brit's dad had given her the square-cut stone when she turned sixteen. She used to say it was like a purity ring, only less creepy and less pure. She always wore it.

"We're waiting on some tests for final confirmation of identity. In the meantime, the family has pulled some strings to keep the fact we've found a body out of the press. There's no reason for her parents to be hounded for a reaction until it's official. But they agreed we should tell you on the off chance that there's a leak. None of us wants you to be blindsided by more hard news. We trust you to keep this quiet."

I nodded. The room tilted again and I whimpered.

"Oh, sweetie." Ms. Harding wrapped me up in her arms. She smelled like oranges. I knew I'd never be able to eat an orange again without thinking of this moment. "I know this is hard. Sometimes when we lose someone, it's hard to accept how final it is." She rubbed my back.

"I want to go home," I said.

Ms. Harding was already reaching for a pad on her desk. "Of course. I'll write a note for you. I'll call your mom to pick you up."

"No, it's okay. I drove in this morning, and she's at work." I stood. I wanted to bolt for the door, but I knew I had to act calm if I wanted them to let me go. "I'll be okay, I just need some time."

Ms. Harding looked ready to argue, but Officer Siegel nodded and opened the door. As I passed her she handed me her business card. "I put my cell number on the back if you ever need to talk."

Jason was at my side the instant the door closed behind me. I flinched. He must have been waiting. "They told you?" he said.

I nodded. "I knew she was gone, but it's still . . ."

His Adam's apple bobbed. "I know. When they hadn't found her body I could almost pretend it hadn't really happened."

His eyes were red and wet. I felt bad for ever thinking that this wasn't hard on him too. He'd done Britney wrong at the end of it all, but he'd been good to her too, for a long time before that. Maybe better than I'd been to Zach. And nobody deserved to suffer through this kind of loss.

Jason walked me to my locker so I could gather my stuff. I could hear the hum of classes going on behind closed doors, but it was like a radio station that you can't quite tune in to.

"I owe you an apology," Jason said. "You were right the other day. What I did to Britney was unforgivable. Me saying that we needed to move on was unfair."

"It's okay. I'm sorry too. I shouldn't have snapped at you or Sara." We stood silently for a moment. "I need to go,"

I said. I couldn't deal with Jason or his guilt right now. I wanted to curl up under my covers and shut everything out.

"Sure. But I wanted to let you know, I'm going to talk to Sara. We need to tell people the truth about us. It's not fair that Beth is getting smeared in this whole thing. If I'd listened to her in the first place and just told Brit about Sara myself, maybe Brit would still be alive today." He choked on the final sentence.

My attention focused and I gripped his arm. "Beth knew about you and Sara?"

Jason nodded miserably. "Yeah. She saw us together. She was furious. She told me Brit deserved to hear it from me, but if I didn't tell her myself, she'd do it. But I chickened out and Beth left town without outing me."

I stared at Jason, trying to connect the dots. Only one thing was clear: the messages weren't from Beth.

The messages weren't from Beth.

The messages weren't from Beth.

He opened his mouth to say something else, but I turned around and left.

I paced back and forth alongside the bed. My brain was like a hamster wheel, spinning around and around. I felt jittery, like I'd drunk an entire gallon of coffee. The messages had to be from Beth.

Britney was dead. They'd found her body. Britney was dead.

Unless Brit wasn't dead.

But the body wore her ring.

But the messages weren't from Beth. And whoever had written them knew Beth very well, and was very interested in the life Brit left behind.

Almost nobody knew Beth that well. And no one was as interested in Brit as Brit was.

I felt the room tilt and I sat down quickly. I was breathing heavily, almost panting.

If the body wasn't Britney's, then it had to be Beth's.

I was starting to panic. I could feel myself clinging to normalcy by my fingernails. If I let go I'd go spinning out of control like a character in a science fiction movie sucked into space from an airlock. I closed my eyes and made myself take a long breath in, counting to six before releasing it. This was beyond my tendency to imagine worst-case scenarios—this was insane.

I could totally picture Britney faking her death. It had all the soap opera drama she would love. It would give her a chance to punish Jason, make her the focus of attention, *and* teach all of us a lesson in how we should appreciate her so much more than we already did. But I couldn't imagine Brit killing Beth.

My phone beeped.

Time for a chat? —B

I sat down at my computer and opened the chat screen. My fingers shook as I typed in my password.

One problem with faking your own death is you can't stick around to see how crushed everyone is to lose you.

God, have you been watching the news? I'm sick of people talking about me, B wrote.

People are worried about you, I typed. **I'm worried about you.** This was an understatement. The last news story I saw had a picture of Beth and the caption *Where is she?* running across the screen.

I'm fine, B insisted. **But it's gotten to the point where I'm afraid to go out because someone might spot me and call in the media. I don't need this hassle. I'm trying to start over.**

A flare of anger burned in my chest. **If you would tell someone where you are, everyone would stop talking about it.**

It's not that easy.

You know what's not easy? Being left behind to deal with all this. Missing your two best friends. Or being DEAD. My fingers jabbed down on the keyboard.

The cursor blinked. B didn't type back. I rubbed my temples.

You're right. The focus should be on Brit. She was lucky to have you as a friend. I'm being selfish. And I miss you too. I wish we could be back in your room hanging out with that huge plate of your dad's famous cookies.

I stared at the computer. Maybe it really was Beth. I hoped so. God, did I hope so.

I missed her. I missed her every day with every atom of my soul.

It came to me in a flash, the perfect thing to say. **I miss you as much you missed Max**, I typed. If it was Beth on the other end, she'd remember the way she'd kissed Roogs's nose and told me about her beloved giraffe. She'd remember the way she'd kissed *me*. She'd know how I felt about her.

Max? God, I can't even remember half the guys I've hooked up with. I hope you miss me more than that!

I sat back and sucked in a breath. This was not Beth. There was no hiding from it.

I know it's been hard. You're the only one who has been really faithful to Brit and me. I won't forget that. Gotta run. She clicked off before I could respond.

I reread all the messages, over and over. It wasn't my imagination. This definitely wasn't Beth. It had to be Brit. There was no doubt.

Which meant Beth was dead and Britney had killed her.

CHAPTER TWENTY-TWO

You know things are not normal when your parents actually want you to go to a party on a school night. They were practically giddy that I asked to go out. They didn't even seem to care where I went, though I doubt they would have been as excited if they'd known that the host's parents wouldn't be home. Apparently Tyler's parents had Cinco de Mayo plans of their own.

Tyler Channing's annual Cinco de Mayo bash was a huge Northside tradition. His older sister had started hosting the parties eight years before, and when she'd graduated, Tyler's older brother had taken the helm, then passed it to Tyler after him. Now it was Tyler's senior year and the end of an era. Judging from the lights, the piñatas, and the live mariachi band, Tyler had gone all out.

While there was a distinct lack of adult supervision, it seemed like everyone under eighteen was there. Less than a month ago, Brit, Beth, and I would have been at the center of the party. Now I didn't even want to be there at all.

I would have stayed home except I'd promised "Beth" this morning to give a blow-by-blow account of the night, with pictures to illustrate. Beth wouldn't have cared about a party like this, but apparently Brit did.

Maybe she'd somehow suspected that Jason and Sara would use this night to make their public debut as a couple. If Brit was hoping that people would boo Jason and Sara or pelt them with garbage, she was going to be disappointed. There had been some whispers and side glances when they came in together, just as there had been at lunch, when she'd sat at his table and he'd draped his arm casually across the back of her chair, but now it was like they'd always been together.

Tyler and his boyfriend, Tomas, were having a dance-off in the center of the living room with Jason and Sara. Jason was as smooth as silk on the basketball court, but he danced like someone was applying an electrical current to his feet. Brit would have been embarrassed by his spastic moves, but Sara was laughing so hard she could hardly stand. I wanted to be mad at them for having such a good time, but it was pointless. There wasn't a person at the party who couldn't tell they were in love.

Tyler pulled Tomas close and kissed him before boogy-ing over to refill the chips and guac. Jason twirled Sara away, then spun her into his arms, and I felt a pang. If Beth were still alive, this party might have been our debut. I could be kissing her, tasting beer or margaritas on her mouth. I didn't like to dance in public, but Beth would have gotten me to do it. Beth was fearless. Of course it never occurred to her she should have feared Brit.

I pushed down another wave of nausea and panic. Until I knew what I was going to do, I had to keep my crazy theory to myself. Brit's messages were solid proof to me, but they were things only Beth and I would know. If I started spouting off about it without better evidence, people would lock me up.

A cheer went up and drew my attention. A giant box with a bright silver bow had been delivered. *TO SARA* was written on the side in block letters. Tyler passed it to her with a flourish.

Sara looked at Jason, her face flushed, but he raised up his hands to claim innocence. "I'd take credit, but I don't have anything to do with it. Tyler said a messenger just brought it to the door."

Sara plopped down on a chair and peeled off the tape slowly. You could tell she was the kind of person who never tore into her Christmas presents with wild abandon. She was a paper saver.

A bunch of people from the party had clustered around to see what the gift was.

"I was going to wrap myself up for you, but I ran out of time," one of the guys from the basketball team yelled out, and I could see her blushing. Jason gave the guy a light punch on his shoulder and everyone laughed.

Sara opened the box and pushed aside layers and layers of pink tissue paper. There was something about the whole situation that felt wrong. I realized I was gripping the beer bottle in my hand and I had to fight the urge to tell her to get away from the box.

She pulled out two stuffed animals, bears with their arms wrapped around each other in an embrace. There was a red satin heart pinned to their chests with "True Love" embroidered on it in curly script. An "aw" went up from the girls at the party. Sara squeezed the bears close while Tyler took a picture.

"What is that?" Tomas pointed at Sara's shirt.

Sara squealed in alarm and began whacking at her chest. There were cockroaches on her. Three or four. Then more. They crawled up her arm, across her neck, even on her face. The people around her screamed and jumped back. Sara had frozen in fear.

"They're in the bears," Jason yelled.

I looked down and saw the seams along the bears' backs were split open and roaches were streaming out.

Jason and Tyler began stomping on the bugs. I could hear the sharp crunch of the shells splitting under their feet. There was a smear of bug guts in the carpet and on the bears, a milky white fluid. Revulsion ran through me.

Sara was crying and shaking. As soon as Jason had killed the bugs and made sure they were all off her, he wrapped her in a hug. Tyler grabbed the box and dumped the bears inside, hustling it out of the room.

A cold certainty sunk into my chest. Britney had sent the box. I could picture her buying the bears, pulling out their stuffing, and replacing it with the live bugs. I didn't even want to know where she'd gotten those. She would have been smiling, imagining Sara opening it.

Jesus, she was sick. I swallowed hard. This was more than being mad, this was psychotic.

A rush of bile filled my throat and for a second I was sure I'd vomit. I squeezed my eyes shut, trying to get rid of the image my brain formed of Britney's mouth curled into a snarl as she accused Beth of betraying her. Lashing out. Hitting Beth.

Hurting her.

Killing her.

I fished another beer out of the bucket of melting ice and went outside. I needed to stop thinking about this. I needed air.

I found Zach and the rest of the Fleshtones doing cannonballs into Trevor's near-frozen pool. Early May doesn't exactly count as swimming season in Michigan, but it didn't seem to bother them at all.

"Bombs away!" Zach bounced off the diving board and somersaulted into the deep end, sending up a spray of water.

When Zach surfaced, he spotted me and climbed out of the pool. He took two steps and jumped onto the patio chair with me.

I shoved him gently in the chest. "You're soaking wet. It's freezing."

"I'm counting on you to warm me up." Zach reached over and grabbed a giant towel from the ground and pulled it over the top of us, making a terry-cloth tent. "Now I have you all to myself." He kissed me. His lips were cold but soft. I shivered and Zach wrapped his arms around my middle. But every time I closed my eyes I pictured the black-shelled bugs scurrying out of the bear.

"You realize that everyone can still see us, right?" I wanted to push him off of me, but I didn't know how to explain what was going on.

"I don't care who sees us." Zach ripped off the towel. "I love this woman!" He yelled into the night sky. An inflatable pool ball smacked him in the head.

"Dude. I have neighbors. Keep it down," Tyler yelled at him.

"I love this woman," Zach said in a loud stage whisper.

I covered his mouth with my hand. "Shhh." I wanted to burrow back under the towel and hide. I felt sick. I couldn't do this with Zach now. There were too many horrible truths in my head.

"I do love you, you know, more than anyone in the world." His eyes pinned me in place and his face was serious as he touched my cheek with one hand.

I felt a flash of panic. We'd never said "I love you" before. Why did he have to pick this moment to try it? "You've had too much beer," I said, trying to deflect him.

"I haven't had any beer," he countered. "I know I'm acting like a spaz, but it's not booze. I love you."

I kissed him. "I like everything about you," I said. "I adore you."

Zach pulled back and stared at me. "Wait a minute. You *like* me?"

I flinched. "That's not what I meant. You know how I feel."

"All this time we've been going out and you *like* me." He turned away from me. "Wow."

I shivered in the night air. "Zach, don't make this something it's not."

He got up from the patio chair. He was hunched over, like someone had punched him in the gut.

I scrambled after him. "Look, this just isn't a good time. Everything that's happened with Brit and Beth has me really messed up. My life is upside down. I can't give any more right now."

"I am trying to understand, I really am, but is there ever

room for me? For us?" Zach's voice sounded pleading.

"Of course," I said. "It's just . . ." My words trailed off.

"Just not now," he said.

I reached for him and he stepped back. I sucked in a breath, as hurt as if he'd pushed me away. I did need him. "Zach—"

"You know, this party sucks. I think I'm going to head home." He swallowed hard and wouldn't meet my eyes. "I'll talk to you later."

He walked away quickly, his gait jerky and uneven. I watched him go.

My anxieties ratcheted up several notches. Zach was my emotional security blanket. I knew I couldn't survive this without him. Without him close, the air felt razor sharp around me.

"Hey."

I turned. Jason and Sara were standing behind me. I wondered how much they'd overheard. Sara's eyes were still red. She'd been crying hard. I would have too.

"Great party," I said. They didn't laugh.

"We wanted to talk to you," Jason said.

"Can I catch up with you guys tomorrow? I think I'm going to go." My throat felt like I'd swallowed broken glass. "I had a few drinks and I don't feel too good," I explained.

Jason fished through his jean pockets. "Look, I haven't been drinking. Sara and I will drive you." Sara nodded.

"You don't have to do that," I said. But I realized I had

no idea how else I'd get home. Zach had driven me here. My parents would pick me up, but I could only imagine their reaction when they smelled beer on my breath.

"It's no problem. Then we can talk on the way. It'll be easier without everyone else around anyway." Jason led the way through the crowd with Sara and me trailing behind him.

I practically fell into the backseat of Jason's car. It was as if someone had found my off switch and flicked it.

I leaned my head against the window. If I squinted my eyes, it made all the lights blur as we sped past, almost like I was underwater. That was appropriate, since it felt like I was drowning.

Sarah turned on the radio to some classical music station. I didn't know if she liked that kind of music or if she thought I needed to hear something soothing.

There was a bump as we pulled into the driveway. I blinked, shocked to find that we were already parked in front of my house. I must have drifted off. I rubbed my eyes. "Thanks for the ride."

Jason twisted in his seat so he could see me. "Kalah. I have to ask you something." He looked at me steadily. "Did you send the bears to Sara?"

I was suddenly wide-awake. "What? No."

"I know you're upset about what I did to Britney, but that was me, not Sara."

"I didn't send them," I insisted. Sara wouldn't even look

at me; she just stared straight ahead, her arms crossed over her chest.

"I get sticking up for friends, but that was messed up," Jason said.

"It's disgusting," Sara spit out.

I wanted to cry. "I'm telling you, it wasn't me. I'd never do something like that." I thought of telling them that it was Brit, but they would think I was mocking them. Or crazy. Or both.

Jason sighed. "Okay, sure," he said. I could tell from their faces they weren't buying it. "I just wanted to tell you that if it was you that sent it, we got the message. You're not happy about us. That's fine. We don't need you to approve of our relationship."

"I swear it wasn't me," I said louder. It was like they couldn't hear me.

He shrugged. "Whatever. It doesn't matter. But you need to know if something like that happens again I'm going to talk to the police. Stay away from Sara."

I opened my mouth to argue, but shut it with a snap. Whatever I said, they wouldn't believe it anyway. Sara's lower lip was shaking. She was acting brave and pissed, but she was scared. She should be. She had no idea who she had as an enemy.

"Fine. Thanks for the ride."

I slid out of the car and slammed the door behind me.

CHAPTER TWENTY-THREE

"Last time I'm knocking," Mom called out. **"If you're** not up in five minutes I'm going to sic Dad on you."

My eye sockets felt like they were filled with gravel. The blankets and sheets were wound around me like a strait-jacket. I hadn't even washed the makeup off my face the night before. My jeans and top from the party lay in a clump by the closet. My normally orderly life was in chaos.

I sat up and caught a glimpse of myself in the mirror. Mascara was smeared under my eyes, making me look even more haunted. I got out of bed and started to put things where they belonged. With physical order restored, I could breathe a bit better.

My phone vibrated on the bed and I lunged for it. *Zach.*

You never said how the party went. Been waiting all night. Want deets! —B

I tossed my phone in my bag. I'd reply later. First I needed to talk to Zach.

I lurked in front of Zach's locker after first period. He hadn't come to my locker before class, and I still hadn't heard from him, despite the two texts I'd sent this morning. I could feel my nerves fraying at the edges. Unraveling.

Warmth slid down my spine as soon as I saw him round the corner. He paused for a second when he saw me. I held out the bag I'd brought.

"My treat this time." I shook the bag when he didn't reach for it. "Honey's. A fried pastry gesture of peace. Consider it a delayed breakfast."

He took the bag but didn't open it. "I shouldn't have left you at the party without a ride. I'm sorry." His words spilled out quickly. "I was out of line."

I could tell he'd practiced his apology. Zach hated conflict.

Being with him was like flannel sheets on a cold night. Warm. Easy. We were going to work it out. I'd panicked for nothing. A couple unanswered text messages and I'd exaggerated it into a potential disaster. "Jason and Sara gave me a ride; it was fine," I said.

"That doesn't make what I did okay."

His hand that was holding the bag was tight. Almost a

fist. I would feel better if he would eat the donut.

"What isn't okay is how I've been treating you," I said. I'd gone over in my head what I wanted to say too, but the words were now stuck in my throat, like they were mired in the thick toffee my grandma makes. I inched closer, hoping he would put his arms around me, making it easier, but he just stood there. "I haven't been myself, and I haven't been fair to you."

"Kalah—"

"Listen," I said, cutting him off. I could tell by the way he said my name, like it was covered in barbed wire, that I didn't want to hear what he was going to say next. "I've been really preoccupied, and really sad, but I need you."

Zach closed his eyes like he didn't want to even look at me. "You don't need me."

"Yes, I do," I said. He had no idea how bad things had gotten. I couldn't handle a murderous Brit on my own.

Zach let out a breath. "But you *don't* need me, that's the problem. You keep me at a distance."

My palms itched. I wanted to grab his vintage *Star Wars* T-shirt and refuse to let go. "I know I've been weird since all of this happened, but—"

"No. It's been longer than that. It started weeks before Beth took off. You were busy more often. You didn't want to talk, not about anything real. You'd kiss me, but it was like you weren't all there. Then Beth left and Britney died and I kept telling myself that I needed to be there for you."

"And you were," I said.

"But I need you to be here for me too!" He looked away.

Panic sliced through me like a shark fin through deep water. "It was just a stupid fight," I said. "We can work through this."

"I think we need some space."

"I don't want space," I said.

"But I do." His voice seemed to echo off the metal lockers behind me.

I felt kicked in the gut. I wanted to reach over and touch him, but it was like there was a wall between us. "Oh." My voice sounded small. "Are you breaking up with me?"

His mouth started to tremble and I felt a flash of hope when I saw tears in his eyes. He wasn't as done with me as he was acting. "This isn't easy for me," he said. "This isn't what I want."

"Then don't do it."

He shook his head. I held up a hand to stop him from saying anything. He wasn't going to change his mind. He'd decided before I ever opened my mouth. All I could do was contain the discussion. Keep it from spiraling further away from me. If I lost him altogether, I wouldn't be able to make it. "Fine, we'll take a break. But don't say it's over. Not over, over. You're my best friend." My voice cracked.

Zach looked resigned. "Okay. A break, not a breakup, but you have to know I can't be around you right now. I really do need space to think."

I nodded quickly before he could change his mind. "Sure. Space."

He held the Honey's bag back out to me. "You want this?"

"No. I got it for you." The bell rang. People rushed past, but I was rooted in place.

"Take care, Kalah."

"You too."

I leaned against his locker when he was gone. I was in this on my own and I'd never felt more alone or scared.

I skipped class. English didn't matter. I needed to keep the conversation with Britney going. I didn't want her to catch on that I knew she wasn't Beth. And I didn't want her to disappear on me again before I could make her pay. I needed to convince her to tell me where she was before word got out that the body had been found. Once the cops figured out that the body was Beth's, this dance would be over. I had to snare her before she thought to get away.

Sorry I didn't talk last night and give party update. Zach and I had a fight. I think we're breaking up, I typed into the chat window.

Oh K, I'm soooo sorry. You'll get through this. Head high.

For a second I actually felt a bit better. Like Brit was still my best friend and could make me forget the sting of Zach's words. As if I wasn't telling all of this to Beth's murderer.

How did the party go before that? Any excitement?

I closed my eyes and saw the roaches scurrying out of the bears. Heard the crunch of their bodies being crushed under foot. Brit wanted all the details. She wanted to know that her gift had been a hit. Screw her.

Nope, at least not that I noticed. I was too focused on things with Zach for most of it.

The curser pulsed silently. **Oh. At least tell me that Zach's not cheating,** Brit wrote. **I want to believe not every guy in the world is a dick.**

No. It wasn't anything like that, I typed back. **He thinks I'm too consumed with missing Britney. That I wasn't spending enough time with him.**

Srsly? Now I am even more convinced you can do better. If Zach doesn't understand how important your girlfriends are then he's clueless.

I wish Brit were here, I typed, each word feeling like navigating a minefield. **She always had the best relationship advice. I would give anything for just one more day hanging out in her basement, for the comfort of that couch and her making me laugh. No slam on you, but she was amazing with this stuff.**

True, but I know what she would say. She'd tell you that you are going to be fine. That Zach's an idiot for not realizing what he had in you.

The fan on my dresser swept the room blowing cold waves of air. The sound was oddly soothing. **Are you in driving distance?** I wrote. **Maybe I could come see you this** weekend, just a quick visit. I could really use a friend right now. I'm so sad about Zach and missing Brit so much.

She paused. **Sorry, K. I wish we could.**

Remember the advice you told me that one time by the sand dunes? I keep trying to think of that.

I can't remember what I said, but if it made you feel better then I'm glad.

My heart folded in on itself, growing harder. I forced myself to type. **I guess I have to just believe I'll feel better until I finally do. What is it you always say? You believe as many as five impossible things before breakfast?**

Exactly! That's the spirit.

Gotta run, parents calling. I clicked off and backed away from the computer as if it might explode.

Beth's all-time favorite quote from *Alice's Adventures in Wonderland* was a line by the Queen of Hearts: "Sometimes I've believed as many as six impossible things before breakfast." *Six.* Even though I knew it was true that this wasn't Beth, I couldn't stop poking at it.

Beth would have also remembered the sand dunes too. We'd gone out there just a few weeks before she left because she wanted to see if we could ride down the giant dune on a sled.

Beth always came up with crazy ideas like that. There was nothing she wouldn't try because she didn't care what other people thought. Beth just wanted to *do* things. To feel things. To suck the marrow from life the way we talked about in English class. Maybe she felt like she had to live twice the life to make up for her brother, or maybe she just had no sense of fear.

I'd found Nadir's metal flying saucer sled buried under cobwebs in the garage and brought it with me. I thought it was a bad idea, but I would have agreed to any of her half-assed plans if it gave me a chance to be alone with her. I wanted to kiss her. Again and again and again.

At first it didn't seem like we'd both fit on the dented sled. It was like trying to seat two of us on a hubcap. Beth had wrapped her legs around me and we both were pushing with our hands, trying to get some momentum.

Suddenly we were skimming atop the sand, spinning in circles, gaining more and more speed. We hit a divot and wiped out. Sand went in my eyes and ground into my clothing. My arm burned where the sand had scoured away a layer of skin. We lay side by side catching our breath.

Beth was giggling. Her hair was half buried and her face was dirty. She was beautiful.

"That didn't go well," I said, spitting out a few grains.

"That's where you're wrong," she said. "It was perfect! Right up to the end."

"You've got an odd way of looking at things," I told her.

"There are always bad bits," she said. "It's about enjoying the good parts in spite of them." Then she leaned forward and kissed me. She pulled back to wipe some sand from my cheek.

I smiled. "I'm pretty sure that was a good bit."

We laughed together and I leaned forward to kiss her again.

Every memory of Beth was like losing her all over again.

And I was going to figure out a way to make Britney pay for it.

CHAPTER TWENTY-FOUR

When I woke up and realized it was Saturday, I was so happy I almost burst into tears. NASA scientists should study the speed that gossip travels in the average high school. It had to be faster than light.

Yesterday the news that Zach had dumped me flew around the school. I didn't even bother explaining that we weren't broken up, we were on a break. But apparently neither did he.

History might have been the worst, because that class Zach and I had together. It's not like he ignored me, or demanded to change seats so we weren't next to each other, but I had no idea how awful it could be when someone you care about is extraordinarily polite to you. I had a new sharp understanding of the term "killing someone with kindness." Every time Zach gave me a stiff smile or said something vague and meaningless, like a conversation he would have with a stranger, it was like being punched all over again. I avoided him the rest of Friday as much as possible. It was the only way to survive.

Melissa and my other team members didn't say anything to me, though I was sure they said plenty *about* me. Not that I expected them to rush to my side in a show of girl power. I'd shut them out in the past few weeks, brushed off every offer to be one of them. Now I had to pay the price. I'd made myself stand up straight and pretend to be fine, pretend to need no one. It wasn't like I'd never been a school pariah before. But I'd never had to feel that way at Northside.

It had taken everything I had to get through the day. Every step down the hall I could feel whispers and pitying looks trailing after me. Rumors sticking to me like mud. I refused to let anyone see me hiding in the bathroom crying. I would act like it didn't bother me. Fake it until it was true.

Now that it was Saturday, all I wanted to do was stay in bed. Pull the covers over my head and never come out. But a waft of sugar and melted butter came from downstairs. My stomach rumbled. I'd skipped lunch on Friday and only picked at my dinner. I heard the clank of a pan on the stove.

I rolled out of bed and pulled on yoga pants. There was no point in being miserable, alone, *and* starving.

"I'm making French toast. You want a piece?" Dad said as I shuffled into the kitchen.

I nodded and pulled out one of the tall stools by the island to watch him work. He slid a plate over to me, the bread topped with warm bananas he'd caramelized on the stove. One of my favorites.

"Your mom told me about you and Zach breaking up."

I looked down. I hadn't planned to tell my parents right away. Not only would they be concerned because I'd lost my first boyfriend, but also they might wonder how much more I could take before I snapped. I was wondering it too. They were already watching me like a bomb squad watches a suspicious package left on a train. It might be fine, but it might blow up, taking innocents out with it.

When I'd walked in the house yesterday and my mom had asked me how my day went, I'd burst into tears. The giant snot bubbles under the nose, hitching chest, sobbing kind of tears. So much for keeping things a secret. My mom had let me cry it out, rubbing my back in slow circles like she used to do when I was a kid.

"I know you liked him," I said to Dad now. I used my fork to pick at my breakfast. My dad tossed a kitchen towel at my head. I tossed it back at him. "What's that for?"

"I did like Zach, but I'm crazy about you. What I want most of all is for you to be happy. How do you not know that?" He rolled his eyes. "And I had you pegged as the smart one in this family."

"Well, that was your mistake right there. I could have told you it was Nadir."

"Your brother is intelligent, but I still would have chosen you as the problem solver." He attacked his French toast. "You want to watch some TV with me later? There's a *NOVA* marathon on and it's going to rain all day anyway." My dad never met a show on PBS that he didn't love. He had a total man-crush on Neil deGrasse Tyson.

"Gosh, that sounds unmissable," I said.

"I weep for future generations and your lack of interest in quality public television. Fine. Pick something you want to watch."

"I don't know if I'm up for it," I hedged.

"We can stay in our sweats all day, no shower. Make popcorn later. Maybe get your mom to go out and get us some ice cream."

I mopped up the syrup with my French toast. At least a TV marathon with my dad sounded better than sitting alone in my room obsessing over losing Zach and what to do about Brit. And with the television on, at least my mom couldn't force me to sit around talking about my feelings. I didn't even know what I felt anymore. I was this giant sucking ball of anger and fear and despair all wadded together.

"I know you're doing this because you're trying to make me feel better," I said.

Dad pointed his fork at me. "See? You *are* the smart one."

I found myself smiling despite myself. "What about some reality TV?"

"Classic movies," he countered.

"Animated," I offered.

"Food channel," he said.

"Sci-fi movies?"

"Sold!" Dad slammed his hand down on the counter like it was an auction. "Fire up Netflix and find us something good. Grab the mail too. Your mom is hoping your cousin's baby shower invite will be in there. I'll be in as soon as I finish the dishes."

I shoved the last few bites in my mouth. I was stuffed. I went out the front door to grab the mail, flipping through the stack.

Amid all the bills and flyers for takeout there was a padded envelope addressed to me. There was no return address.

I turned the package over in my hand. My name was printed in tiny, precise block letters. There was a place where the ballpoint pen had torn into the paper slightly, exposing the plastic bubble-wrap liner.

My dad was humming in the kitchen, but he sounded so far away. Part of me wanted to take the package in to him, tell him that it scared me.

My dad had always taken my phobias seriously. When I was little he would carefully inspect under my bed and closet for monsters. He would encourage me to be rational, remind me that I was only afraid because I was imagining the worst, but the worst almost never happens.

I knew, rationally, that I shouldn't be afraid of this package. It wasn't a bomb, or a bloody finger wrapped in a rag, even if it was from Brit. Britney thought I was on her side. There was no reason for her to send me a creepy care package of bugs. As Nadir would say, I was seeing zebras.

I tore the envelope open along the side. A wad of pink tissue paper plopped out. I unfolded it carefully. The tiny pocket watch pendant I'd given Beth dropped into my hand. The silver was cool to the touch at first, and then warmed to match my skin.

I shuddered as hard as if it had been a pile of centipedes in the package instead of a charm. I couldn't help but see it as a warning. This had been around Beth's neck. Britney must have pulled it off Beth's body.

I turned the silver pendant over with the tip of my finger. A pocket watch was a perfect symbol. I was running out of time.

After one movie I begged off, telling my dad that I needed a nap so I could slip upstairs and be alone. I slid Beth's pendant onto one of my chains, and when I put it over my head, it hung right above my heart. That seemed fitting.

Maybe Brit sent it to be nice. Maybe she sent it as a warning. It didn't matter. It was mine now. I squeezed it to give me strength.

I sent a quick invite and waited.

Hey.

I got your gift, I typed. **I love it.**

I knew you would. You needed a pick-me-up after the mess with Zach. Besides, I felt bad about our conversation the other day. I was only thinking about myself, and you were focused on Britney. I thought this was a way to make it up to you.

How generous of her to give away Beth's things. I sat on the edge of my bed and tried to figure out what Brit would want to hear. What would convince her to come home and get caught. **It's still so hard for me to believe she's dead.**

I know. She was a good friend.

She was the best. But it's more than that. Brit was going to do big things. It's a loss for everyone, not just us. Think about what she could have accomplished at Cornell.

She only got in because of her family, Brit typed.

She got into Cornell because she deserved it! Maybe her family connections got her application to the top, but you and I both know Brit would have ruled that place by the time she graduated.

She would have, wouldn't she?

Hell yeah. Cornell wouldn't have known what hit them. It's such a waste, I said. **Speaking of, what are you going to do with yourself the next four years, and the next forty?**

What are you, my mom?

Sorry, but won't things kind of suck for you in the future

without even a high school diploma? I know you weren't on a path to rule the world like Brit was, but it seems kind of dumb that you're giving up college and everything. I know you wanted to get away from things, but did you really end up someplace better? I was laying it on thick, but I needed her to worry about those things if she wasn't already. **Oops, gotta go,** I wrote. I turned off the chat program. Let her stew on that for a while.

I leaned back against my pillows and rubbed the pocket watch pendant between my fingers.

Think about it, Brit. The world needs you. You can't disappear. C'mon, you bitch, imagine that we all can't live without you. Come back to us.

Come back so I can get you.

CHAPTER TWENTY-FIVE

I told myself it didn't count as breaking and entering since I knew the code to unlock the door. Brit's family kept losing the key to the nanny suite, so they had one of those locks put on the basement where you punch in the numbers. I'd seen Brit unlock it hundreds of times. She'd even told me the code. Back when I thought we had no secrets.

Britney's parents always spent Saturday afternoons volunteering. I had the place to myself. I closed the door behind me and felt an instant chill. The last time I'd been down here, we'd all been together. It was almost as if there was a transparent overlap of another world where the three of us were still in the basement suite. Beth flopped on the sofa, Brit sitting at the bar painting her nails, me sitting on the carpet, flipping through a magazine, and the music thumping in the background, the TV on but muted.

The room smelled dusty and stale, like it had been closed up since Brit disappeared. Dust motes kaleidoscoped through the window light that cut through the room.

There was a stack of magazines against the side of the sofa and an unfolded blanket heaped in the corner. I peeked in the bathroom. Brit's makeup and nail polish were lined up on a silver tray. No splotches of eye shadow or powder on the granite counter. Britney and I had a desire for order in common.

I opened each of the bathroom drawers. It was hard to tell, but I was pretty sure a few things were missing. Britney's favorite lipstick shade was MAC Please Me, a pink that she knew looked perfect with her skin tone. My fingers ran over the tubes. There wasn't a single one of that shade in there.

I opened the closet in the living room. Most of Brit's clothes were up in her room, but she kept a bunch down here too. The wood hangers clicked together as I brushed my hand across the cloth. Something caught my eye. I shoved the other hangers to the side and stared. It was Beth's cardigan. Her blue one. The one she'd worn on her birthday.

I pulled it out and inhaled deeply. It still smelled faintly like her, a mix of rosemary, mint, and hints of vanilla.

Beth had worn it that day, because it was the exact same shade as the enamel teacup charm I'd bought her.

More proof that she'd been here that night. I pulled on the sweater. I wanted it.

I ran my fingers over the bookshelf. Brit wasn't a big reader. Most of the books on the shelf were things that had been assigned in English classes, fat paperback romances, and her favorite paranormal books.

On one shelf there was a small glass bottle, almost like an empty perfume bottle tied with a red ribbon. I picked it up. There was a pressed metal tag tied to the neck. *DRINK ME.* I turned it over in my hand. This had to belong to Beth too, I was sure. I shoved it in my bag.

I turned in a slow circle. If I was honest I wasn't even sure what I was looking for. Did I think I'd come in and somehow develop a Sherlock Holmes–like ability to spot the whispers of what had happened using only the smallest clue as a map? Did I really think evil would leave a fingerprint? Or that Britney would have been so obvious as to leave a giant bloodstain in the center of the carpet as proof? There wasn't going to be yellow police tape across the door and a chalk outline of a body. But it was still a crime scene.

Beth had come here to tell Brit that Jason was cheating, but Brit already knew. She knew he was cheating and she was sure it was with Beth. She must not have allowed Beth to speak. She might have attacked Beth as soon as she came in, hitting her over the head with something heavy. Or whatever happened might have been an accident. Maybe when Beth denied being with Jason, Brit shoved her in frustration, catching her off guard. I imagined Beth falling back, her mouth opened in a perfect O. There were a lot of sharp corners in the room. The fireplace, the iron-and-glass coffee table, the edge of the granite bar counter.

Once Britney realized Beth was dead, she would have freaked out. Revenge is sweet, but a dead body in a pool of blood isn't. But what did she do then?

That's when I noticed it. The giant walk-in wine fridge. My hand was shaking as I reached for the handle. The seal made a gasping sound as the door pulled open. The air inside the fridge was freezing. Perfect for chilling your chardonnay, pinot grigio, or Diet Coke. Perfect for chilling your best friend's corpse. Morgue cold. Goose bumps rose up on my flesh.

I turned in a slow circle. Britney could have mopped up the blood and dragged Beth in here. Kept the body from rotting until she could get rid of it smartly. No wonder she hadn't wanted us to come down here that afternoon I came over to help with the student council packets. She hadn't wanted to socialize so close to Beth's corpse.

The pieces clicked into place like a tumbler in a lock. Brit had lain low for the weekend, biding her time, and making a plan. She'd deposited money into Beth's account, and sent a few texts from Beth's phone before disabling it. She'd skipped school the Tuesday after Beth supposedly took off so she could check into a hotel using Beth's ID, and withdraw money again using Beth's ATM card, someplace far enough away. She'd encouraged the rumors about where else Beth could be, and acted like she'd heard from her, so people wouldn't worry.

Did Brit think that with Beth out of the way, Jason would be hers again? She must have. But all along, just in case, she probably had a Plan B. Then when things with Jason still blew up, she put it into action.

She probably researched the tides to choose the right spot for dumping the body, in a place where it wasn't likely to surface. But just in case it did, she made sure it was otherwise unidentifiable and put her own ring on it. She dumped Beth's body off the cliff, left her car with the suicide note on the beach, and went off to start over with Beth's ID somewhere else.

Bitch.

I walked out of the wine fridge and spotted Brit's unicorn figurine on the end table, something you'd see in a place of honor in a nine-year-old's bedroom. I remembered Brit going on about how she'd had it since she was a kid. I used to think it was cute that Brit—pulled-together, sophisticated Brit—still had her unicorn. I picked him up. If only he could talk. Maybe he could tell me what had really happened, how it had all gone down.

I was furious with Britney. Both because I was sure she had done something to Beth, my Beth, but also because she'd put me in this situation. I'd loved Beth, but Britney had been one of my best friends too.

Now Brit was making me choose. If she'd murdered someone else, killed Jason or Sara, I would have been appalled. Sick. But I would have stood by her. I could imagine an alternate future where Beth and I, dressed in our best clothes, supported Brit during a trial. Yes, she'd killed someone, but we would have testified that at the core she was a good person.

I would have found a way to understand, even if I didn't approve. But Brit had chosen to kill the one person I could never forgive her for hurting. She'd taken Beth, and so I was losing them both. That somehow made it even worse.

There was crack and a searing hot, stabbing pain in my palm. I dropped the unicorn. The pressure of my fist had snapped off his horn and it had stuck in my flesh. I used my fingernails to pull out a sliver of porcelain and sucked on the wound. The coppery taste of blood filled my mouth. Just when I'd thought Brit couldn't hurt me any more, she'd found a new way.

I put the damaged unicorn back on the end table. There was nothing here and it was time to go.

I knocked on the open door. Officer Siegel had been focused on her laptop and seemed surprised to see me standing there, even though I'd called ahead to make sure she'd be there on a Saturday. She motioned me into her office. Calling it an office was a bit of an insult to real offices. I was willing to bet it had been a closet at some point. There were no windows and not even room for a full-sized desk. Instead there was a small table and two chairs. With the door closed behind me, it felt like the walls were closing in.

Of course, maybe it was supposed to feel like an interrogation chamber.

"You ever play Solitaire on that?" I asked her, motioning to the computer.

"Nope."

So much for small talk. I focused on trying not to pick at my fingernails and tried to figure out how to bring up what I needed to ask.

"You want a Diet Coke?" She reached down between her feet and opened a small cooler. "I keep a stash in here."

"Sure."

She popped the tops on two and passed one over. "I'd offer you a glass, but I'm sorta lacking in the Martha Stewart department."

"No problem." Our knees bumped under the table. "Can I ask you something?" I asked.

Officer Siegel took a long drink from her can. "I figured you didn't come down here for the ambiance."

"Is there any more news on Brit's body?"

She paused. "Any particular reason you're asking?"

"I've just been thinking about it. The media made such a big deal about how she would likely never be found, and then she was."

She rolled her eyes. "The problem with a twenty-four-hour

news cycle is that people have to fill the space. They find something to talk about even when they've got nothing to say. The story is starting to die down, but when it goes public that we've found her body it's going to explode all over again. The department brought in an expert on these types of deaths, and I hope he'll handle most of it." Siegel tapped her fingernail on the corner of the laptop.

"And he said the body seemed . . . normal? For a suicide?" I pressed.

"He said it wasn't unusual."

Now I was confused. "Is that the same thing?"

"Law is funny. People are found not guilty, but that doesn't mean they're innocent. There's a lot of gray zone in my work. What we know is that the expert states that given the way we think Britney died, the angle she would have hit against the rocks and the water, and the expected tides, plus the encounter with the motor boat, it's *reasonable* that her body would look the way it did. I know it's hard to take, but we're lucky that she was found. Gives her parents a bit more closure."

"So they didn't have any doubts when they identified her body?" I tried not to look too interested in the question, but I had to know. I understood that a body in the water would break down, but it hadn't been years. Shouldn't they still have known their own kid? Beth and Brit didn't even have the same coloring.

"My understanding is that when her dad came down to

the morgue, the coroner showed him a few pictures, but he didn't see the body directly."

"Why not?" I asked.

Officer Siegel leaned back and her chair creaked a protest. "Like I said, Britney's body was significantly damaged. Especially her face and head. There was no reason to put him through that. They cropped some photos to show him what they thought he might identify."

My stomach rolled.

"Ms. Harding's a better person to talk to about this, but you have to accept that Britney's gone. We have a suicide note, a shoe that washed up on the beach, a girl who was emotionally destroyed that her boyfriend was cheating on her, and a body wearing her clothing and jewelry. I'm sorry, Kalah."

"Of course," I said. But Brit could have faked every one of those things. I could picture her putting those details in place. Planning.

"The DNA test will confirm everything, of course," Siegel said.

My fingers started to tingle. "When will that happen?"

"The state lab is backed up, but we should have results any day now. Once that happens, we'll go public with the news. I'm sure you'll hear about it instantly."

Officer Siegel had no idea how much the story would explode. A countdown clock appeared in my mind. Once the police discovered the body wasn't Brit's and the media caught wind of it, Brit would know the jig was up. She would disappear forever.

My ears started ringing. I had to figure out some way to convince Britney to come home before the body became public and she vanished completely.

I had to make her believe she could get away with it. That she could still come back because there was no body, so there was no crime. That she could trust me with the truth that she was still alive. That even if Brit returned, no one would ever know Beth was dead.

Or I needed some kind of proof of what she'd done. All I had now were suspicions and circumstantial evidence. The note I found in Brit's locker, a sweater, and a few chat sessions wouldn't be enough to send the cops on a nationwide manhunt. Even once they realized the body they'd found was Beth's, that wouldn't mean they'd believe me that Brit wasn't dead too. If she didn't come back on her own, she had to give me some kind of evidence, something I could take to the police.

It sounded impossible, but I couldn't help believe I should be able to convince her. Disappearing had been an adventure, but Brit would get bored quickly with a life on the run. She was already bored. That's why she still cared about what was happening back home. It seemed more fabulous than wherever she was now.

Dying was exciting. Being dead was dull.

Britney was emailing me because she missed her life. She

already wanted to come back. She couldn't survive without being the center of attention. All I needed to do was tip the scale, make returning irresistible. Brit was smart, and she'd planned her escape carefully, but I had an advantage.

Britney didn't know that I knew the truth.

I stood and downed the rest of the Diet Coke. "Thanks for answering my questions."

"Of course. Not knowing is often harder for people," Officer Siegel said.

A laugh slipped out and I tried to cover it with a cough. "I'll see you around."

"Kalah?" Officer Siegel called. "If you need something, or if you're in trouble, you should feel free to call me."

"I'll be fine."

I'm not sure either of us believed me.

CHAPTER TWENTY-SIX

If Buckingham Palace had a doorbell, it would sound like the one at Brit's house. I stood on the front porch, listening to the sound of the chimes echoing through the giant foyer, bouncing off the marble floors.

Brit's mom opened the door and looked at me. She had a glass of white wine in one hand. There were deep black circles under her eyes. They looked as if they'd been carved into her flesh.

"Well, hello, Kalah."

"Hi, Dr. Ryerson. I wondered if I could talk to you about an idea."

For I moment I thought she was going to say no, but then she opened the door wider. "You know you're always welcome here," she said stiffly.

I followed her into the kitchen. There was a bowl of marinated olives on the counter. There were also a couple of takeout containers that she was in the process of emptying into a dish to be heated up. The place was far from an episode of *Hoarders*, but it was a mess compared to how it usually looked. There were crumbs on the table, and the kitchen towel hanging on the oven door was stained and limp.

Dr. Ryerson pushed the olives toward me, but I shook my head. Their salty scent filled my nose. The stereo was on in the living room playing some kind of opera, deep drums and mournful cellos. I wondered if Brit's dad was sitting in there in the dark.

"How are you?" I asked, stalling to see what sort of mood Brit's mom was in.

Dr. Ryerson took a drink of her wine. Her lipstick had bled into the lines around her mouth, which seemed deeper than I remembered. "We're holding up as well as could be expected."

"I was thinking about Britney's things," I said carefully, lacing my voice with sympathy. "I know when my dad's sister died, my mom said one of the most difficult things was figuring out what to do with her clothing. Britney always had the best outfits." I gave her a significant glance, like I knew all along it was she who'd been the fashion guru behind Britney's look.

She tilted her chin up and looked wistfully off to the side. "I raised her to understand that quality lasts."

"People at school always loved what she wore. We all sort of looked up to her, admired her style."

Dr. Ryerson looked down her nose at me. "Are you asking if you can have Britney's things?" The fact that she found this immeasurably tacky was written all over her face.

I put my hand on my chest. "Gosh, no. Not for me. But knowing how everyone loved Britney's style so much . . . well, I thought we could auction off some of her things and use the money for the foundation."

Dr. Ryerson put down her glass of wine.

This was make-or-break time. "Some of the things could probably bring in a lot of money, like that jacket she got in Chicago—"

"She has those Kate Spade handbags," her mom added. "And that one Italian leather tote too." Then her face clouded over. "It has a couple scratches on it."

"People wouldn't care about that," I said quickly. "You know, because they were *hers*."

Dr. Ryerson's finger spun around the lip of the wine-glass, her ring catching the light. "It would be a lot of work," she hedged. "Someone would have to catalog and take pictures of everything. I'm not going to have people crawling all over her things."

"I could do that," I offered.

"Are you sure?" She gave me an appraising look.

"I'd be honored to help Britney's foundation in any way I can." I hoped my voice sounded sincere. "Helping other kids reach out in their time of need is what Brit would have wanted."

Doctor Ryerson's eyes were glassy with tears, and I felt a flash of guilt. It wasn't her fault her daughter was a sociopath. At least, not her fault entirely.

"Let's do this." Dr. Ryerson gave a sniff and blinked rapidly. I reminded myself if anyone should feel bad about upsetting her it should be Brit.

"If it's okay, I'll take a couple pictures now with my phone so I can post a teaser about the auction and start drumming up interest around school and online," I said.

"You know where Britney's room is, so I'll let you pop up on your own. I still find it hard to go in there." She reached over and squeezed my hand. "Thank you."

I didn't have anything to say to that. I squeezed her hand back and grabbed my purse off the floor.

I slipped into Britney's bedroom. As always, it looked like it was taken right out of a magazine spread. I pulled open Brit's closet and took a moment to drink it all in. There are people who live in apartments that are smaller than Britney's walk-in. It had drawers, shoe racks, and a floor-to-ceiling mirror with a light that you could turn to different settings to see how your outfit would look in daylight versus evening. Each of the drawers had a lavender sachet tucked inside so her things would smell fresh.

I pulled out Brit's newest purse, arranged it on a bright pink scarf with some designer sunglasses, and took a picture. I grabbed a few other things and did a quick photo shoot. I sat on the tufted bench in the closet and uploaded the photos to our school events page with an announcement, and hummed under my breath. Another piece was in play.

Monday morning I got to school early. I scanned the street across from the student parking lot. The school administration had forbidden reporters from being on school grounds. For the first several days after Brit's supposed death, there had been a collection of vans with satellite dishes and small white tents set up clustered across the street. Now it was quieter, but there were still a couple of reporters around. They'd probably been stationed there just in case Beth finally came back or Brit's body was found. Or maybe they were hoping another student would jump.

I spotted the guy who'd approached me on the steps that very first day after Brit was gone. The one I'd almost hit with my car. Derek, he'd said his name was. I jogged over.

Derek was sitting in a metal folding chair that was sinking into the ground. He had a cigarette hanging out his mouth, and he paused every so often to tap the ash into a dented Mountain Dew can that was balanced on his crotch. He raised an eyebrow when he saw me.

I passed him one of the flyers I'd made the night before. His eyes skimmed over it.

—246—

"An auction, huh?"

"The Ryerson-Matsons and I are hoping to raise money for Britney's foundation. I thought you might want to promote it."

"Maybe." He dumped the cigarette butt in the can where it went out with a hiss. "Does it come with a statement from the dead girl's best friend?"

Classy. "It could."

Another reporter who had been listening in elbowed her cameraman and approached. "Would you mind if I filmed your comments?" she asked.

I bit my lip. "I don't know." I didn't want to come across like I wanted the limelight, but I'd been counting on an on-air opportunity. What good was the show if Britney couldn't watch it?

The woman crunched her face into an expression I think she hoped would mimic concern, but actually made her look constipated. "Think how a few words on television could help spread the news about your auction thingy."

I'd barely nodded before a bright light was shoved in my face.

"Tell us about your relationship to Britney," the reporter said. Derek stood behind her with his recorder.

I fingered Britney's scarf that I'd tied on that morning. I knew she'd recognize it instantly. "I like to think I was one of Brit's best friends, but I know I failed her."

"Can you tell us what you mean?" The reporter had

almost perfectly square white teeth. Her smile reminded me of one of those creepy wind-up monkeys with cymbals. The kind Stephen King wrote stories about.

"Britney always seemed so perfect. And she was special, she really was. Everyone looked up to her. I think most of us wanted in some way to be like her. The problem is, she wasn't perfect; she was human like the rest of us. Even those of us who loved her best—we never realized how much she might need us too. We let her down. *I* let her down."

"Do you blame yourself for her suicide?"

I forced my voice to shake and looked down as if I was about to break into tears. "People keep talking about why Britney killed herself, but they're missing what's important. They're focused on the last thing she did in her life instead of looking at the whole picture. Brit made one horrible mistake. One I know she would take back if she could. Don't judge her by that one desperate decision. I don't."

They let me say a few words about the online auction, and I nodded to show I was done. When the camera light went out there was still a white dot in the center of my vision. A blind spot.

I spelled my name for Derek and for the woman from the cable show. Derek passed me one of his cards in case I wanted to talk to him again.

That's all it was. One bad decision. Regrettable. Not something Britney would have done in normal circumstances. Certainly nothing for her to ruin her life over. Didn't she know her other best friend would be here for her?

Come back, Brit.

Believe me.

Come back.

I was going to have to run to make it to homeroom on time. I grabbed my bag and turned to sprint, then jerked to a standstill. Zach was across the street, staring at me. He must have seen me standing in front of the camera. He looked at me like I was a slimy bug he'd discovered when he turned over a rock. Before I could reach him, he turned and walked away.

I didn't bother to chase after him. He wasn't interested in listening, and there was no way he'd believe the truth.

WTF?! B's parents are selling her stuff??? Like, all her possessions, everything? How could they?

I smiled at the screen and sipped the lemon spice tea my mom had brought up to my room to help me sleep. I kept thinking about how we should do something for Brit, something nice in her memory. I think she'd really like this, I wrote.

I don't know, she typed.

To be honest, I think her parents need the help. They're not doing so great. You can tell they're just sick about all of it. I think they regret being so hard on her all the time. Her mom said something like they wish they had a chance to do it all over.

They wanted to push her, Brit wrote, so she could be the best.

It looks like they pushed her too far. And anyway, Brit was the best.

I saw you on TV. What you said about her was really nice.

Ugh. I hate those vultures, but I had to do something. It's like people here are already forgetting her, I typed.

What do you mean?

You don't know because you're not in school, but it's like people are all ready to move on. They have the attention span of gnats. Get this: they're talking about changing the prom theme. People don't want the one Brit picked because they think it might be too depressing.

Oh.

And you should see Jason and Sara, I wrote. I see them walking the halls holding hands and making out like they're auditioning to be cover models on a romance novel. They make me sick.

She'll be sorry. Once Jason goes away to college in the fall he'll drop her flat. Sara's going to discover that no one trusts a bitch who would steal another girl's boyfriend, Brit wrote.

Unless Jason doesn't go away. I heard he's thinking about deferring admission and taking classes here in town for a year or two, I lied. I hate that by dying, Brit let them win.

He got into an elite university and he'd go to some rinky-dink community college for Sara? What is it about her? Does she piss glitter or something?

I didn't respond. The curser blinked on the screen. I pinched the pocket watch pendant and waited her out.

You still there? Brit asked.

I waited another minute. Patience.

Kalah?

I have to talk to you about something, I wrote. You know I love you and I want you to come back . . . I let the dots trail across the screen.

But?

But I'm mad at you. I've tried to not be. I don't want to be, but I am. We're best friends, and that means I have to be honest with you.

What did I do? I told you, I'm sorry I abandoned you.

It's not that. It's what you did to Brit, I wrote.

But that was Sara.

Yes, but Brit told me that she confronted you about Jason after you left and you cut off all contact with her. If you guys had just talked then she wouldn't have taken that last step. Can't you see how you ignoring her just made it seem even more like you were the one who had betrayed her?

Brit should have known I wouldn't do that, Brit protested.

You can't blame her for believing you and Jason might have been hooking up. What was she supposed to think? You used to push her buttons all the time. Annoying her was funny to you. The idea of you being with Jason isn't completely ridiculous. It's not like someone already having a girlfriend was enough to stop you from fooling around in the past. You knew how much Jason meant to her, and you couldn't be bothered to reassure her because you were so busy with your fun new adventure. Britney deserved better than you gave her. You were a shitty friend, Beth.

I know, she wrote.

I wish I'd told her when I had the chance that I'd have done anything to help her through what happened with Jason. I wish she knew that even though she's gone, she can still always count on me.

Brit always knew she could rely on you.

You don't know that. We'll never know what she thought. I missed the chance to tell her, to make sure she knew without a doubt that I would always have her back, no matter what.

My fingernail snapped as I jammed down on the keys. I tore the broken part off, wincing at the sharp pain. What I was writing wasn't a total lie. While trying to convince Britney that I was her closest friend in the world, I might have uncovered another truth. I was still mad at Beth too.

Beth had known Brit was upset, and upset for good reason, but she'd laughed off Brit's anger and protected Jason instead of telling the truth right away.

And I was mad at myself too. I'd been so focused on Beth I hadn't seen how close Britney was to the edge. I hadn't wanted to get mixed up in another one of their fights.

If I hadn't been so busy obsessing over Beth and trying to figure out what to do about Zach, then maybe I could have stepped in and defused things before this all happened.

Before things were forever fucked.

I picked up Roogs and buried my face in his fur. I needed to stay focused. I took a few deep breaths and then went back to the computer.

Sorry, I typed, slower this time. I had to get that out. I didn't want it to be between us.

I'm glad you told me, Brit responded. Now we can move forward from here. No secrets.

No more secrets.

CHAPTER TWENTY-SEVEN

When I got home from school the following day, I went up to my room and stopped short in the doorway, my body on high alert. Someone had been in my room.

It wasn't trashed. No one had dumped out my desk drawers or thrown everything in my closet onto the floor, but it felt wrong. Things were just slightly out of place, moved only enough to be noticeable to me.

I was compulsive about the things I kept on my dresser. I liked them arranged a certain way. My field hockey trophy needed to be lined up square with the upper corner. The silver hairbrush that belonged to my grandma had to be sitting horizontally, directly below the trophy, next to my jewelry box. The small ceramic bunny my dad gave me when I was five had to sit at an angle so I could see his face when I was lying in bed. Yes, it was weird that it had to be like that, but it was like that. Always. But not now.

I slowly turned the bunny so he was at the correct angle. I hoped that would make me feel better, but I still could feel the wrongness of the room. The bedspread, which I always tugged all the way up, was folded back a few inches. My mouth tasted funny, almost electric, as if I'd been sucking on pennies. I stepped forward slowly, like I thought someone might be lurking in the closet, waiting to attack.

I reached for the things on my desk, but I was almost afraid to touch them. My fingers hovered above where my papers were still stacked, but I was almost sure they weren't in the same order. The window blinds were open all the way. I never left them like that. Never.

Thinking someone would break into my room just to rearrange things a touch was paranoid. Nuts. A prickle of sweat broke out under my arms.

Not someone. Britney. Somehow she knew I was lying to her, and this was a warning of what she could do.

I had to calm down. Brit couldn't have broken in. She was too far away. The things out of place were just a coincidence, or a trick of the imagination. There had to be another explanation.

I started organizing my room. I needed things to be back the way they were supposed to be. It felt as if my skin was smoldering beneath the surface, all itchy and wrong.

I shook out my folders and reordered the papers, tapping them each six times before tucking them back in.

I ripped the sheets off the bed. I didn't want to sleep on them. I hated the idea that Brit might have been here, looking through my things. I shoved the sheets into the bathroom hamper and pulled a clean set from the closet.

I twisted the blinds almost shut, trying to get the right angle. When I couldn't get it at first I almost started crying in frustration.

When everything was back the way it was supposed to be I thought I would feel the tiniest bit better, but I still felt horrible. It being right now didn't undo the wrongness that had been there. My heart was racing.

I sat down and tried to do the deep breathing that I'd learned years ago with Dr. Sherman. But I was shaking harder, breaking down. It wasn't working. I could feel control slipping out of my grasp. It felt like I was hanging off the roof of a hundred-story building and my fingers were sliding off one by one.

My breathing was coming faster. I worried my heart might explode out of my chest.

I dialed the phone. It took me two tries to hit the numbers right. When it went to voice mail I jammed the off button and called again. And then again. I gripped the phone like it was the only thing holding me in place.

"Kalah, I meant it when I said I needed some time," Zach said instead of hello when he finally picked up.

"Help," I gasped. I couldn't get enough air in my lungs to say more.

"What's wrong?" Zach's said, his voice instantly concerned. "Wait, never mind, where are you?"

"Home," I whispered.

"Do you need me to call the cops? Or an ambulance or something?"

"No. You."

"Stay on the phone. I'm close to your place. I'm on my way." I could hear him grabbing things. "I'll keep talking to you until I get there, okay? You don't have to say anything, just let me know you're there once in a while."

I gripped the phone like it was a life jacket and my ship had just gone down. I couldn't focus on what he was saying, but he kept talking in a soothing voice, keeping me from sinking. I heard his car squeal into the driveway within minutes.

"Kalah?" Zach yelled as he came through the front door. His feet pounded up the stairs. My door flew open and he spotted me on the floor. I must have looked as bad as I felt because his eyes grew really wide. He crouched down next to me. "Are you hurt? Should I call nine-one-one?" His hands patted my sides as if looking for a bullet wound.

I shook my head. Every nerve in my body was on high alert. "Panic," I gasped out.

"Panic attack," Zach finished. I'd told him about them, but he'd never seen one. Even though I knew it was all in my mind, it felt impossible to stop it. I was trembling and sweating. It seemed possible I might die.

Zach looked scared, but he sat down on the floor and pulled me between his legs so that my back was against his chest, and wrapped his arms around me.

"Try to breathe with me," he said. He took a long breath in and held it for a beat before letting it out. I tried to match it but couldn't. My entire body was shaking. "Shhh, you're okay. I got you," Zach murmured.

I tried to tell him I was sorry, but I couldn't get the words out.

"Don't talk. Don't think. Just breathe. We're going to get through this together." He took another deep breath in and out. I did the best I could to clear my thoughts and parrot his breathing. Time slowed down.

I closed my eyes and slowly felt myself start to calm. My heart no longer felt like it was straining out of my chest. I relaxed into Zach. His familiar smell helped. I became more aware of how close we were, how the heat of his body warmed mine. Zach's thumb slowly rubbed the back of my hand.

I sat forward, putting some space between us. "I'm better now," I said. I was embarrassed and grateful and mad at myself all at the same time. Why did I have to have this problem? Why could no part of me be normal?

Zach leaned against my bed. He let out a shaking breath. "That was freaky."

"Sorry." I pulled my knees up and rested my chin on one. My shirt was stuck to my skin with sweat. Great. No better way to see your ex-boyfriend than while having a panic attack and sweating like a freak.

I tried to explain. "I wouldn't have called you, but my parents are at a cooking class. Nadir is too far away to do anything. I didn't know who else to call." The fact that there was no one else in my life that I could reach out to said a lot about how shitty things were going. "Thank you." I felt a chill where his warm body had touched mine just seconds before.

Zach shrugged uncomfortably. "I don't mind that you called." He looked like he minded. He looked like he wanted to disappear through the floor, which made two of us hoping for a magical way out of this awkward situation. "What happened?" he asked.

"It's a panic attack. They just happen sometimes."

Zach raised his eyebrows in disbelief. "Out of nowhere?"

No way I was telling him that I was freaking out because I had a feeling that Britney had been in my room. He'd think I was losing it.

"I'm okay now," I said instead. Part of me hoped he would push, that he'd beg me to tell him what was going on. I wanted to tell him everything. I needed him on my side.

Zach stood. "Okay. If you say so."

I crossed my arms over my chest. Zach knew me. He had to know I wasn't okay. But he didn't want to be messed up in this.

If he could play it cool, so could I. "I should get started on my homework." I pulled on my sleeves. "I really appreciate you coming over. I know you didn't have to."

Zach looked like he wanted to say something but couldn't figure out what it was. He nodded and moved toward the door. "I'm sorry I was a jerk when you first called," he said. He was practically halfway out the door already.

"Don't worry about it. You came when it counted," I said. I mentally willed him to stop being so stiff and formal. To ask me why I'd talked to the reporters. To ask me what was wrong.

Zach smiled weakly. "You can always call me if you need to." But it was obvious he hoped I wouldn't.

Zach started down the stairs, then stopped and turned back. "I hope you know what you're doing," he said.

I smiled instead of answering.

As soon as I heard the front door close I started crying. I cried until I couldn't anymore. I went to the bathroom and splashed cold water on my face. I crawled onto my bed, pushing the set of clean sheets onto the floor. I wrapped the duvet around me and turned on my computer screen. I would go through all the chats with Britney. Reassure myself I hadn't said anything to give myself away. Then I'd forget this and move forward.

When the chat program opened I thought I must have done something wrong. I shut it down and opened it again.

The history section was empty. All of our talks were gone.

Vanished.

I clicked open the deleted items folder. Nothing. My breath slowed down. I clicked on the sent folder. Also empty. I leaned back against the pillows. Where were all the messages?

Above my desk I had a cork board. Directly in the center was a piece of paper listing all my school and personal passwords. I used the same one for email and chat, and for most of my social media stuff. Brit wouldn't need to have seen the Post-it, though. We'd all known each other's passwords at some point.

How could I have been so stupid? I should have realized she would access it. What else had I screwed up? What other messages in my history had she seen?

I wondered if I could get into her account. I typed her new user name and the password she'd always relied on in the past. It was declined. I tried Beth's, but that failed too. I tried switching the numbers in it to Brit's birthday and then the day she started dating Jason. Declined. I typed in the date she'd "died." This time a window popped up.

> You've exceeded the number of password attempts for this account. If you've lost your password, enter your email and it will be sent to you.

Shit.

My hand shaking, I picked up my phone and dialed Nadir.

"Hey, sis," he said picking up. "How's it going?"

"Not great."

"I was thinking I might come home this weekend," he said. His voice didn't contain any of the usual teasing.

I closed my eyes. I wanted my big brother to come back and fix everything, but I knew he couldn't. "You don't have to do that. You're getting ready for exams. I'll be okay. But I needed to ask you something."

"Whatever you need."

"Do you know how I can recover lost chat transcripts?"

He paused. I could tell he hadn't expected that question. He was likely wondering who was left for me to chat with. "It depends on the program. Open it up and I'll see if I can walk you through it."

I knew having a computer whiz for a brother would come in handy. "I'm looking at it now."

"Have you checked the history and the trash?"

"Seriously?" I asked, annoyed.

"Hey, when I help Grandma with computer stuff I start by making her double-check that the computer is plugged in. Which often solves it."

"Yes. It's turned on and the chats aren't there. They're not in the trash, they're not in the history, and they're not anywhere else I can see."

"I'm sorry, Kay-Kay, but that means they're gone. Unless the other person saved them. You're using a web interface, so they're not stored elsewhere on your computer."

He had me open the settings tab. There was a box checked that said *delete all chats after sign-off*. "There's your problem right there."

"But I didn't want that. I never checked that option," I said.

"You might have selected it by accident. Happens all the time."

"I didn't change it," I said, my voice louder. "I would remember if I had. I'm not delusional."

Nadir was silent.

"Sorry. I didn't mean to snap."

"Maybe the default settings changed. Whatever it was, those chats are gone."

It wasn't the default. Britney had deleted them. I was sure of it, and it was my own fault. It never occurred to me to change my password.

Beth underestimated her too. Beth had assumed she could manage Britney, and look how that turned out.

"Thanks for trying to help," I said.

"No problem, what are big brothers for? Look at the bright side—it was just some chats. At least you didn't lose a term paper or anything important."

I had no way to tell him I'd lost everything.

"I have to run to class, but let's talk later, okay? Think

about me coming for a visit. It's not just for you; I could con Mom into making some *kadhi*."

"Mom would make you whatever you wanted."

"That's because I'm her favorite son," Nadir fired back.

"Yeah," I said.

"Wake up, little sister: you're supposed to point out I'm her only son."

I managed a small fake laugh and hung up.

Did I really think Brit would hurt me? Not hurt, *kill*.

Killing Beth over Jason was a crime of passion and betrayal. If she came after me it would be about covering her ass.

I wanted to believe Britney wouldn't go that far. But it felt like I'd been warned.

CHAPTER TWENTY-EIGHT

You know it isn't a good day when there's a cop at your doorstep. Even if you're the one who invited her.

"Hi," Officer Siegel said. She had on jeans and a crisp white blouse. She must have been off the clock.

"Thanks for coming." I stepped back so she could come in.

"Hard to take a pass with all that mystery."

"I didn't want to explain everything on the phone. I thought this would be easier."

"Who's here?" Mom came around the corner, wiping her hands on a kitchen towel. She smiled at our guest.

"This is Officer Siegel. She's the liaison officer from my school."

My mom's smile tightened and she shot me a quick look before reaching out her hand. "Nice to meet you. I'm Amina."

"Alex," Officer Siegel replied. I don't know why I was surprised she had a first name. "Kalah invited me."

They both looked at me. "I want to talk to all of you."

"Well, then let's go into the living room. I'll get Kalah's dad. Can I make some tea, maybe coffee?" My mom had gone into hostess mode.

"No, thank you."

"All right. Then we'll join you in a minute." She walked away.

I led Officer Siegel into our living room. She peered at the display of family photos.

"Officer Siegel?" My dad strode in, my mom trailing behind. She was still holding the kitchen towel. "I'm Scott."

They shook hands. My parents both sat on the sofa and Officer Siegel took the leather club chair. I kept standing. They all stared at me.

I took a deep breath. I'd written down what I wanted to say in a bullet-point list to make sure I came across as rational as possible. I'd even practiced in front of the bathroom mirror. I felt the list in my pocket ready to be pulled out if needed. "I've gotten myself in a situation and I need help."

"Maybe you should talk to your parents first," Officer Siegel said, holding up her palms as if to stop what I was going to say. "I'm not here in any kind of official capacity, but I wouldn't want to blur any lines."

Did she think I was going to confess a crime? I saw my mom reach for my dad's hand. She looked pale.

"There are no lines to be blurred," I said. "This isn't about me, at least not directly. It's about Britney and Beth. I've uncovered what really happened and I think I'm in danger." I cleared my throat. I had to come across as more confident and calm. "I'm *sure* I'm in danger."

"Kalah," my dad said, his voice resigned.

"Someone broke into the house earlier today, They were in my room." I threw the words down like a gauntlet. Officer Siegel leaned forward. I had her attention now.

My parents exchanged a glance. "Honey, is this about your panic attack?" Mom asked. "Zach called me."

"He's worried about you," Dad added.

"Panic attack?" Officer Siegel asked.

"Kalah has some challenges with anxiety," my mom said.

"I had an attack because I realized she'd been here," I said. "She broke in and rearranged things in my room. It was a threat. She wanted me to know, to put me on guard that she could get to me."

"Beth broke in?" Officer Siegel asked, her eyebrows drawn together in confusion. "Are you saying you think Beth did something to Britney?"

"No, Britney did. Let me explain," I said.

"Oh, honey," my mom said. Her voice was so sad. Officer Siegel looked away, almost embarrassed.

"I'll check the alarm. Maybe we can clear this right up."

Dad got up and went to the kitchen.

"After you left for school I put some laundry in your room," my mom said. "I'm sure I moved some things. I remember tilting your blinds for a bit more light."

"It wasn't just that," I said, but suddenly I was uneasy. Had I been mistaken?

Dad was back a second later. "There's no record that the alarm went off."

I pushed aside frustration and dropped into a chair. I had to stay calm. "We all knew the codes to each other's houses. She wouldn't have set off the alarm."

"Kalah, the alarm records any time anyone comes in and out of the house. After your mom set it this morning, the next time anyone came into the house was at three. That would have been you." Dad's voice was even, but I could see the tension in his face.

"It's not just the alarm. I've been getting messages."

My mom's eyes filled with tears. It wasn't the reaction I'd expected. Dad's face was neutral, but he was gripping my mom's hand.

I could feel panic burbling up, like bubbles in a boiling pot. I had to get back to my bullet-point list.

"Kalah, I'm not sure you're seeing this situation objectively," Dad said gently. "It's understandable. You've been through a lot."

Officer Siegel nodded and I felt the panic increase. She didn't believe me either. I'd lost her before I even got started.

"I see the situation fine. You need to listen to me," I said. "There's been a crime."

Mom stood and I could see the effort she was making to pull herself together. "I'm sorry you came all the way out here, Officer Siegel. I think Kalah's concerns are something we should explore as a family, and with her doctor. If there's anything we need to share with the police, I can assure you we'll do that."

Officer Siegel stood too. "Of course." She squeezed my shoulder as she passed me. "I'll see you at school."

My dad and I didn't say anything while we waited for Mom to return. I felt tracks of hot tears cutting down my face.

When Mom came in she sat on the ottoman right next to my chair. She took both my hands in hers. "We're going to help you through this."

I shook my head. "You don't believe me. You think I'm crazy." Bitterness soured my voice.

Dad came over. "It's not that we don't believe that this feels real for you."

"It feels real because it *is* real," I said.

"Honey, sometimes you see things that aren't there," Mom said, her voice soft.

I sucked in a breath. No matter how softly she said it, it was still a low blow. "This was nothing like that. I'm not crazy."

"I said that the wrong way. I'm not saying you're

—269—

hallucinating. You're not. I'm saying you're sensitive. You always have been. You might have misread the situation. Misunderstood motivations. Then you started to fill in the missing information with a worst-case scenario and suddenly it's overwhelming."

"It's not like that," I said.

"You lost your two best friends," Mom said. "Of course you're grieving. And grief can make even the most healthy, stable mind do wild things. The heart too."

"We'll make you an appointment with Dr. Sherman," Dad said. "And we'll keep talking together. We're glad you told us."

I stood. I should have known I'd never be free of my past.

At my old school there had been a girl in my class who I'd thought was my friend. But being Madison's friend was like pledging a sorority. She put me through test after test— hazing me, really—to make me prove how much I wanted to be near her. And when I'd passed all the tests, she'd laughed in my face and humiliated me in front of everyone.

I wasn't her friend; I was her puppet. And when she pulled all my strings, they'd snapped.

That's when I'd started having panic attacks, needing to count things, and tapping to feel calm. It got so bad, my parents noticed, and sent me to see Dr. Sherman. In the end, my parents and Dr. Sherman made the decision to have me change schools so I could have a fresh start. But a fresh start didn't mean they believed I was stable.

I needed proof.

"Hey." My dad caught my elbow and made me turn around. "Whatever's happening, I want to make sure you know this. Your mom and I love you. We will always be here for you. We supported you before, and we'll support you now."

I nodded and they both hugged me. "I love you guys too," I said.

I could feel them staring at my back as I went upstairs. They loved me, but they didn't believe me. Just like before. They never saw me as bullied. They believed the school administrator, who'd made it sound like I'd stalked Madison, made a whole relationship up in my head, and done crazy things to get her attention. That I'd basically chased her down, stuck to her side. Been a groupie until she'd been forced to be mean to get rid of me.

It wasn't like that. That hadn't been a figment of my imagination. And this wasn't either.

CHAPTER TWENTY-NINE

Trying to act normal was exhausting. My parents kept me home from school and I spent all day pretending to be regular, everyday Kalah. Every word felt practiced and scripted before it left my mouth. I talked about getting back to field hockey. How I would feel better when I got back to my routine.

My parents visibly relaxed as the day went on. It wasn't that they were stupid; it was that they wanted to believe I was going to be all right. They were willing to suspend disbelief because cooperating with my lie was easier than dealing with the truth. Just because they wanted to believe I was okay, that didn't mean it would be easy for me. I was going to have to keep up this charade for days, maybe weeks.

If I made too much of a change too quickly, they would be suspicious. That's why I snapped at my dad over lunch when he finished all the deli turkey, and stormed upstairs to my room. Let them think I was still high-strung.

I hadn't slept much the night before. Sleep was becoming an elusive luxury. One I fantasized about, but nothing I hoped to actually obtain. I'd lain in bed and wanted to work up a rage at my parents for not believing me, but if I was objective, I couldn't blame them. All I had was a story. A bizarre story. If I heard it from someone else I wouldn't have believed it either.

I had to find proof that Brit was still alive. Something that would make people listen. To actually hear me. Even once the DNA tests proved the body was Beth's, that didn't mean they'd believe me that Brit wasn't also dead. I had to lure her back.

I sent her a message. **You free for a talk? I had a huge fight with my parents. Could really use a friend.**

As soon as she replied, I would print out the message. I thought about changing my password, but if Britney wasn't already suspicious of what I knew, she would be if I did that. I had to act normal. I had to act like things were fine.

I glanced at the clock and wondered if I should send another message to say it was urgent. We were heading out for dinner soon. It was Dad's idea. My mom wasn't a total vegetarian—she'd eat the occasional bite of chicken or fish, but our house was a no-red-meat zone. If my dad wanted to fulfill his cravings for steak, he had to do it at a restaurant. I wouldn't be able to check my phone while out with them. I'd be too busy playing my starring role: happy, healthy daughter at loving family dinner.

I checked the online news feeds. I was turning into an addict looking for a hit, bracing for news that Beth's body had been officially identified. Maybe when that happened they'd start searching for Britney. But most likely, when the news hit, Brit would just vanish.

I had to hunt her down before that.

I rooted through my bag and found the business card the reporter, Derek, had given me. I flicked the edge with my fingernail. The first time I'd met him outside the school, he'd hinted how he wasn't crazy about popular girls. He'd wanted dirt on Brit.

I put his name into the search bar. He was a freelance writer. His articles appeared mostly in local papers around the state, but he had at least a few in national magazines. His bio at the end of the articles described him as an investigative reporter.

"Five minutes! Or we'll be late for our reservation," Dad yelled from downstairs.

I flicked the card. Maybe I didn't need to find Brit myself. Maybe Derek would do it. All he needed was a nudge in the right direction. This was his job. He was a trained professional.

My foot was tapping. I stopped it. I should think it

through before pulling him in. Except there wasn't much time. They'd know about the body any second now. After that, Britney would disappear.

I picked up my phone and put it down. Derek would have caller ID. This had to be anonymous.

I quickly set up a new email account and typed in the address from his card.

> FROM: koncerned@gmail.com
> TO: derek@diriven.com
> RE: Matson Story
> You have questions about Brltney and you're right to have them. Things aren't what they seem. Ask yourself, if she weren't dead, where would she be?

I read over the email and hit SEND. If he took it to the police they could likely trace it back to me, but I didn't think Derek would do that. I didn't out-and-out accuse her of anything. My goal was to make him curious.

Curious enough to do some poking around and find the story of the century.

"Let's go, people," Dad shouted. "I hear a cow calling my name."

I yanked off the sweater I'd worn all day and pulled on a different one. Clean was as good as it was going to get. I put on some lip gloss and headed downstairs. I wasn't even remotely hungry, but I was going to have to pretend.

"Looking foxy," Dad said as I came into the kitchen.

"No one says *foxy*, Dad."

"Really? That's a shame." He whistled when my mom came down the stairs. She winked at him.

My cell rang just as Dad grabbed his car keys off the counter.

"Ignore it," Mom said, but I'd already picked it up. I had this irrational fear that it was going to be Derek, who'd somehow figured out the email was from me. The caller ID said unknown.

"Hello," I said.

"Kalah?"

My heart stopped in my chest. My ears filled with a loud buzzing sound.

"Kah-bear? Is that you? I'm ready to come home now."

Britney was back.

CHAPTER THIRTY

Hospital waiting rooms are designed for maximum discomfort. The plastic chairs in this one were shaped with something other than a human butt in mind. The magazines were all at least six months out of date, and the coffee tasted like it was strained through an old T-shirt. Instead of getting his steak, my dad had to make do with a stale ham sandwich that tasted like the plastic triangle container it came in.

The clock ticked off another minute. There was a TV attached to the opposite wall showing Headline News. We'd seen the same stories cycle through two or three times already, so everyone was ignoring it.

I wondered how long before the media heard about this headline.

Things had happened quickly after Britney had called. My tongue had lost all ability to shape words, so I'd passed the phone to my mom. Brit was apparently crying by then, but able to say where she was. My mom made my dad call for an ambulance on his cell while she stayed on my phone with Brit. As soon as we knew the paramedics had her, we jumped in the car to meet them at Munson Hospital.

My mom called and called Brit's parents until they finally picked up. They must have broken every speed limit in town getting to the hospital.

After all, it's not every day your daughter returns from the dead.

Brit's parents had rushed in, sweeping past us with a quick thank-you before disappearing down the hall.

Because my mom worked at the hospital she'd pried some information from the nursing clerk. Britney had a few injuries, but nothing major. The nurse thought she was underweight and was clearly disoriented. They were running a tox screen on her in case she'd taken something or been drugged.

I'd already chewed my thumbnail down, exposing the tender flesh underneath, and I was working to complete the gnaw-manicure on my other fingers. It's a good thing I wasn't planning to hold hands with anyone soon.

I practically bounced out of my seat when I saw the police arrive. This was it. This was my moment—Beth's moment. The moment when Britney would finally get the handcuffs she deserved.

Two male officers with stern expressions walked past with Officer Siegel trailing behind them. I fought the urge to dance around her chanting, "I tried to tell you!" They didn't say anything to us.

After another hour and another four repetitions of the same headline cycle, Brit's mom finally came out into the waiting room. We all stood like she was the president. She reached over and squeezed my shoulder, which was pretty touchy for Brit's mom. It was practically a hug. Dr. Ryerson wasn't known for showing a lot of affection.

"Britney is doing well," she announced.

We all stood there, waiting for more. She was doing well? That's all she was going to say? How about explaining where her "dead" daughter had been for the past few weeks? Or what Brit might know about the body everyone assumed was hers?

Maybe the cops were still interrogating her. Maybe they hadn't told her parents yet.

"We're all so glad to hear that," my mom said.

"Thank you for calling for an ambulance. Britney's quite disoriented. When she didn't get an answer when she called us at home, she called the only other number she knew by heart." Dr. Ryerson gave me a small smile.

"She was afraid she was going to run out of change for

the pay phone before she could reach anyone." Dr. Ryerson's lip shook with emotion. I thought of pointing out that Britney could have called collect, or gone inside and asked the guy if she could use his cell. If Britney couldn't remember how to sweet-talk some gas station attendant, she was seriously not herself.

"This all must come as such a shock," my mom said.

Dr. Ryerson swallowed. "Not completely. The police called us this morning. They told us that Britney's DNA didn't match the body."

I wanted to pump my fist at the sky. I couldn't wait to hear how Brit was going to explain that away.

"At that moment, we couldn't help but hope she might still be alive." Dr. Ryerson nodded to me. "The police will want to speak with you as well."

I crossed my arms over my chest. "I'm looking forward to talking to them too," I said.

"We'll do whatever we can to help," Dad said.

"Britney's been through a terrible trauma, but we're going to get her the best help possible to get through this."

"Where has she been?" I asked. I wanted to know if she'd already been questioned about Beth's murder, or if her parents were making her stay silent until they could get her a lawyer.

It was amazing—I'd done it. I'd convinced her to come back. She must have thought it was safe, that Beth's body would never be found. I couldn't wait to see her squirm.

"We don't know where she's been. We believe Britney has PTA," Dr. Ryerson said.

"You'll have to excuse me—I'm not up on my medical terminology. What's PTA?" my dad asked.

"Post-traumatic amnesia," Dr. Ryerson said. "It's common after a head injury. The condition is characterized by disorientation, confusion, memory difficulties, and emotional liability. Britney has a textbook case."

I'll bet she did. "So she doesn't remember anything?" I pressed. Did she think she'd get a lighter sentence if she had amnesia? Maybe she thought that excuse would play better with a jury.

"Not as much as she would like." Brit's mom smiled weakly. "It's very common. She's missing both the actual traumatic event as well as events before and after. It's important we don't push her too fast or too hard. This is a difficult time for her."

"Excuse me, can we speak with you?" one of the cops we'd seen earlier asked. He motioned for all of us to take a seat. I sank slowly into the uncomfortable plastic chair. "I know this is an emotional time, but we want to get some statements while everything is fresh." He gave a juicy sniffle.

"Of course," my mom said.

"Any of you need anything, maybe some coffee?" He turned to Officer Siegel. "Why don't you run down to the cafeteria and get some fresh coffee for these folks." The only sign that Officer Siegel wanted to punch him in the face for treating her like a waitress was a twitch above her eyebrow. I was glad when everyone shook their head no, but I could tell the other cop had wanted to get rid of her. "I'm Detective Cabot. Can you tell me what time the call came in?"

"It was just after five," my dad said. "We were headed out for dinner."

Detective Cabot scribbled something in his notebook. "And how did you know it was Britney?"

"I recognized her voice," I said.

He nodded like I'd said something deep. "Can you tell me what she said on the phone?"

My mom recounted their conversation. Officer Siegel watched me, trying to read my reaction. Detective Cabot slapped his thighs when Mom finished and heaved himself up.

"Okay, then. We might have some more questions for you later." Detective Cabot jammed his notebook back into his inside jacket pocket.

"That's it?" I asked. Clearly watching television and movies had given me an overinflated sense of the police's ability to do a basic investigation.

"Yup. Things are fairly straightforward," the detective said.

Was he joking? This was straightforward? Unease fluttered through my gut.

Officer Siegel saw my expression. "Britney was able to tell us a few things."

"Such as?" I demanded.

Officer Siegel looked over at Brit's mom, who waved her hand, apparently giving permission to tell us. Maybe this was our reward for taking Brit's call and sending the rescue party.

Officer Siegel met my eyes. "On the day she disappeared, Britney's intent was to commit suicide. She reports she was in a state of despair. The only person she told was Beth, in an email that she'd thought Beth never received."

I blinked. This was bullshit. By that time Beth was already dead.

"She has some snippets of memory of Beth trying to stop her," Officer Siegel continued. "After that she doesn't remember much. We believe that's when Beth tried to intervene and there was some kind of accident."

"But Brit doesn't know what happened," I repeated.

The detective hitched his waistband up. "What we think is most likely given the injuries to the girl's body is that Britney was about to throw herself off the Point, when the other girl—"

"Beth," I interrupted. "Her name was Beth."

"Right. Beth. Most likely Beth tried to stop her and they both ended up going over the edge together. Both girls hit their heads, but tragically only one of them survived the fall."

"So where has Britney been?" I demanded. Were we supposed to believe she'd been wandering the woods all month?

"PTA," her mom explained. "In her disoriented state, she must have picked up Beth's ID and assumed that was her own identity. Given the level of emotional upset and Britney's desire to harm herself, it's possible her brain found it easier to accept that she was someone else. Her mind couldn't cope with what had occurred, so it gave her time. She was scared and hurt. This was a major trauma. Basic fight or flight. She hid."

I stared at Officer Siegel, wondering if she was buying this. Her face gave away nothing.

"Slowly things started to come back to her," Dr. Ryerson said. "You have to understand this would have been very confusing for her. Because she believed she was Beth at first, and had no medical attention, or support, it took some time for her mind to—I guess you could call it reboot, to the reality of her situation."

Detective Cabot was nodding as Doctor Ryerson talked. I couldn't believe he was swallowing it. Did anyone really believe a word of this bullshit?

But I'd forgotten the most basic truth of all: that pretty little rich girls are always believed. People expect evil to look ugly.

"We hope Britney will be able to give us more details eventually. We're going to keep her here overnight for observation, but she should be able to come home tomorrow," Dr. Ryerson said. "We're lucky that she's in overall good health."

"Thank goodness," my mom said.

Dr. Ryerson nodded. "We don't want this to drag out. Britney's been through enough, and the whole situation is so . . . sordid. She wants to get back to normal life as soon as possible."

"What about Beth?" I pushed.

"We've asked the lab to put a rush on confirming the body's hers," Detective Cabot said. "Then her family can put her to rest."

My mom put her hand lightly on my back.

"So, that's it," I said, my voice flat.

"Not entirely. Britney wants to see you." Her mom smiled at me like I'd just won the lottery.

CHAPTER THIRTY-ONE

Britney's the only person I know who could make a hospital gown look stylish. Her parents had arranged for her to have a private room. Flowers had already been delivered, a giant bouquet of red and gold tulips by the window. The room smelled like a mix of antiseptic and Dr. Ryerson's perfume.

I stood by the door.

"Hey," Britney said faintly. Her eyes fluttered open, her dark lashes like spider legs. "My mom said you were here." She pulled herself up and leaned against the recently plumped pillows. There was an IV needle in the back of her hand. I liked the idea that she was tethered to the bed in some way. "Come on in, I'm not going to bite," she said.

"You're back," I said, stepping closer.

She laughed softly. "I guess I am."

I stared at her. "Your hair is brown." It was the same shade as Beth's.

"I know." Brit pulled on a lock of hair, staring at the end as if she were surprised about it too. "It's another mystery. One more thing I don't remember. I'm going to get it changed back to blond as soon as I can. It's not really me."

I wanted to slap her. "Why did you send me those emails?"

Her eyes widened. She looked like a character in a fairy-tale book. "What emails?"

I felt my jaw tighten. "You emailed me, saying you were Beth. We chatted. A lot." I watched for a crack in her expression. Nothing.

Her hand went to her mouth. "I did?" She blinked twice. "I have to be honest: a lot of stuff is still really blurry. But apparently I thought I was Beth. Are you sure I sent them?"

"Who else?"

"I don't know. This whole situation seems so unreal." Britney leaned forward. "Can you bring them to me? Maybe if I read them it will help me get back some of the missing time. You know, shake something free."

I could see why they'd believed her. She was a good actress. "I don't have them anymore."

She sighed and slumped back. "Damn. Those might have helped." She rubbed her temples like she was getting a massive headache. "You have no idea how scary all of this is. I just wish I could remember something."

"Me too," I said. She sounded so earnest, I was almost starting to doubt what I knew. But there was no part of our chats that had sounded confused or disoriented, or however PTA was supposed to impact her.

Brit smiled weakly. "My mom told me how amazing you were at the funeral, and trying to help with the foundation." She brushed some hair from her face. "I guess everyone has wondered at some point what people would be like if they were gone, what stories others might tell about them. I suppose the silver lining of this situation is I now know who I can count on."

Britney began to cry, or at the very least her eyes watered. Big crystal tears tracked down her face.

No one cries that pretty, I thought. I remembered how she'd sobbed when she'd had the fight with Jason. That was real emotion. This was an act.

"They told me about Beth. I can't believe she's gone," she said.

I didn't even know what I was supposed to say to that. "Me neither," I answered honestly. I couldn't believe any of this.

"Beth was my best friend." Britney's voice shook. She reached over and grabbed my arm, her nails digging in. No matter how weak she might look, her grip was strong. "All we have is each other now."

I tried to pull away, but she held on to my wrist. It made me uneasy to have her touching me. More than that, it repulsed me.

"You're my very best friend now," Britney said fiercely. "I'll never forget what you did for me."

"Okay, girls." A doctor popped her head in the doorway. "Britney should get her rest."

Brit let go of my wrist and put her head back down on her pillow, once again looking wan. I stepped back quickly out of her reach. I couldn't help but wonder if she believed her own bluff.

"I knew you'd have my back," Brit said.

"That's what friends are for," I replied. She didn't even blink.

I stepped out of her room and into the hall. It felt for a second as if my legs might not hold me, so I leaned against the wall. Nurses and orderlies rushed past, pushing carts or carrying files. It felt like I'd walked back into the real world. Britney's room was a portal to an alternate universe, where nothing makes sense or even tries to.

I felt unbalanced. Maybe I really was crazy.

Officer Siegel walked up and leaned against the wall next to me. "How does she look to you?"

"She says she's tired."

"I imagine she is." Officer Siegel watched the nurses and doctors bustle by. It was hard to tell if she meant anything by that.

"How come you're not in charge of the investigation?"

"Investigation." Officer Siegel snorted. "I guess you could call it that. There are a few reasons. One, Britney's parents and I didn't exactly see eye to eye on some issues when her apparent suicide first happened. Also, I'm just a beat cop. They always involve a detective for this kind of thing. I think my supervisor figures the way I handled her parents early on proved I don't have the communication skills needed to carry a case like this."

"Really? I think people skills is one of your strengths," I said. As soon as the words were out of my mouth, I worried I might have crossed a line, but Officer Siegel actually smiled.

"My personality can be an acquired taste." She glanced at me. "I'm not allowed to interview Britney. They think I'll upset her. And with her parents being good friends with the mayor, along with both of our state senators, that means no one wants to upset the little princess."

"Do you have things you want to ask her?"

"There are a few things I wouldn't mind getting clarified. Technically we should have talked to her before her parents did, but that's not how things went down."

"I had some messages," I said softly. "Online chats that were supposedly from Beth. But they couldn't have been. They must have come from Brit."

"That's what you were trying to tell me and your parents."

I nodded. "I didn't believe it was Beth. I mean, I did at first, but then I knew it couldn't be."

"Can you send them to me?"

"They were deleted. It might have been the chat program, but I think Brit did it. Could you get some kind of warrant to retrieve them from the company?"

Officer Siegel shook her head. "A warrant requires more than a suspicion. Besides, chat records wouldn't prove anything. You could have had them with yourself."

"I didn't do that," I said.

"I didn't say you did. I said I couldn't prove it." Officer Siegel sighed. "We know Beth died from a blow to the head. What we can't prove is how it happened. Britney's story of Beth trying to stop her and falling also matches the evidence."

"They'll know more from the autopsy, though, right?" I asked. An image flashed in my mind of sophomore-year biology class, when we pinned frogs to wax trays and dissected them, their organs looking sort of plastic and purple under the fluorescent lights. I swallowed hard. I needed to be careful. Very careful. I knew how Britney dealt with betrayal.

Still. Brit was smart, but she must have messed up somehow. There must be a fiber or hair that would raise alarm bells. Now that they knew there was reason to be suspicious, they'd look more carefully at Beth's body.

Siegel's expression made me nervous. "There won't be a full autopsy. The body was cremated."

I closed my eyes, wanting to block out reality.

"The body should never have been released until the DNA tests were back, but Britney's parents pressed the county to allow them to lay her to rest. Someone's likely going to lose their job over it."

"So now they'll never know how Beth died." I wanted to slide down the wall and curl into a fetal ball. I thought when Brit came back I was close to the finish line. That I was going to win. That this whole horrible situation would at least end with justice. But it wasn't going to. It was a marathon with no end. I'd keep running until my lungs shredded and my bleeding feet gave out. Brit was going to get away with it.

"There was a preliminary autopsy. I know they did a tox screen and the doctor would have looked over the body then. But everyone was so sure it was a suicide, and the body was in the water for some time. No one knew they should be looking for anything suspicious." Officer Siegel shrugged. "Now everyone wants to sweep this ugly situation right under the rug, along with any hints that things weren't done correctly."

I wiped a tear off my cheek. It was so unfair to Beth. She'd done nothing wrong, certainly nothing to deserve this. They'd carved her up, they'd cremated her, but they never even really saw her.

Officer Siegel handed me a Kleenex. "Beth's beyond any pain or humiliation now."

My grandma would have told me the same. Hindus believe the Atman, or spirit, is what is immortal. The body, and the pain that goes with it, is just temporary. I wished I knew what I believed.

"Do you buy into the idea of heaven?" I asked. I wanted to have faith that Beth was someplace better. She deserved so much more than how things had turned out. She deserved justice.

"I don't know. I know I want to," Office Siegel said.

"What would it be like?"

I liked that Officer Siegel took time to think about it. She didn't give me a flip answer. "I think it would be different for every person. For me, it would be like this old ski cabin my grandparents used to have in Canada. I'd sit inside with a nice fire and some hot chocolate. It would smell like pine trees. There'd be a couple dogs with me on the sofa, a fluffy blanket, and it would be almost perfectly quiet. Just the soft hush of snow falling outside."

I considered that. "I think mine would be one of those perfect spring days. Where I'd be outside lying on the ground and it would be warm from the sun. It would smell like fresh-cut grass and dirt." In my mind I pictured Beth lying next to me. Her hand reaching for mine, our pinky fingers linked as we watched the clouds float past.

"Nice," Officer Siegel said. "What about Beth's idea of heaven?"

"I don't know," I admitted.

"Try."

I closed my eyes for a second. "I think it might be a tea party. Earl Grey and scones. A giant Alice in Wonderland tea party with the Mad Hatter, the White Rabbit, and the Cheshire cat, the whole gang swapping weird literary quotes with each other."

"Then that's how you should picture her."

And so I did. I could see Beth laughing the way she always did, with her head thrown back as if she didn't have a care in the world, her front tooth just slightly crooked. She'd daintily select a cookie from a silver tray like she'd done in my bedroom. "Don't mind if I do," she'd say. "After all, it's my unbirthday." I imagined her taking a big bite, crumbs spilling down her shirt as she winked at me. I couldn't help grinning for the first time since I'd known Beth was gone for good. And then I realized Officer Siegel was watching me, a faint smile of reflection on her own face.

"Siegel! Let's get a move on." Detective Cabot called, heading toward the waiting room. He turned around without even waiting for her to respond.

"That's my exit cue." She took a few steps down the hall. "Just remember, if you have your head down, sometimes you can run right into something. Take care."

I met her eyes. I couldn't tell if she was saying good-bye or warning me.

When Officer Siegel pushed through the swinging doors at the end of the hall there was an explosion of camera flashes and people yelling out questions.

The world was ready to welcome Brit back. Their star had come home.

CHAPTER THIRTY-TWO

Beth's parents didn't have a funeral for her. At first I thought maybe they were hosting a small, family-only kind of thing, but they didn't even do that. I didn't know you could bury someone without doing *something*, but apparently you can. Or maybe they didn't bury her. Maybe they just kept the ashes in a can.

Some parents are naturals at the whole mom-and-dad thing. They leave notes in their kids' lunch bags. They run alongside them on the sidewalks to teach them how to ride bikes, and don't freak out if they accidentally grind Play-Doh into the carpet. I know not everyone gets good parents, or even decent parents, but it seemed *any* parent should pull together a funeral for a dead daughter. I was disgusted with

Beth's mom and dad, but my mom told me to go easy on them.

"To bury one child is an unimaginable hell, but for them to lose both—" My mom's voice broke and she shook her head violently, as if to whip the thoughts from her mind. "I can't even fathom it." She bustled around the kitchen. She'd organized a brigade of neighborhood families to make meals for Beth's parents and to make sure their yard got mowed. "Now isn't the time to judge what they're doing," she told me. "Now is the time for us to try to think of what we can do for them."

I was sitting on one of the stools watching my mom. "What about Beth?" I asked.

Mom came over and hugged me. She smelled like curry and spices from cooking. "It's not the size of the funeral that matters." She pulled back and tapped my chest. "It's the size of the hole they leave in our hearts when they go. There is no greater compliment to Beth, and the person she was, than the fact that you miss her."

"I loved her," I said, staring down at my hands.

"I know you did," Mom said.

"No. Not like that. I *loved* her," I said, looking up. I was surprised the words were out of my mouth. I hadn't planned to say anything, but I couldn't stand the way everyone had pushed Beth aside. You couldn't turn on the television or pick up a newspaper without seeing Britney's picture smiling out. Beth wasn't a story. She was dead and gone, but not for me.

My mom's eyes filled with tears and she came quickly around the island and wrapped me in a hug. "Oh, Kalah, I am so sorry." I could hear the pain in her voice. And how she loved me.

I sobbed into her chest. She stroked my hair and let me cry. When I finished she went to the sink to wet a handful of paper towels, and pressed them gently to my face. "I didn't know," she said. "I had no idea."

I sniffed. "I didn't want you to know." I took another paper towel and blew my nose. "I didn't want anyone to know."

Mom tucked a lock of hair behind my ear. "Love can be confusing at the best of times. I can't say I understand what you're going through, but I want to."

"I'm not sure it matters now. Beth's gone." My breath kept hitching in my chest.

"It matters that you loved her. That's never gone."

I nodded. I didn't trust myself to say anything else without starting to cry all over again.

"I'm going to make us some tea." Mom put the kettle on the stove. She opened the cupboard and pursed her lips. "Mint or chai?"

"Mint," I said.

She pulled out the tin and swirled hot water in the teapot, getting it ready. She grabbed some honey. It relaxed me to watch her. She moved through the kitchen like a ballet dancer. "I'm glad you have Britney back in your life," she said.

Hearing Brit's name was like a sliver of ice through my chest.

"I know I was critical of her at times, but I also know how important friendships can be. You two will both do better knowing you have each other to get through this."

I nodded again.

Mom turned and smiled. "Good friends are everything."

I stayed home from school. The official story was that I had a cold, but the truth was I wasn't ready to face the world and my parents weren't interested in pushing me.

I'd decided to have my own service for Beth. I went to Lighthouse Park.

The beach was empty of people but full of stuff. Now that people knew that Beth was the one who'd died, they'd turned the spot into some kind of shrine for her, leaving notes and tokens and flowers there. People thought she'd died at the Point saving Brit. I knew she hadn't died there, that she'd been murdered in Britney's basement, but this was still where she'd kissed me for the first time. I felt closer to her here.

I crouched down near the driftwood log where people had left candles and gifts. I put down the bouquet of bright gerbera daisies I'd bought—red, orange, yellow, and hot pink. There was a huge bouquet of dark roses already there. I read the card.

With our deepest condolences, the Ryerson-Matson family.

I plucked one of the rose heads from the stem. The velvet-soft petals bruised as I crushed them in my hand. I let go and they sprinkled down on the ground. I brushed my hand against my leg. I had to remember why I came.

I pulled out Beth's copy of *Alice in Wonderland*. "I thought I should say a few words," I said into the wind. "It seemed to me you wouldn't want me to give some kind of big speech, so I thought you might like this better." I cleared my throat and found the places I'd marked with a Post-it note.

> "The sun was shining on the sea,
> Shining with all his might:
> He did his very best to make
> The billows smooth and bright—
> And this was odd, because it was
> The middle of the night.
>
> The moon was shining sulkily,
> Because she thought the sun
> Had got no business to be there
> After the day was done—
> 'It's very rude of him,' she said,
> 'To come and spoil the fun!'
>
> The sea was wet as wet could be,
> The sands were dry as dry.

You could not see a cloud, because
No cloud was in the sky:
No birds were flying overhead—
There were no birds to fly.

In a Wonderland they lie
Dreaming as the days go by,
Dreaming as the summers die."

I closed the book. There wasn't any sound other than the wind whispering in the long beach grass. "I was going to tell you, if I ever got up the guts, that I love you." I felt a little silly talking to the empty air, but I forced myself to keep going. I wouldn't be able to move forward if I didn't try to find some way to tell her what I felt.

"I like to think that you knew, but I still wish I had told you. I didn't say anything before for all sorts of reasons. Because I was afraid you might not feel the same way. Because I was afraid you might think I was being weird, all mushy and overly emotional. Because maybe you were just messing around and I was making it into something it wasn't. Because I was confused about Zach and my feelings for him. Because I wasn't sure if loving you meant I might be gay and if I could even handle that.

"Basically, it comes down to all the stuff I was afraid might happen if I told you. It never occurred to me to be afraid of what might happen if I *didn't* take the chance. I assumed we had all this time, but I was wrong.

"This is sort of a bitch of a way to learn that regretting stuff you didn't do is worse than regretting stuff you tried and failed at. The point is, now I'll never be able to tell you." I glanced down at the log, remembering sitting there with her, sharing her dad's bourbon. Clueless of what was going to happen. "Nothing against this conversation, but it doesn't really count.

"I wanted to tell you that knowing you, loving you, made me a better person. I want to be the person you deserved. This might seem stupid, but when we first started hanging out I thought of you like some kind of modern fairy godmother come to life. You were beautiful and smart and brave, but you weren't the type to wait for anyone else to rescue you. The fact that you noticed me and seemed to like me, it made me like myself better. If you could find me interesting, then you must have seen something that I hadn't seen yet, maybe hadn't realized yet."

I bent down and brushed a clump of rose petals off the log. "I'm so sorry I didn't get a chance to do this right." I closed my eyes and let myself remember the sensation of her brushing the sand from my lips before that first kiss.

I stood and took a deep breath, trying to clear my head. Part of me wanted to let this tragedy end here. There wasn't going to be any easy solution to what had happened. No one was interested in digging up the truth. Not Britney's parents, or mine, not the police, not the teachers at school, not the media. Everyone liked the story the way it was.

I wanted to go back to a time when all I worried about was pop quizzes and field hockey and whether it would be better to get a job at the mall for the summer or try for a position as a camp counselor. I wanted to have concerns that were everyday and simple and not about death and lies. I didn't want to think about what would happen if Brit realized I knew the truth.

But as much as I wanted to shut the door and declare it as past tense, I couldn't forget Beth that easily. I couldn't pretend that I didn't know what Brit had done. Brit had killed Beth, and she was getting away with it. The only person who could fix that was me.

Sooner or later Brit would slip up. She would make a mistake. She would give something away.

And I would be right by her side when she made that mistake. I would use it to bring her down.

This had to be Brit's fantasy come to life. There was a giant banner in the main hall with foot-high letters painted in blue: WELCOME BACK, BRITNEY! She was standing by her locker holding court. Her hair was back to the perfect shade of blond, and it looked like she'd had a blowout this morning. No doubt she wanted to look good. She had a media image to keep up.

I'd seen Britney on TV last night. She'd done a personal interview with a reporter from CNN. She'd sat on her parents' sofa, sandwiched between them, perfect Swarovski crystal tears hovering in each eye. The lights of the camera glinting off the new highlights in her hair.

"Beth was like a sister to me." Brit had covered her heart with her hand. She'd had a manicure, a tasteful pale pink. "I wish I could remember more, but I know she died trying to save me. She's my hero."

I'd watched the TV, the remote clutched in one hand, pushing back a wall of rage.

"I plan to honor my best friend's memory by living my life to its fullest. I know that's what Beth would want." Britney had faced the camera and smiled through her tears.

I watched Brit now from the front door of the school. She reminded me of a silent movie actress, big eyes and lots of dramatic hand motions as she spoke to her admiring fans. She glanced over and spotted me at the doorway. I sensed she'd been waiting for me to show up. It was now or never. Showtime.

"Brit-Brit!" I yelled out.

"Kah-bear!" she called back, throwing both of her arms in the air.

We ran toward each other like one of those slow-motion scenes in cheesy movies. I did my best not to flinch as we hugged. Her bracelets jangled in my ear.

"I'm so glad you're back. You have no idea how much I missed you," I gushed, squeezing her tight. This was the only strategy I had. I was going to be Britney's new best friend. I had to make her believe everything I'd told her in those chat sessions was real. That I would be there for her no matter what.

I'd be the most devoted best friend she'd ever imagined, until I found a way to destroy her.

There were only two people who knew what had really happened to Beth and one of them was dead. I needed Brit to trust me. To let down her guard. I needed to give her space to slip up. Brit had to believe I was the loyal BFF she'd always wanted. I had to almost believe it myself if I was going to fool her. This was a serious trip down the rabbit hole.

We broke out of the hug. "C'mon, guys, give Brit some space." I motioned for people to back up.

"What are you, her personal bodyguard?" Melissa said.

Brit narrowed her eyes at Melissa and threw her arm around me. "No, she's my best friend. You should try getting one sometime."

I burst into a huge smile. Melissa's face turned tomato red. Britney poked Melissa in the stomach. "God, don't get mad. I was just joking."

I laughed like I thought it was the best joke in the world, and Melissa was forced to laugh too. No one could afford to be on the outs with Britney.

"I should get to class," Brit said to the crowd, making a pout with her glossy lips. "You guys have no idea how behind I am. I'll catch up with all of you at lunch." She waggled her fingers at them as we stepped away.

I walked with her down the hall, our arms linked like we were headed down the yellow brick road together. She looked over her shoulder to make sure we were alone. "God, it's exhausting. All these people want something from me. I'm just trying to get my life back, you know?" She sighed like it was all too much.

"You're a celebrity," I told her. "Everyone's going to want a piece of you."

There was a quick twitch at her lips. "Lifetime called my parents. There's a producer there who wants to do a movie of the week about my story. About how I was distraught and Beth saved me, and then I thought I was her, and how eventually I found the courage to fight and get my own memories back. There have been some talk shows in touch too."

"Wow. A movie."

"My mom says it's tacky." Britney tossed her hair. "I don't want to exploit what happened, especially not Beth's death. I don't want to make it into some kind of circus."

"But your story could really help people," I urged. The more often she told her story, the more likely it was she would mess up. Be inconsistent. Let something slide. "Maybe you should even think about writing a book, or doing an article, maybe for *People* magazine or something. It's important for you to share." I pulled out the big guns. "Beth would want you to."

She glanced at me out of the side of her eyes. "You think?" I nodded. She pulled me over to the lockers so we were out of the rush. "I thought maybe you were mad at me," Brit said. "At the hospital you seemed, you know, weird. Then you didn't call the last couple days or anything."

I let myself tear up, just a bit, not too much. "I am so sorry. I was being horrible. All I can say is that I had sensory overload. I thought you were dead, and then you were back, and that meant Beth was dead." I stared down at my shoes, like I couldn't meet her eyes.

"Of course." She squeezed my arm. "Trust me, I know all about sensory overload. I feel like I've been on some kind of emotional roller coaster."

"But you had real trauma. I don't have an excuse." I took a deep breath. "It's just, when you were writing to me, I really thought you were Beth." I needed her to trust me. That meant I had to be vulnerable. "There's a secret I need to tell you."

Brit's mouth pinched. "Sure."

"Beth and I . . . we were a thing. Nothing official, of course. And I still had Zach. But there was something between us, once or twice. Whatever it was."

Brit shifted her weight, her eyes widening. She hadn't seen that coming. It probably made her wonder what else she'd missed.

Almost instantly I could see her pulling herself back together, tucking in the rough edges, figuring out how she could use this knowledge to her advantage. There was no way she'd admit she hadn't known. "I know," Brit lied. "Beth told me. I was happy for you guys."

I let out a breath. "I'm glad you already knew. I didn't want any secrets between us." I made myself smile. "If I was acting weird, it's just because realizing Beth was dead was like losing her all over again. It's still hard."

"Beth was amazing, and you and I are never going to forget her," Brit vowed.

I hugged her. "I know we won't."

The bell rang and Brit sighed like school was already boring her. "I should go. All I need is to be marked late."

As if we didn't both know that the teachers would never mark her down. They'd likely be falling all over themselves to make sure she didn't have to make up too much work. "I'll see you at lunch."

Brit reached out and touched my elbow. "You know, it means the world to me to have you in my corner." Her eyes locked with mine. "If I didn't know I could trust you, I don't know what I would do."

My mouth was too dry to answer so I nodded. As I did, a flash of blue at her neckline caught my eye. Her hand reached up and touched the small blue teacup hanging on a thin chain. My breath seized in my chest. I watched her disappear down the hall.

ACKNOWLEDGMENTS

I have a confession to make. I always read the acknowledgments first when I get a new book. I want an inside peek on how an idea became an entire novel. Here's your behind-the-scenes view.

I first have to thank Rachel Coyne for getting me into this book and my new agent, Barbara Poelle, for making sure I crossed the finish line.

To say this book wouldn't have existed without the amazing editorial support of Anica Mrose Rissi and her assistant, Alex Arnold, is not an understatement. They cajoled, cheered, pushed, and pulled until this book was completed. When I was certain I'd written myself into an impossibly deep rabbit hole they were there to help me through. I can't thank them enough.

Writing a book is a fairly solo activity, but publishing requires a team. The group at HarperCollins is amazing. Special thanks go to Katherine Tegen for her fearless leadership, Joel Tippie with Amy Ryan and Barb Fitzsimmons for the amazing cover. Ro Romanello, Lauren Flower, Alana Whitman, and Onalee Smith for their support in spreading the word, and copy editors Janet Robbins and Bethany Reis for saving me from misused commas and other random errors. For everyone else at HarperCollins that I am forgetting, I owe you cupcakes.

I am indebted to friends and family who support me in my desire to make things up for a living. Special thanks to those who did some early reading of this manuscript and also talked me off the ledge as needed: Jennifer Ochoa, Joelle Anthony, Jamie Hillegonds, Terra Elan McVoy, Joanne Levy, and Serena Robar.

My dog, Cairo, made sure I came out for fresh air occasionally and loved me even on the days when the writing went badly. Never underestimate the power of a dog to make everything seem okay.

Most of all, thanks go to Bob. There is no one else I would rather be on this adventure with than you.

JOIN THE
Epic Reads
COMMUNITY

THE ULTIMATE YA DESTINATION

◀ DISCOVER ▶
your next favorite read

◀ FIND ▶
new authors to love

◀ WIN ▶
free books

◀ SHARE ▶
infographics, playlists, quizzes, and more

◀ WATCH ▶
the latest videos

◀ TUNE IN ▶
to Tea Time with Team Epic Reads

   Find us at **www.epicreads.com** and **@epicreads**